Blasquez

The TWENTY-SEVENTH Day

E. P. DUTTON & CO., INC.

NEW YORK

THE 27th DAY

by
John Mantley

to my mother

The

TWENTY-SEVENTH

Day

1

As far as it could be ascertained from later inquiries, the first person to hear an extraterrestrial voice on earth was Jonathan Clark. It happened between four and five o'clock* on the morning of July 18, 1963.

Jonathan, a first-string reporter on the Los Angeles *Telegram,* had returned from the fights about midnight with several double bourbons under his belt and a glow which was not entirely the result of alcohol. His boy Dynamite had dropped the champ in the middle of the ninth, with as sweet a right cross as he had ever witnessed, and the upset had augmented his financial status by an even twenty dollars. He opened the door to his Pasadena apartment feeling so smugly triumphant he decided he was big enough to tackle the impasse in his novel which he had craftily avoided for almost two weeks.

By four the glow of both bourbon and triumph had faded and the inspirational ideas which had flowed out on an alcohol mist began to seem just a little transparent. He ripped the tenth consecutive sheet out of the typewriter, crumpled it into a neat ball, and lobbed it out of the circle of lamplight in the general direction of the wastepaper basket. There was a muted ping from the darkness. Bull's-eye! Jonathan permitted himself a scowl of satisfaction. He spun around in his swivel chair to reach for a cigarette and a voice spoke out of the darkness of

* Pacific Standard Time.

the room behind him. The voice was rich, full, and resonant, and it said, "Excuse me."

As far as Clark knew, he was completely alone in the house. It was four o'clock in the morning, the door of his second-floor apartment was locked, and the door to his study was closed. He had heard no noise and the last thing in the world he expected was the sound of a voice practically at his elbow.

He jumped visibly and spun around in his chair to stare into the shadows from which the voice had come. It is still his impression to this day that he actually *saw* nothing in this first moment, but he had a sensation, an indefinable feeling, that there was *something*. The sensation made his skin crawl uncomfortably. After a pause, in which his thrumming nerves vibrated back into an approximation of control, he found his voice: "Who's there?"

The disembodied reply came back quietly: "My name is of no importance. I am sorry to disturb you, Mr. Clark, but I must ask you to come with me."

Jonathan Clark was impetuous. He had the reputation among fellow reporters of exploding into action in situations where most men would have preferred to step cautiously. The entity in the shadows might or might not be holding a gun, but at the moment Jonathan didn't give a damn. His sense of privacy had been outraged. The muscles in his jaw bunched angrily. He tensed. In one sudden movement, he was out of his chair, trying for the light switch on the wall. There was a simultaneous flicker of movement in the dark shadows of the room and for the first time Jonathan had a glimpse of his intruder. He was arrested in mid-movement. His face betrayed a mixture of amazement, awe, and something which might have been horror. The shadow of the visitor fell across his face and the deep voice said gently and not unkindly, "I'm afraid, Mr. Clark, that it is not quite that simple."

At almost the same time that Jonathan Clark was being disturbed in his Pasadena apartment, some six thousand miles away, at approximately two o'clock in the afternoon,* an unusually attractive young lady by the name of Eve Wingate, clad in a brief bathing suit, was float-

* Greenwich Mean Time.

ing languidly in the clear waters off the beach of Torquay, England. The sun was hot. It shone down out of a cloudless sky, and beyond the bay the sea was a smooth, aching blue. There was no intimation in the clear brightness of the day that an event of historic porportions was in the making. On the shore, a group of Eve's companions were engaged in a strenuous game of beach ball, from which she had just escaped.

She watched them dispassionately for a few moments, then swam diagonally away from the beach toward a small headland projecting into the sea some fifty yards down the shore. When she reached the headland, she decided, on a sudden impulse, to explore the beach beyond the rock. There is no means of knowing whether the decision was prompted by her own volition or induced by the intelligence that awaited her. Whatever the reason, she made up her mind and paddled slowly around the edge of the promontory out of sight of her companions. A few minutes later, she got to her feet in the light surf and walked out of the water to the unmarred sand of a deserted cove. To her left the rock angled slightly inward away from her line of vision so that she was not immediately aware that she was not alone. She came a few steps up the beach, her bronzed body glistening with tiny rivulets of water. She took off her bathing cap and ruffled the short auburn curls, tossing her head to clear the moisture from the tendrils which had escaped beneath her cap. And then she saw it. For an endless second, she, like Jonathan Clark, was frozen into immobility. The chords of her throat worked. No sound escaped her lips. Quietly she crumpled to the sand. A shadow, grotesque and angular, slid slowly over her body and the second contact of the Aliens had been made.

At the moment that Eve Wingate decided to explore the beach beyond her headland, a waiter in Heidelberg was filling the glass of the toastmaster at a distinguished farewell luncheon. The toastmaster removed his gold-rimmed spectacles, placed them carefully on the tablecloth in front of him, and raised his glass as the fifty renowned scientists in the room fell silent. "To our departing guest," the toastmaster began, "to the individual whose contributions to science will be remembered as long as man pursues his insatiable quest for knowledge; may his genius flourish even more brightly in the new world than it has in the old. Good luck and Godspeed, Professor Klaus Bochner." The last syllable of the name was drowned in a chorus of bravos and an explosion of applause. At the table of honor a short, round-faced man with a halo of white hair reluctantly rose to his feet. He adjusted his spectacles and tugged nervously at his right eyebrow in a gesture familiar to most of the men present.

"My friends," he began in a heavy German accent, "you–you know I am no good at making speeches. I only would like to say 'thank you' for–for everything. I am sorry to leave, but I–I must, and if I do not go soon, I will miss my plane." He hesitated, floundering, and then went on, "After so many years of waiting, I would hate to miss America. I am told by many of you that things move so fast there that I–I am beginning to be afraid it may vanish by way of the Fitzgerald contraction before I arrive."

There was a roar of laughter, the scraping of chairs and the professor found himself surrounded by a group of Europe's most redoubtable names in the world of science, wringing his hand and offering their best wishes on his departure. With difficulty he freed himself and made his escape to the open air. There on the gravel path leading to the driveway he heaved a sigh of relief. Receptions, particularly receptions in his honor, always unnerved him. He took a deep breath and began to walk toward the drive where his car would be appearing any moment.

He had covered perhaps half the distance to his objective when a voice spoke from behind him. It said, "Dr. Bochner?"

The scientist turned in his tracks. "Yes?" He spoke the word before he was conscious that there was no one on the path. He gazed about him curiously. On either side, the walk was flanked by enormous pines alternating with neatly tailored bushes taller than the professor's head. As a result, although it was just after midday, the path itself was in shadow streaked with narrow triangles of light where the sun broke through. He began moving slowly back up the aisle. "Did someone call me?"

"Yes." The voice came from the shadows at the base of a nearby pine. The professor peered shortsightedly at the tree while he fumbled in his breast pocket for his spectacles. Before he could find them the voice spoke again. "I'm deeply sorry, Doctor," it said, "but I'm afraid I will have to ask you to postpone your visit to America."

"Postpone," repeated the professor. "But why?"

"Because it will be necessary for you to come with me."

By this time the professor had succeeded in getting his spectacles out of his case and nervously slid them over his nose. His brow creased with perplexity. "You will forgive me," the voice continued, "if I remain where I am, but I prefer not to be seen by anyone other than yourself." Then, for the first time, the professor saw. His look of perplexity gave place to one of wonder which slowly grew into an expression that was almost pure excitement.

"But of course," he said agitatedly, "of course. Certainly! My plane is of no significance whatsoever. *But what,"* he added breathlessly, as the shadow crossed his face, *"what could you possibly want with me!"*

A few minutes later at the farthest limits of Russian power in Asia, another encounter took place. In the darkest hours of the evening a young Russian soldier by the name of Ivan Godofsky was on guard duty at a highly secret military installation in Vladivostok. As part of his regulation equipment he was carrying an automatic weapon similar to the British Sten gun. Sometime during the late hours of the watch, he heard a noise in the darkness of the courtyard opposite him and was accosted in Russian. Since he saw no one, he challenged the voice and, instead of the required password, was rewarded by the sound of measured footsteps approaching him. He made a second challenge and, when it too was ignored, fired the entire clip of his automatic rifle into empty air. The Russians, with customary thoroughness, know the bullets were fired into empty air because the place where they were fired was enclosed and every bullet was subsequently recovered.

The fifth and final encounter took place on a small Chinese farm near the village of Ho Chin in the foothills of the Kunlun Mountains in the province of Tsinghai, China. A few minutes before the incident, the farm had been looted and burned. The Communists insist that the attackers were brigands; there are others who insist they were Communist hirelings. Whatever the story, the owners of the farm and their teen-age son were shot. Two older brothers were abducted and an eighteen-year-old girl by the name of Su Tan was raped. Her clothes were torn and she was badly beaten; presumably she was believed dead.

She was left lying on the ground outside the flaming lean-to which had once served as a barn. It was with this Chinese girl that the being or beings from outer space made their fifth, and, so far as is known, the last of their individual contacts with the people of Earth.

It is remarkable in retrospect to realize that the abduction of five people in five different locations throughout the world could have been carried out without a single witness. The fact remains that it was done. In the light of later revelations, the reasons for the lack of an immediate hue and cry are self-evident, but the manner in which the contacts were made and the subsequent revelations about the meeting between the Aliens and these five citizens of the Earth still stagger the imagination. It appeared impossible, on the basis of our understanding, that the meetings actually took place, because, so far as we know, none of the victims ever left the earth. They never left it, that is, according to our limited conception of time, but perhaps the story is better told without conjectures, exactly the way it happened.

2

Eve Wingate remembers nothing from the moment she crumpled on the sands of an English beach until she regained consciousness under circumstances which came close to inducing a state of extreme shock. She awakened to find herself lying on a couch, still clad in her bathing suit, her body dripping wet as it had been when she emerged from the sea. Her left leg and side were covered with damp sand and her forearm and elbow were red and painful where they had rasped the beach as she fell. She sat bolt upright, staring around her in terror.

She was in a room of strange and incredible beauty. The floor was a deep sea green, so vivid in color and so resembling the surface of the ocean itself that she had to touch it with her toes before she could believe it was actually solid. It was warm and resilient beneath her bare feet and, when she stood up, it absorbed the moisture from her soles without leaving a trace. She looked across the floor to where it was broken by the base of a column and caught her breath as her eyes traveled upward. The column was a mighty feather of spume surging up out of the emerald floor. It was so perfect in conception that any second she expected it to come crashing down in an explosion of white thunder. It was as if some inhuman sorcery had forced that mighty welter of water up out of the ocean depths and then frozen it at the precise moment of its most breathtaking grandeur. There were six identical columns arranged in a circle and their tops disappeared into a mist of pale frosted light. A soft radiance in the faintest pastels shone through the mist so that, from her standpoint, the impression was that of being imprisoned in the heart of a diamond . . . a giant crystal whose outer facets were filtering rainbows into its heart.

Eve tore her eyes away from her surroundings and made a desperate effort to get herself under control. Her body had a strange feeling of lightness, but other than this she seemed to be unhurt and relatively rational. Her sole link with reality came with the discovery that she was not alone. Around her, on couches similar to her own, arranged at the bases of the circular group of columns, were four other human beings. All of them were sleeping. She forced herself to approach the nearest figure and found herself looking down at the immobile face of a young Chinese girl. There was blood trickling slowly from one corner of the girl's mouth and the shoulder of her dress was torn loose, revealing raw ugly scratches that could not have been made more than a few moments previously. For a second, Eve thought the girl was dead, and then she noticed the rhythmic movements of her breast beneath the torn quilting of the gown. Eve fought the speculations which forced themselves into her consciousness and hurried to the next couch. As she leaned toward the young soldier who lay there, her thigh touched the barrel of the gun which was resting beside him and she cried out in pain. The metal was red-hot. There was panic inside her now. The last faint hope that all this might be a dream was gone. The angry red weal on her thigh was not of the stuff of which dreams are made.

The next couch bore the figure of a small man in late middle age. He had a round, almost cherubic face with apple-red cheeks, a blunt little nose, and a halo of white hair around his bald pate, and he was, incredible as it seemed, wearing spats. Eve had a definite sensation that this face was familiar–very familiar–but in her anxiety she could not remember where or when she had seen it before.

The last couch revealed a tall and not unhandsome young man. He had unruly dark blond hair, a good mouth, and a square determined chin softened by a deep cleft. But the nose was the outstanding feature. In some uncanny fashion, it managed to fit, even to complement, the face, but it was overlarge and it looked as if it had been chiseled out of granite by a sculptor in a hurry. It was a strong and egotistical face. Under any other circumstances it might have been appealing. As it was, the only reassuring fact was that it looked, if not English, at least Anglo-Saxon. It slept on blissfully unaware of Eve's presence. She felt tears of hopeless confusion coming into her eyes and she sank down to the side of the couch, her heart pounding. She was close to hysteria, when the man beside her stirred. She remained where she was, too terrified to speak or even to move. She saw his eyes open. For a long second, they gazed upward to where the ceiling seemed to melt into silver nothingness. Then suddenly the man sat upright; his eyes ranged about the room, and finally came to rest on her in furious astonishment. It was probably the first time in history that a young man's eyes had rested on Eve Wingate in a bathing suit without taking the slightest recognition of anything but the fact that she was another human being. He opened his mouth twice as if to speak and closed it both times without saying anything. Finally he noticed the other figures and made a move to get up. Eve found her voice.

"It's no use," she said huskily. "They're all asleep."

The man looked at her perplexed, in the manner of one who doesn't understand something and doesn't quite know why. "Who are they?"

"I don't know. There's a Chinese girl over there who's been beaten; a Russian, at least I think he's a Russian; and a little old man who looks familiar, but I . . ."

Jonathan got up from his couch, looked at the soldier and the girl, glanced briefly at the third figure, came back and sat down. "What are they doing here? Where are we?"

She shook her head.

"All right, then, what are *you* doing here?" His voice was angry.

"I tell you, *I don't know!* I woke up just before you did."

He put a hand over his eyes and rubbed them, then shook his head and took his hand away. The room was still there—the girl was still there. He let his mind go back to that split second before he lost consciousness and an impossible idea exploded in his brain. He looked sharply at the girl.

"Look," he said, "did you see . . . ?" His voice trailed off into nothing. He couldn't put it into words. He shook his head again.

There was a pause. It seemed to go on forever. The insane, impossible idea came back demanding to be accepted. He pushed it aside. The girl was staring at him, expecting him to do something. He made an effort to bring himself back to reality and found himself seeing the girl for the first time. His eyes took in the brief two-piece bathing suit which, by concealing a little, emphasized a lot. She was slightly above average height and her face was framed with damp close-cropped auburn curls. Her eyes were a deep clear green under enormous lashes, and she had that indescribably beautiful complexion which is the heritage of most English women. At the moment, however, the fierce tension in her face and body told him that she was almost at the breaking point. He searched for something to say, feigning a calmness he was far from feeling. The sound of her accent impinged on his inner ear. "You're English, aren't you?" he managed finally.

The banality and unexpectedness of the remark brought her to herself. The faintest suggestion of a dimple appeared in her left cheek and she showed small, perfect teeth in the ghost of a smile. "How did you guess?"

He pulled at the lobe of his ear in embarrassment. "I had to say something." He held out his hand. "I'm Jonathan Clark."

Her small hand was swallowed in his enormous one as she extended it. "And I'm Eve Wingate." The attempt at lightness in her voice was belied by the trembling of the fingers Jonathan held in his own. She made no effort to withdraw her hand. It was as if she sensed in Jonathan something solid and indestructible to which she could cling.

He extricated his hand. "Take it easy," he said. "It will all work out somehow. We can't both be having hallucinations. There's got to be some explanation."

"I agree with you, Mr. Clark." The voice had a strong German accent. They swung around to see the little man on the neighboring couch sitting up smiling at them. "Excuse me for intruding," he continued, "but we seem to be thrown together whether we like it or not." He rubbed a plump hand over his bald pate in a gesture of obvious embarrassment at their stares. Jonathan looked at him wonderingly.

"Now I know I'm crazy. You're Professor Klaus Bochner!"

The professor blushed. "I'm afraid so."

Eve looked from one to the other. "Not *the* Professor Bochner," she exclaimed, and then rushed on to cover her confusion. "But of course you are. That's why your face looked so familiar! I'd have known immediately if all this weren't so—so . . . Professor, what in the name of heaven are we doing here?"

The professor shook his head and began to tug at his right eyebrow. "I'm afraid I don't know any more about that than you do, but if we are to accept the facts . . ." He broke off and turned to Jonathan. "I hope you will forgive me," he said self-consciously, "but I couldn't help overhearing your conversation. You started to ask the young lady if she had seen something before she arrived here. You didn't finish the question and she didn't answer it, but I gathered from both your attitudes that she *had* seen something and so had you. Something that one could scarcely explain away as a normal visual experience?"

Jonathan's eyes met Eve's. Hers were wide and frightened. Her lower lip trembled and she nodded her head.

"We saw something," Jonathan admitted grimly.

The professor nodded and his eyes took in the two recumbent figures on the couches. "I think we can take it for granted that the same thing happened to all of us."

Eve gasped. "Then you saw something too?"

"Yes."

"But it just *can't* be possible."

Jonathan stood up abruptly. "Let's stop beating around the bush," he said angrily. "What we're all afraid to say is that we think we've been kidnaped by bug-eyed monsters." He glared first at the professor and then finally at Eve. "Isn't that it?"

Eve swallowed. "I—I suppose so."

"Well, damn it, we all know that *can't* be true, so there has to be some other explanation. . . . *Well, hasn't there?*"

The professor began massaging his head. It was, like the eyebrow tugging, an unconscious gesture which generally brought restrained smiles to the faces of his colleagues. It was lost on the two young people in front of him. After a moment he stopped rubbing and spoke quietly. "I know it is all so highly improbable that the mind refuses to accept the facts. But what else can we do but accept them? All of us, or at least the three of us here, were visited by entities which defy description in our normal frame of reference. If your experiences parallel my own, you remember nothing from the moment of encounter until you awakened here in this room, which, I am sure, is like no room that any of us has ever seen." Jonathan stopped pacing and Eve sat very still. "There is another very disturbing fact about all this," the professor continued. "Unless I am mistaken, we come from all over the world." He looked at Eve. "For instance, young lady, may I ask where you were when this happened?"

"I was on the beach."

The professor's smile was unexpectedly mischievous. "So I noticed," he said. In spite of the situation Eve blushed. "But where?"

"At Torquay on the south coast of England."

The professor turned. "And you, young man?"

"Pasadena, California."

"And I," said the professor, "was leaving a scientific meeting in Heidelberg to catch a plane for America. All of which should make the time interval extremely interesting. What time was it, young man, when you received your–ah–visitor?"

Jonathan frowned. "About four-thirty in the morning, I guess–the birds had just started to sing."

"And you, young lady," said the professor, "what time would you say it was when you were taking your swim?"

"I don't know precisely, but it must have been about half after twelve."

"Yeees!" said the professor somewhat absently and lapsed into silence.

"Well?" Eve prompted after a reasonable interval.

The professor started, shook his head again. "I left the reception at Heidelberg at exactly one-twenty," he said thoughtfully. "Now, if I remember my zones correctly, there should be eight hours' difference between Pasadena and Torquay, and about one hour's difference between Torquay and Heidelberg."

Eve gasped. "Then that means that this happened to all of us at about the same time."

"It seems probable," the professor said and turned to Jonathan. "You said it was about four-thirty in Pasadena. What time is it now?" Jonathan glanced at his watch and looked up dumfounded. Without saying anything he lifted his arm and held the instrument against his ear. When he spoke, his voice was somewhat strained. "It says twenty-seven minutes past four and it hasn't stopped running." He held out the watch for their inspection. "Look!" The second hand was pulsing regularly as if trying to break some invisible barrier.

There was a hush and then Eve whispered, "Professor, when I awoke I was still wet. And that Chinese girl over there, her mouth was bleeding. And the Russian boy, I burned my leg on the barrel of his gun. Look." She pointed to the red mark on her thigh.

"But it's impossible!" Jonathan stormed. "If what you're saying is true, it means we were brought here from all over the world in a matter of seconds."

"There seems to be no doubt about it," the professor said softly.

There was a sound from the opposite side of the room and all three turned to see the Russian standing by the side of the couch, looking at them with the same shocked and bewildered eyes that had characterized Eve and Jonathan on awakening. And, at almost the same moment, the Chinese girl moved quietly and sat up.

Then, from the emptiness of the room, a rich, resonant voice spoke.

3

"Ladies and gentlemen, now that you are all awake, permit me to interrupt you long enough to explain your presence here and to apologize for the peremptory manner in which you were brought to us. The reasons, as you will hear presently, are, I hope, serious enough to warrant somewhat unusual methods." The professor made a movement toward Jonathan and Eve. "There is no need for you to interpret, Professor," the voice interrupted. "Each of you is hearing these words in his or her native tongue."

The professor spun around. *"Mein Gott,"* he said. "You are hearing it in English?" Eve nodded in unison with Jonathan. "And you in Russian?" the professor asked, turning to the soldier. It was not quite clear whether the Russian understood the words but he certainly understood the question. He nodded his head violently. "And I in German," the professor marveled. "Incredible!"

"My disclosures to you," the voice continued, "will make you the most sought after, the most responsible, and perhaps the most hated people on Terra. On you, fortunately or unfortunately, however you choose to view the situation, will depend the future of your world, and possibly of ours. It grieves me deeply that you should be burdened with this responsibility without your wish or consent, but there was, and is, no other alternative. You were selected almost entirely at random from several of the greater earthly nations by five of my youthful colleagues. Lest it should disturb you to be in doubt as to your whereabouts, you are, as some of you have already surmised, the guests of a race that is not of the planet Earth. You are on a space ship from the heart of the Galaxy. You are traveling through space at such a speed that no measurable time interval has yet passed on earth, to which you will presently be returned, completely unharmed." As the voice paused to allow the five to absorb the import of what it had said, there was a stunned silence. Then Jonathan broke the stillness.

"May I ask a question?"

"Ask."

"If all this is not some kind of a hoax, why can't we see you?"

The voice replied in the same controlled register. "If it will make this interview any easier for you, something will be arranged." There was a soft whirring, and a section of the wall at one end of the room slid back, and the group, as one, gasped in overwhelming surprise. Seated on an enormous chair on a low dais, backed by something that resembled black velvet, was an overpowering figure. But the fact which had drawn the incredulous reaction from all of them was that the figure was human. It was a man! A man whose perfectly proportioned body dwarfed Jonathan's six-foot frame to the proportions of a midget. There was a massive leonine head with perfectly chiseled features complemented by a short crop of tumbling silver curls. He was dressed in some dark, shimmering material whose texture rippled like swiftly moving black water. But what was most impressive about the figure was neither its size nor its perfect features, but an aura of intellect which emanated from it in such tangible waves that the five people of earth were struck by a feeling which was akin to awe. The eyes were a deep unearthly blue, giving the face a look of infinite warmth and gentleness.

"You asked that one of us be present at this interview," the figure began. "Since my natural shape would undoubtedly have caused some consternation among you, I have tried to put before you a figure to whom you can speak without feeling a sense of revulsion. I realize that my proportions are somewhat larger than those of a normal human being, but in other respects I hope I meet with your approval." The figure on the dais smiled ever so faintly. The effect was magical. "I will take your silence for agreement," he said gently. "Only the eldest of our race are truly skilled in what you earthlings might call metamorphosis, and the clumsy attempts of my young associates to contact you in human form must, in some instances, have been quite terrifying. The young lady, I believe, found herself confronted by a being about eleven feet tall with green hair and a third eye which, if I am correctly informed, kept drifting around at will."

There was a choked syllable which bore a faint relation to the word "Yes" from Eve.

"For this, young lady, I apologize, and also to the rest of you. It was an unforgivable breach of good manners, to say the least. Your contours, I may add, are almost unique in the Galaxy, and are not easy to duplicate. Only one of my agents had the good sense not to try to approximate human shape and appeared in his natural form. The professor received him with somewhat less shock than the rest of you. You must realize by now that we are not of your world. We come not even from your universe, but from another sun in this Galaxy, from what the people of earth call 'the stars.' My people and my world existed billions of years before your earth was born, and now my universe is dying. Perhaps this is as it should be; in everything there is a cycle of birth and death. One world dies and another is born. And yet, I think I need not remind you that among all races, as among almost all individuals, the most basic instinct is that of self-preservation. It is in some ways much easier to accept one's own death than it is to accept the end of one's race and heritage. That is the reason for my presence here. Within thirty of your earthly days, our sun is going into Nova, which means the total destruction of our planet and our civilization. We must, therefore, find a new world to which we may emigrate and our time is short."

"An invasion!" The two words tumbled from Jonathan's lips over the indignant outburst of his companions.

"No." The single word cut off further protests. "At least, not in the sense you mean it, young man. Your people are only now contemplating travel in space. It may interest you to know that all the planets in the Galaxy old enough to have produced life, and capable of supporting it, are inhabited. Thus the problem of finding a new home is not an easy one, and we have no time in which to prepare a dead world for habitation. For this reason, we have been observing your planet for several hours, though your governments stubbornly insist that our 'star ships' are the result of mistakes and mass hallucinations."

"For several hours!" the professor said. "But the first reported sightings date back to the year 1600."

"You must forgive me," the voice explained, "I meant for several of *our* hours, which is to say, in the neighborhood of four hundred earthly years."

"Incredible." The professor did a swift mental calculation. "Then your life span must be about half a million years!"

"Yes." The word sounded slightly apologetic.

The guttural voice of the Russian broke in for the first time. When he had finished speaking, the presence replied in a slightly firmer tone. "No, my son, I am *not* deliberately evading your question. I will say again we have no intention of invading your planet. Our ethic does not permit us to invade or destroy another civilization, even at the risk of the total extinction of our own. However, we have observed that since the inception of your race you have indulged in a form of self-destruction which you call War and at this moment, having made the initial conquest of the atom, you are at last in a position to wipe out not only yourselves, but all life forms on earth. There is no intelligence within the cosmos strong enough to predict the absolute future of any race, but we know that the probability of your total eclipse by atomic war is very close to one hundred per cent. Therefore, we have approached the Galactic Council with a plan. The Council has approved this plan on the basis of the fact that, at this time, our race is infinitely more valuable to the Galactic Union than yours. The Council has given us permission to put into your hands weapons which will materially facilitate your urge to self-obliteration without harming your beautiful planet or its wealth of flora and fauna with lethal radiation. The weapon is not explosive, so it will have no effect whatsoever on the planet itself or on your homes, factories, or other constructions. This weapon will be lent to you for a period of twenty-seven earthly days. If, by the end of this time, you have not used it, it will automatically become harmless. Your race will live and mine will probably die. We shall attempt no form of external coercion to induce you to use the weapon we have given you. If any pressures are exerted, they will come from your own people."

The professor stepped forward. "May I ask a question?"

"Certainly."

The professor frowned. "I want to be quite sure that I follow you. As I understand it, you are going to give us a weapon capable of destroying the human race, and you expect us, *without external coercion,* to use this weapon against each other?"

The figure on the dais nodded almost imperceptibly. "I can understand your incredulity, Professor. We, too, find the proposition that any race would knowingly destroy itself untenable, but our computers, fed on the records of your racial history, insist that there is a better than 50 per cent possibility of this weapon being used within twenty-seven days, if it is put into your hands now. We wish you to understand that we do not hope this catastrophe will come about; we merely–expect it. On the other hand, if you can resist the internal forces of aggression for twenty-seven days, we will depart. You will forgive me if I sound callous in my bluntness, but I have no time for subtleties. Yes, Professor?"

"You spoke of a Galactic Council–what is this council?"

"A body comprising the greatest intellects of thirty thousand intelligent worlds."

The professor swallowed. "Such a meeting was called to consider *our* problem?"

The Alien nodded gravely. "And *ours,* Professor."

The professor shook his head, trying to stretch the fingers of his mind around the concept of thirty thousand worlds peopled by intelligent life, and then, with an obvious effort, forced himself back to the immediate problem.

"Let me be clear on another point. If we do use this weapon against each other and destroy life on earth, you will then occupy our planet?"

"That is correct."

"Suppose that only a portion of the population is eliminated, what then? Will you still take over the earth?"

"The Galactic Council has decreed that, unless two thirds of your planet is freed of human life, we may not enter. Should this happen, we will share the earth with the remaining third, but they will remain completely free of us and our domination."

Eve's voice was tense with emotion as she spoke, "I'm almost afraid to ask this question, but–to whom are you intending to give this weapon?"

"To each of you."

"Oh, no!"

"What if we refuse to take it?" Jonathan said, a sharp edge of anger in his voice.

"Then it will be given to the rulers of all your nations. At the advice of the Galactic Council, we offer it to you five first–because it has been said, with some justice, that it has never been the people themselves that cause a war, but their leaders. If you refuse to accept this charge, we have no choice but to put the weapon in the hands of those who, I am afraid, will be less scrupulous about its use."

"The ultimate ultimatum," whispered the professor.

"Will you accept it?"

The professor glanced inquiringly at the other four. It was Jonathan who answered. "Look, you can't just ask us to make up our minds whether we will accept the responsibility for our entire race like that. You've got to give us time to discuss it among ourselves."

The leonine head of the Alien surveyed them thoughtfully for a few seconds. "Very well," he said finally. "However, I must remind you that for me and my people time is running short. I shall give you a period which will seem to you the equivalent of one earthly hour. By then, you must reach a final decision to accept the weapon. Otherwise, I shall be forced to take the alternative and place it in the hands of your various governments. Should you reach a decision before the allotted time, you have only to call. I shall leave you alone."

The large panels of the walls slid slowly into place, returning them to privacy. The five of them stood motionless, overcome with the immensity of the message they had received. Finally, Eve found her voice. "Professor, do you really think all of this is–is possible?"

"If we are to believe the evidence of our senses, I don't see what other construction to put upon it. It is highly unlikely we are all having the same hallucination."

"I don't believe it," Jonathan broke in, but his tone held more anger than conviction. "I'll admit it looks that way, but it's got to be some kind of a hoax, particularly all that hogwash about no time having passed on earth."

The professor took out his glasses and began to polish them absently. "The extreme relativity of time could make your stand on that specific point a little dangerous, Jonathan."

"You mean," Eve said, "that such a thing is actually possible?"

The professor shook his head uncertainly. "Only the lack of a sufficiently powerful fuel for our rockets prevents us from running into the weird phenomenon of time warp."

"You mean that wasn't just hokum he was talking?" Jonathan interjected.

"Not necessarily. We know today, for instance, of the opposite kind of time warp, namely, that time, as we measure it, slows down as the speed of motion increases."

"I can't believe it," Eve exclaimed. "You mean to say that if I drive my car at one hundred miles an hour, time is actually passing more slowly for me than if I were walking?"

"Well, yes," the professor answered, "except that at such slow speeds the change is so small as to be immeasurable. However—" He broke off, staring thoughtfully into space.

"However?" Jonathan prompted.

The professor started. "Excuse me, I'm afraid my mind was elsewhere. However, for a person traveling at or near the speed of light, which, as you know, is just slightly over a hundred and eighty-six thousand miles per second, the difference in time flow would be so great that, during what would appear to him as the passage of one year, something like two hundred and fifty million years would pass on earth."

"You can't be serious," Eve said.

"If this is true, how come the public doesn't know about it?" Jonathan demanded.

The professor sighed. "Unfortunately, a large portion of the public isn't interested."

"Then it is possible," Eve exclaimed, "for a couple of million years to have passed back on earth, if we were traveling fast enough."

"Not quite," the professor replied. "We have not been here long enough for more than a few hundred years to have passed, even at the speed of light. The thing that puzzles me, however, is that the kind of time warp we are talking about seems to be in the wrong direction—unless . . ."

"Unless what?" Jonathan said.

"Unless the theory held by some is true."

"And what is that?"

"Simply that if time slows down as it approaches the speed of light it should stop entirely as the speed of light is reached, and go backward once this point is passed. Up to now, this theory has seemed to me to be thoroughly implausible, but, if the Aliens have somehow succeeded in surpassing the speed of light, it is not inconceivable that they might be able to return us to earth before this whole thing happened or at least to make the time lapse during our absence almost imperceptible. If it is true that they come from another star system, there can be no doubt that they have developed some sort of hyperspace drive to bridge the millions of light years between their planet and ours, though how this can be managed without converting their ships and themselves into pure energy is beyond me."

The professor lapsed into silent contemplation of the problem until Eve interrupted. "Professor, Jonathan, let's forget about everything else. We've only got an hour. Are we going to accept this horrible bomb, or aren't we?"

The professor came out of his reverie. "Precisely, my dear," he said. "The point is, do we have any choice?"

"Wouldn't it be better to let them give it to the governments as they suggest? At least they'd know what to do with it."

"Would they?" Jonathan said gloomily. "Look where they've put us already with a weapon far less powerful than this one. Do you really believe they're capable of not using it, or are you just ducking the responsibility?"

"That's not fair," Eve protested. "I didn't ask to be brought here. I don't want the responsibility for the rest of my race on my shoulders."

"*You* don't want it?" Jonathan's tone was caustic. "Do you think the rest of us are turning handsprings for joy? Why is it that all women have to assess every situation in terms of personal inconvenience?"

Eve's eyes flashed fire. "I've always heard that Americans were the rudest people in the world. You've just proved it."

"Oh, for the love of Mike! We're sitting on a volcano and all she can think of is that I'm rude."

"I've got plenty of reasons. You've done nothing but snarl at that man up there ever since you saw him."

"What do you want me to do?" Jonathan countered. "Kiss his feet because he wants to help us kill ourselves?"

"If all Americans are like you, thank God your government isn't getting the weapon!"

"I suppose Her Majesty's people would know exactly how to handle it!" said Jonathan bitingly. "You've always been a peace-loving little group—ever since you started collecting the world!"

"You dropped the atom on Hiroshima—we didn't!"

"Please, please," the professor broke in. "Do not quarrel. We have so little time. And both of you are right. Miss Wingate, I am sure, expresses all our sentiments when she says she does not want the responsibility. And you, Mr. Clark, also have a point when you say we have very little choice in the matter. If we are agreed that the weapon should not be placed in the hands of our respective governments, then we must perforce retain it among ourselves."

Eve was still smoldering, but she tried hard not to show it. "Couldn't we make a pact?" she asked. "I mean, couldn't we decide among the five of us here to keep this a secret and not reveal to anyone that we have the bomb, or whatever it is, until the twenty-seven days are up?"

"The three of us could," Jonathan said coldly, "but what about him?" He looked toward the Russian, who was sitting alone on his couch, hands on knees, gazing at the floor.

"For that matter, what about her?" Eve countered, pointing to the Chinese girl. "She looks as if she had every reason to hate the whole world. But that doesn't mean we can't try. Does anybody speak Chinese or Russian?"

The professor and Jonathan both shook their heads.

"Then we can't even ask them if they'll join us."

"What good would it do?" Jonathan demanded. "How do we know the Russian wouldn't agree to the plan and then give the bomb to the Central Committee as soon as he got back to earth? How do we know any of us will keep our word?"

The professor put his spectacles on, took them off again, breathed on them, and slipped them back on his nose without wiping them. "We don't," he said after a long pause. "But, on the other hand, if we could make an agreement, as the young lady suggests, it would at least be a step in the right direction."

Jonathan turned his head and looked at the Russian. Eve and the professor followed his gaze. Suddenly Jonathan stood up, crossed the room, and stuck out his hand. "We're all in this together," he said to the soldier awkwardly. "I'm Jonathan Clark."

The Russian looked up from the floor and saw the outstretched hand. He understood the gesture. He got to his feet, his face creased in the beginnings of a smile. He squeezed Jonathan's hand warmly.

The reaction took Jonathan by surprise. He made a broad gesture of invitation toward the professor and Eve. "Won't you join us?"

The Russian approached Eve and held out his hand. "Ivan," he said eagerly. "Ivan Godofsky." His face had lost the grim and anxious look it had worn up to now. Eve saw that he was scarcely more than a boy–a frightened one. She had somehow pictured all Russian soldiers as stone-faced automatons. This pink-cheeked, self-conscious youth could easily have been her brother and she felt a wave of compassion well up in her.

"Eve," she said. "Eve Wingate," and pressed his hand firmly between her own.

The Russian turned to go through the ritual again with the professor, and Eve gave Jonathan a cold stare. "Well, you made it four," she said. "I'll see if I can make it five." She got up and went over to where the Chinese girl sat alone on her couch. Her method of approach was simpler than Jonathan's. She took the Chinese girl by the hand, smiled warmly, and led her over to the assembled company. There she pointed in turn to the professor, Jonathan, and the Russian, and spoke their names. At each introduction the Chinese girl took the proffered hand timidly and whispered, "Su Tan."

"Well," said Eve, "here we are. What's next?"

Jonathan grunted, stepped a foot or so away from the group, and bent down, pointing to a nonexistent object on the floor. He threw up his hands, shouted "boom!" and staggered backward. He pointed again at the original spot and said, "Bomb. Understand?" He looked at the

Chinese girl and Ivan. He held out his hand palm upward and pointed to it. "Bomb. Get it?" They nodded.

"I have an idea," Eve said, forgetting her pique in the excitement. "I'll try to take it away from you and you resist. Haven't you got something that could represent the bomb?" Jonathan fished in his pocket, brought out the stub of a pencil, and laid it on his palm.

She pointed to the pencil. "Bomb," she said. "Boom!" And made a gesture of explosion. They nodded. Then she turned back to Jonathan and reached for the "bomb." Jonathan closed his hand over the pencil, put his arms behind his back, and shook his head in negation. Eve looked around, saw the Russian's gun leaning against the couch. She picked it up and pointed it menacingly at Jonathan.

"Go easy with that thing!" he whispered. "It might go off!"

She smiled icily. "Don't be such a coward," she said. "I thought all Americans were heroes."

Out of the corner of his eye, Jonathan saw the professor trying to suppress a smile. It occurred to him that he would derive considerable satisfaction from being able to wring this girl's lovely little neck, but, before he could put the thought into words, she rammed the gun muzzle into his stomach muscles. He closed his eyes and winced. When he opened them, she was smiling demurely.

"Yes?" she said innocently.

Jonathan gritted his teeth and swung his head back and forth in melodramatic refusal, still holding the pencil behind him.

"Fine," Eve said in the tone of a tolerant teacher approving a backward student. "Now give the pencil to the professor."

Jonathan glared. He was on the verge of a beautiful explosion. He opened his mouth to tell her exactly what he thought when he felt the professor's fingers touching his arm. Reluctantly, he handed over the pencil. Eve turned away to point the gun at the professor, who drew himself up to his full five feet three inches and shook his head back and forth so violently that the halo of white hair stood out almost horizontally. Then, with an almost courtly gesture, he turned and offered the pencil to Su Tan. The Chinese girl took it silently and when threatened with the gun, closed the delicate olive fingers and moved her head almost imperceptibly. When it was over, she stood quietly holding the pencil until Eve gently removed it from her fingers and passed it to

Ivan. The boy stared at it for a long moment, and then his eyes came up to meet theirs. His face was pale and he moistened his lips with the tip of his tongue. It was painfully apparent that, for Ivan, this was no simple decision. Eve felt a sudden terrifying emptiness in the pit of her stomach. For the first time, the enormity of the decisions they were all making so blithely struck home. If anything went wrong now, the repercussions would be world wide, and for Ivan they could well be fatal. He glanced down at the pencil again and Eve felt the gun growing heavy in her grasp. She began to think he was going to refuse when suddenly he reached out, grasped the muzzle of the weapon and placed it against his chest.

"Nyet," he said.

Eve exhaled in relief and tossed the gun to the nearest couch, then took the boy's hand understandingly. Suddenly, a third hand was placed upon theirs. Eve looked up to find the professor smiling gravely.

"You were fine," he said. He looked toward Jonathan. "Both of you."

Jonathan glared for a moment and then abruptly grinned wryly. He took a step forward and placed his hand on theirs. "All for one and one for all," he said.

Their eyes turned toward Su Tan. She was standing as if in a trance, her face expressionless, her eyes distant. Then, as if some sixth sense had told her she was observed, she moved her head slowly in their direction. She saw the four clasped hands and came toward them. Like a small green-gold butterfly, her hand drifted down to rest on theirs. A strange, almost primitive rite, yet there was no mistaking its meaning. They were pledged to a common cause. The world's first pact among its simple peoples to preserve the dignity of man.

The professor broke the silence. "I think we have done all we can. Shall we announce our decision?"

"Yes," Eve said. "Let's get it over with. You call him, Professor."

The professor walked to the center of the room. In a loud, clear voice, he said, "We have decided. We accept your charge."

As the professor finished speaking, the lights in the enormous room began to dim until the scene was lit only by a faint glow which seemed to emanate from the panels concealing the Alien's dais. Unexpectedly, in front of this panel and backlit by its glow, five shadowy obelisks rose silently out of the floor. At the apex of each obelisk was a small, square platform surmounted by a dark semicircle. When the platforms had raised themselves to approximately the height of a high table, all motion stopped. Then with startling abruptness, a lance of light seared down from the ceiling and flared on the central platform. The dark semicircle surmounting the platform was now a translucent bubble of iridescent beauty enveloping a small black box. As they watched, four more shafts of light pierced the gloom until each obelisk was bathed in a pillar of brilliant incandescence. The panels concealing the Alien's dais whirred quietly backward revealing the Alien still seated.

"People of Earth," he said, "you have shown courage. It has ever been one of your greatest assets. On the pedestals before you are five small boxes. You will each take one of them."

The group moved forward hesitantly. In their concern over whether or not to accept the Alien weapon, it had not occurred to any of them to consider what form the weapon would take. The realization that it was probably contained within the tiny receptacles before them was deeply disquieting. Sensing their uneasiness, the Alien smiled.

"The boxes are perfectly safe. You may accept them with confidence."

The reassurance was not entirely convincing. If the Alien had spoken the truth, the boxes they had been asked to handle contained sufficient power to destroy the human race. For the moment, only Jonathan managed to overcome his reluctance. He moved forward until he stood directly in front of the central obelisk. The iridescent bubble surrounding the box resembled nothing so much as the films of soap he had so often blown with a pipe when he was a child. He stretched a tentative hand toward the bubble and felt a strange tingling in the tips of his fingers. He advanced a hand a little farther and found to his intense surprise that it was impossible to touch the opalescent surface. He tried again. It was as if he were pushing against a stone wall. The more he strove to advance his hand, the stronger the tingling in his fingers. That was all. He raised his eyes questioningly toward the Alien, who was watching him with interest.

"Forgive me, Mr. Clark. I could have forewarned you, but I preferred to let you see for yourself. That particular box belongs to Miss

Wingate. You will find that your hand can only penetrate the force field of the box attuned to your own electrical impulse. The one to your left is yours, Mr. Clark."

Jonathan moved over to the adjacent obelisk and this time his hand passed through the force field without the slightest resistance. He withdrew the box and looked at it as the other four moved into their places. For a brief second before Eve took the box on her pedestal her eyes met Jonathan's, then resolutely she lifted the box through its translucent shield and stared at it. It was light, surprisingly so, because the material comprising it was obviously quite thick and looked like black jade. It had a transparent cover of some clear plastic and beneath the cover, resting on what appeared to be a type of spun glass, lay three intricately worked golden capsules. Before she had time to examine them further, the Alien spoke again.

"You hold in your hands," he said, "the power of life and death. The properties of these boxes may very well seem like magic to you, but I assure you they operate on strictly scientific principles, though," the voice continued with a trace of gentle amusement, "the science is somewhat more advanced than your own. Each box, as you have seen, contains three golden capsules. Each capsule has many thousands of times the energy of an X-bomb, which I understand is your present most powerful weapon. Each capsule has a circular destruction area the diameter of which is exactly three thousand statute miles. As I said before, they are completely harmless to anything except human life and there is no dangerous residual radiation. Within their lethal area there is no possible method of protection known to the people of Earth which will permit them to escape instant and painless death. Each capsule is so designed that the ultimate responsibility for the release of its lethal energy is solely yours. Each of them is tuned to the electrical impulse of the owner. There is no possible way for this box to be opened except for the owner to wish it opened. It operates on the owner's particular encephalographic waves. You may take my word for it that there is no force on earth capable of opening one of these boxes without your consent. Once it is opened, however, the rest is simple. You have only to remove the tiny spindle at the end of each capsule, speak loudly and clearly the latitude and longitude of the target, and the energy will be launched. Thus, though you and you alone can open these boxes, any hand can pull the spindles and any voice can dispatch them to their target. Once this has been done, there is no way of recalling the bomb. I think further directions are unnecessary."

"And within twenty-seven days," asked the professor, "they become useless?"

"That is correct."

"One more question, please," the professor said. "Do we have your solemn word that if we succeed in keeping the peace for twenty-seven days, earth will be free of invasion forever?"

"You have my word, Professor, that neither my people nor any other of the known worlds will usurp your planet by forcible or other means as long as you still inhabit it. But I cannot guarantee that another may not come from outer space in search of conquest."

Ivan said something in Russian and the voice replied. "I mean, my son, that on the basis of the habitable planets already discovered, we know that the Galaxy must contain countless billions of intelligent worlds. In fact, every planet in the Galaxy capable of supporting life has produced intelligent life, but no nation or group of nations could begin to explore all the worlds even of this Galaxy. It would be like trying to count, one by one, the sands of the sea. As you encounter new individuals each day of your life, each galactic year we come into contact with hundreds of new worlds about whose existence we had no previous knowledge. Some of the life forms are ruthless killers. These our science has, so far, permitted us to deal with. But some day there may rise into space a race as heedless as your own with power even greater than ours. I leave you to imagine what the results of such an event might be."

"How do we know this whole thing isn't just a trick?" Jonathan said. "How do we know these bombs will really work?"

"I know of no way in which to prove this to you, since this particular weapon is not explosive. I could, of course, by the use of a different type of bomb, cause a gigantic explosion on some dead planet or even, if you like, on your own moon. But if you are truly skeptical you would merely believe I had created an optical illusion to support my falsehoods. No, my son, I am afraid you will just have to take my word for it that these tiny projectiles house a power undreamed of by earthly minds. In any case, the question is somewhat specious, because, if you firmly believe the capsules are worthless, they can do no harm one way or another. Are there any further questions?"

There was a pause while he waited for an answer. When no one spoke, he continued quietly, "People of Earth, I am sorry this meeting should have caused you unhappiness. I hope you will try to understand in the difficult days to come that it was not our wish to place you in this position. Now, if you will forgive me, time is short. If you will be kind enough to return to the couches on which you wakened, you will be sent back to Earth. Do not be frightened. The journey will be instantaneous and harmless. Thank you." The Alien stood up. Seated, he had been an imposing figure. Standing, he was overpowering; almost eleven feet of perfectly proportioned man. He smiled once, softly, and for all his grandeur, somewhat pathetically. Then the panels slid into place and masked him from sight. Silently, one by one, the five people of Earth walked slowly back to their couches and lay down. The lights dimmed, a deep hum began to pervade the room.

Suddenly Eve's voice came out of the darkness. "Jonathan, I'm scared. Jonathan, I forget your last name. Where do you live?"

"Clark," Jonathan said. "Pasadena, California."

Eve heard the last syllable of the word "California" as she was lying crumpled on the white sands of Torquay.

4

Eve's first reaction on awakening was one of intense relief. The white sand, the blue sky, her position on the beach, and the absence of anyone else in her vicinity convinced her that she had fallen asleep and had had a terrifying dream. The illusion ended suddenly when she found clutched in her right hand a small black box through whose transparent cover three tiny golden capsules glittered ominously.

For perhaps a minute she stood there gazing at the indisputable evidence that she really had undergone the experience she remembered. In the distance beyond the intervening headland, she could hear, faintly, the shouts of her companions. Any second one of them might swim around the rock in search of her and discover her holding the box. It was vitally important that no one see it. She had to get rid of it and quickly. She glanced upward. There was no one on the cliff above her, and the cove was deserted. She turned and ran up the beach to where the cliff and headland met and, kneeling down, began to dig. She was half panicky now and perspiring from effort. Suddenly she stopped. This was no good. The whole plan was ridiculous. Granted, if she dug deep enough, no storms could uncover the box and in this deserted cove the chances of a child digging it up were a billion to one.

But supposing something happened and the existence of the boxes was discovered? If the pressure became great enough, she might be forced to tell the authorities what she had done with the capsules.

Buried here they could always be retrieved and this was precisely what she didn't want. She must find a hiding place less accessible than this. She looked out toward the horizon. Swim out to sea? No. That left a margin for error. She couldn't get far enough out to be sure the box wouldn't wash ashore in a storm. But the sea was the answer. The Alien had said there was no power on earth capable of opening the box except her own mental waves. That probably meant it was indestructible.

If she couldn't, then, burn it, pulverize it, melt it, or vaporize it, she could at least put it where no one could ever find it. At the bottom of the ocean–far enough out and deep enough down so that no human agency could ever locate it and no storm or tide could hurl it back to the beach. Not ever! Well, perhaps in a hundred years, or a thousand, but certainly not in twenty-seven days. After that, it didn't matter. The box would be useless.

She stood up and pushed the tiny black box down as far as she could into the top of her two-piece bathing suit. Then she hurried across the beach, dived into the surf, and swam as strongly as she could, back around the rock to the beach where she had left her friends. Obviously, no great length of time had passed, because they were still pursuing the same game of beach ball from which she had escaped a few minutes earlier. She ran up to one of the young men.

"Harry," she said sharply, "is your motorboat running?"

He turned to her, surprised. "Yes. Why?"

"I want to use it." She brushed past him, picked up her purse from a beach blanket, and took out a coin. Harry frowned, confused by her voice and manner.

"You want to use the boat *now?*"

"Yes–right after I make a phone call."

He stared at her. "Look here, Eve, are you all right?"

"Of course I'm all right."

"But, I—"

"Harry, I haven't time to explain now. I must make that phone call!" She left him and ran up the beach toward the phone booth near the road. The beach ball bounced off his shoulder and somebody shouted, "Come on, Harry–wake up!" He waved an impatient hand in the direction of the voice and then started up the beach after Eve.

The phone booth was reached, from the opposite direction, by a portly, lobster-colored gentleman a fraction of a second before Eve arrived.

"Please," she accosted him, "do you mind if I go first? It's terribly important."

The pompous-looking gentleman eyed her bathing suit disdainfully. "I should just about think it was," he said meaningfully.

Eve was in no mood for argument. She put one hand against the gentleman's chest, shoved, and ducked into the booth. Thrown off balance, he staggered backward, stumbled, and sat down forcefully in the sand. A group of bathers nearby laughed loudly. The portly gentleman's face purpled with indignation. He scrambled to his feet and yanked open the door of the booth.

"Come out of there!" he shouted. "Come out of there, you shameless baggage! I'll have you know this is a free country and I was here first!"

Despite Eve's struggles, he dragged her bodily out of the booth.

"Let me go," she panted. "Let me go! I tell you it's a matter of life or death."

"We'll see about that," the portly man said righteously.

"We will indeed!" The voice was Harry's. He dropped a heavy hand on the portly man's shoulder and spun him around. "The young lady told you it was a matter of life or death. What more do you want?"

The portly man was almost apoplectic. "So now we have bullying!" he said. "Well, fortunately we have laws in this country to deal with ruffians like you." He shook Harry's hand off angrily and strode off through the gathering crowd of onlookers.

Inside the booth, Eve had gotten through to the long-distance operator.

"Can I help you?"

"Yes, please. I want to make a transatlantic call to a Mr. Jonathan Clark, Pasadena, California."

"Yes, madam. Do you have the address, please?"

"No, no I don't. But I must reach him immediately. It's a matter of the utmost urgency!"

"Will you spell the name, please?"

Eve felt a sense of frustration rising in her. "I don't know.

C-L-A-R-K . . . C-L-A-R-K-E . . . How many ways can you spell Clark?"

"And the first name?"

"I told you–Jonathan."

"That was Pasadena, California?"

"Yes, yes. Operator, *please,* this is desperately important."

"We will try, madam. What is your number, please? We will call you back."

"You *can't* call me back!" Eve almost shouted. "I'm in a public call office and there's someone waiting. I tell you this is a matter of life or death!"

"One moment. I will consult the supervisor."

"But, operator——" The line was dead. There was nothing to do but wait for her to return. Eve's mind spun with frantic conjecture. What if Jonathan had gone out? What if he had no phone? What if he lived in a hotel or a boardinghouse? Supposing his phone wasn't listed? The possibilities of not getting him seemed infinite.

After what seemed an eternity, the operator came back on.

"What is the nature of the emergency, madam?"

Eve caught her breath. "Mr. Clark's brother has been seriously injured in an accident. He may not live."

There was a few seconds' pause, then: "Very well, madam, we will take your call. Can you give us a number to which we can refer the charges?"

"Yes. Kensington 41881." Out of the corner of her eye, Eve saw the portly gentleman coming down the steps to the beach, gesticulating wildly to a constable. "Operator, *please* hurry."

The circuit closed. The constable and the portly gentleman stopped momentarily while the latter pointed down the beach toward the booth, then came on again. Harry (bless him) left the crowd and went to meet them. Halfway to the booth, a three-way argument began. After a minute or two, the group moved a few feet closer to the booth and stopped again. Another eternity later, the operator came back on.

"Go ahead, please."

Her heart leapt. "Jonathan?"

"Hello? Hello?" The voice came through sharp and clear.

"Jonathan! Thank God I've found you! It's Eve."

"Who?"

"Eve–Eve Wingate. Don't tell me you don't know who I am."

There was a fractional pause during which her heart almost stopped beating. Then he said, "I know. Look, be careful. Don't say anything. You don't know who may be listening."

The constable opened the door of the booth. "Sorry, miss, you'll have to give up the telephone to this gentleman."

Eve turned to him desperately. "One moment, officer, please!" She pulled the door shut, said into the telephone, "I know. Jonathan, I can't talk any more now, but I'm coming to California. I know someone who can get me a reservation on the midnight plane from London. I'm leaving tonight. Jonathan, I'm sorry I was rude to you before. I––"

The constable took the receiver out of Eve's hands firmly and placed it on the hook. "You'll have to come with me, miss."

Eve turned and came out of the booth. "I'm terribly sorry, officer. I know this gentleman was here first, but this call was a matter of the utmost urgency."

The portly man was still fuming. "She pushed me and her companion here threatened me. They're ruffians, both of them. I order you to arrest them!"

Someone in the crowd said, "Oh, really!" and a second voice said, "Why don't you make your call if it's so urgent?"

The constable turned to Eve. There was the suggestion of a twinkle in his eye.

"Please, officer," she pleaded, "it won't happen again. I promise you!"

"Very well, miss. I think we can overlook it this time–unless of course this gentleman wants to come down to the station with me and lodge a formal complaint."

The latter hesitated for an instant, then stamped past them into the phone booth in high dudgeon.

Eve smiled. "Thank you, officer." She and Harry pushed through the crowd and started back down the beach. Harry was silent for a few moments, watching her, then he said:

"Eve, what happened to you out there in the water?"

"Nothing."

"Then why are you so upset?"

"I'm not upset. Really, I'm not."

"Then perhaps you wouldn't mind telling me why that call was so urgent."

"I can't."

He glanced at her stiff profile, then brought up his hand and opened it. "Could it have anything to do with this?"

Eve stopped dead in her tracks and went pale beneath her tan. Her hand flew instinctively to her bosom. "Where did you get that?"

"It is yours, then?"

She took the box from him, clutching it so hard her knuckles whitened under the pressure. She looked exactly like a well-dressed woman Harry had once seen caught in the act of shoplifting.

"Yes, it's mine. Where did you get it?"

"I found it on the sand outside the call office. You must have dropped it when you were struggling with our friend."

She bit her lip in an agony of self-reproach. She had sworn to conceal the existence of the box and within a few minutes, by sheer stupidity, she had managed not only to betray its possession but to surround that possession with suspicion.

Harry's voice intruded. "Who gave you that box–what's the significance of those gold cylinders? What is there about them that's troubling you?"

She made a brave attempt at control. "Harry, I know this must all seem very peculiar to you, but I promise you I'll explain it all one day. Till then, you'll just have to trust me."

He stared at her, deciding there was nothing to be gained by pressing her further. "All right, Bernhardt, but perhaps you'll tell me why you want my boat?"

"I just want to be by myself for a while." The lameness of it rang hollowly in her ears and she blushed in embarrassment.

"Oh, now, really, Eve. That is a bit thick, you know."

She decided she had only one weapon left and was ashamed of herself as she used it. "Of course, if you don't *want* to lend me your boat, that's perfectly all right."

"The car is over here," he said quietly.

At the dock, he helped her into the launch. "You're sure you don't want me to come along?"

Her smile was a little strained. "No, thank you, Harry. You've been awfully kind."

"Not at all!" The voice had an edge of anger. "Is there anything else?"

She stopped, hesitating.

"Well?" he prompted.

"Harry, there is something, but I've been so beastly I'm afraid to ask."

He softened then. "What is it?"

"It's an awfully big favor and you'll have to grant it without asking any questions–and without any explanations whatever."

"It's getting to be a habit. Go ahead."

"You have a New York bank account, haven't you?"

"Yes, I have."

"I–I need some American money."

"How much?"

She swallowed. "About twenty-five hundred dollars."

It is to Harry's credit that he managed to answer. "When?"

"Today. This afternoon. I'll give you a draft on my London account to cover it."

"You want a check or an American Express money order?"

"A check, if you don't mind."

He looked at her then, trying to catch her eyes, but she avoided his gaze. He sighed. "All right. I'll have the check for you when you get back. But, Eve—"

"Yes?"

"I don't know what this is all about, but don't–don't do anything foolish."

"I won't. Thank you, Harry." She pressed the starter and the launch roared into life. Harry cast off the bowline and she waved to him as she pulled away from the dock.

She drove out of the breakwater at full throttle. The prow knifed through the smooth sea like a great mahogany cleaver flaying back the blue skin of the ocean, the bow wave curling off like two ribbons of creamy white fat. From time to time, a mist of spray cleared the top of the glass windshield and touched Eve's face with cool tentative fingers, but she scarcely noticed. She kept the launch driving until the gas was exhausted and the engine sputtered and died. Then she turned and looked back. The land was a long way off. Far too distant, she thought approvingly, for anyone to be able to see her figure in the boat, and the nearest vessel was just peeking above the starboard horizon. She released the wheel, walked to the gunwale, and looked down into the blue-green depths. She took the black box and leaned out over the water.

For a long second, she held it above the sunlit surface; then, with a sharp intake of breath, she released it. There was a tiny splash and a little jet of spray as it hit the water. She saw it again for a brief instant sinking slowly—almost reluctantly. Just before it disappeared, a vagrant ray of sunlight caught the white plastic surface, dazzling her eyes. Then it was gone. She stood there for a full minute trying to follow its progress in her mind, picturing it slipping, sliding, dropping down through the fathoms into the weed-drenched darkness and coming to rest in some crevice of the ocean floor where not even the most concentrated search could ever find it. A shiver ran through her. It was done. One threat to the human race was finished. She had made an idiot of herself by letting Harry see the box, but it didn't matter. It couldn't matter now. She felt as if a tremendous weight had been lifted from her shoulders.

On the roof of the Yacht Club, Harry Ward-Bellows III withdrew his eye from the powerful marine telescope and rubbed his chin reflectively. He was more confused than ever.

5

Su Tan returned to earth as did the others in exactly the same position in which she had left it. She arose slowly from the ground where she had been lying. The barnlike structure near her was burning furiously, throwing macabre shadows into the night, and the heat of it scorched her skin. She moved away awkwardly, walking with difficulty. Her head throbbed feverishly from the blows she had received and the salt-sweet taste of blood was in her mouth. Her viciously abused body sent shrieking protests to the brain against every movement of her limbs. With a dull sense of wonder, she remembered briefly that she had felt no physical pain during the entire episode aboard the great machine from the sky. She put the back of a small hand to her mouth and it came away smeared with blood which looked black and unreal in the light from the flames. Thirty feet from the barn, she stumbled and almost fell over the body of her brother. There was no need to assure herself that he was dead. She walked away from the spot in the direction of the house. Above her, ragged black clouds scuttled across the face of the moon, alternately plunging the area beyond the light of the flames from cold harsh moonlight into semidarkness. The roof of the house had gone up in one splash of flame but the mud walls were still standing, bleak and sightless silhouettes against the night sky. Outside the door of the house was a second body. Her father lay where he had fallen, his neck twisted at a sickening angle.

Behind her one of the timbers in the barn crashed down with a muffled explosion, sending a welter of burning sparks into the sky. She neither moved nor flinched. Outwardly it appeared she felt nothing. No tears coursed down her cheeks; no sign of anguish broke the immobility of her face as she gazed at her father's crumpled figure. Only in the dark almond pools of her eyes was there a flicker of something infinitely fragile, splintering away.

She moved slowly around the body and stood in the doorway of the little mud dwelling which was the only home she had ever known. The wooden door had been smashed open and hung in splintered uselessness by one hinge. A tiny tongue of flame was licking quietly at a crack in one of the corner beams near the top of the wall. As she watched, it flickered and went out. She remained there on the threshold limned against the night while memories of her past slid in unhurried succession through the corridors of her mind. They were not pleasant memories. They spoke of privation, of cold, and of gnawing hunger; of sickness, of war, of sudden death. Together they made up a great, vague shadow which hung like a pall over all of her people, whispering of the ultimate futility of everything–even of life itself. There had never been time for laughter, or tenderness, or peace. Of the rare moments of warmth in human relationships she had known, perhaps the most moving had been the brief hour she had just spent with four people whom she would never see again. An overwhelming sadness welled up in her, blinding her momentarily to the knifing pain in her body.

She turned and looked out across the earth to the horizon where the first almost imperceptible light of dawn was beginning to brush the sky. Out there were the countless millions she had never known–the races who did not know or care what had happened to China and her people, the China her father had told her was once the greatest nation on the face of the earth–a China that now groveled in misery and famine beneath the heel of evil and ruthless men–men who this night had taken the lives of those closest to her and destroyed the body that might one day have borne her a son. For the first time, a film of tears touched her eyes. The destruction of the tiny life she might some day have borne moved her more deeply than the grim reality which surrounded her. She turned slowly and entered the house.

On a shelf in a corner which had served as a kitchen lay a long homemade knife with a rough bone handle. The blade had once been broad but years of honing had worn the metal to a thin curved sliver with a needle-sharp point. Su Tan approached it. In the hand that she stretched out to grasp it, there was no sign of trembling. She turned to face the miniature shrine of Buddha across the room. She took a few steps toward the shrine and knelt down. Her lips moved in inaudible prayer.

She raised a hand to her bosom and pushed once, twice, firmly. She made no sound as the knife entered her heart. After a second the body crumpled to the floor. Beneath the transparent cover of the black box there flared for a second a light of incredible, blinding brilliance. When it had faded the box was unharmed but inside, where the three capsules had been, there were three tiny mounds of soft gray powder.

6

Professor Klaus Bochner found himself standing in the pathway staring into the now empty shadows at the base of the pine tree. No sooner had he oriented himself than he raised the black box which, like the others, he was holding in his right hand. He peered at it excitedly until he heard his car churning the gravel of the driveway, at which point he thrust the box surreptitiously into his pocket and hurried down the path to where his limousine was drawing up. The chauffeur greeted him and saw him comfortably ensconced in the back of the car.

"I think we'll have to hurry, Hans," the professor said blandly. The chauffeur nodded with resigned understanding. For a man who spent most of his waking hours concerned with the theories of space and time, he thought, the professor showed a marvelous disdain for getting anywhere in space at a designated moment in time.

As the car slid smoothly into the brighter sunlight of the street, Professor Bochner assured himself that Hans was occupied with the traffic, then, with trembling fingers, he took the box out of his pocket. He remembered the Alien had said that there was only one way in which the box could be opened. It was actuated by its owner's encephalographic waves. Fantastic! The professor held the box in front of him and gazed at it steadily. The lid clicked open.

He took one of the capsules out of the box, laid it in the palm of his hand and peered at it through his bifocals, his brow furrowed with concentration. The chauffeur glanced back at him through the rear-view mirror. What was the old duck up to now, he wondered. He was peering at something in his hand like a puzzled owl. The chauffeur knew that look well. He knew he could drive the professor right past the airport and end up any number of hours later in Paris, Vienna, or Rome, and the old boy, on arriving at the end of the journey, which should have lasted twenty minutes, would look vaguely around for an airplane. He was very fond of the professor, but he could not help wondering how one so absent-minded, so gullible, and so totally unconscious of the savage nature of the modern world could have managed to survive, let alone come to be acknowledged as its most brilliant scientist. Hans recalled how the professor had once given him not only the wrong hour but the wrong day on which he was to drive him to accept the world's most coveted scientific award. Only frantic calls from the society, the embassy, and various friends had succeeded in getting Professor Bochner to the august reception three quarters of an hour late.

In the back of the car the professor was still enthralled with his new toy. He had discovered the golden spindle which primed the bomb and it was only with the greatest difficulty that he restrained himself from removing it to examine its nature. He could see nothing, of course, except the exterior surface of the capsule which, though fascinating, told him very little. He dug his hand into his pockets in search of a magnifying glass which he felt sure he had brought with him.

The search uncovered several lengths of string, a cork, a few scraps of well-scribbled paper and the lint-covered core of an apple which he thrust absent-mindedly back into his pocket as security against some future famine. He decided he must have forgotten the magnifying glass and held the capsule close to the window. It reflected the light almost like a diamond. On the underside there were, embedded in the metal, tiny crystals which looked very much like precious gems; red, blue-white, and green, they glittered in their setting, winking the light back at him tantalizingly. On the opposite side of the capsule, the metal was deeply but so delicately worked that only examination under a microscope or a powerful magnifying glass would reveal whether the tiny incisions were functional or decorative. The professor felt highly frustrated. He debated with himself the advisability of asking Hans to return to the laboratory where he could examine his treasure at leisure and with a proper instrument, but he quickly gave up the idea. Hans was stubborn; there was no other word for it. He knew perfectly well that Hans would refuse to take him back to the laboratory. Hans would explain with the patient control that people invariably adopted toward difficult children that he had been instructed to take the professor to the airport and that there he was going to take him. If the professor insisted, Hans would simply turn into a mute. His face would assume a ridiculous mask of dogged determination and he would proceed to his destination through hell, high water, and dense traffic. It was a ritual which irritated the professor intensely, and the most embarrassing part of the whole thing was that Hans, with unfailing and obnoxious regularity, turned out to be right.

The car drew up to the terminal with twelve minutes to spare. Hans hurried to open the door. The professor, caught napping as usual, just barely managed to get the capsule back in the box and the box closed before Hans opened the door. But, as the professor hastily attempted to thrust the box into his pocket, he fumbled and the box fell out of his hand, bounced off the edge of the floor board by the open door and out into the roadway, where it jumped back under the car.

The professor looked a little upset, not because he feared the immediate danger of explosion, but because he had a rather strong impression that it would be better if no one knew he had the box. He scrambled up from the seat and bent over in an effort to reach the box before Hans. But Hans, who had seen it fall, had the advantage. He was already bending down to retrieve his employer's possession when the professor made his move. The passers-by were then treated to the remarkable spectacle of a six-foot chauffeur on his hands and knees outside the open back door of the limousine while an excited, cherubic-faced little man with a thatch of white hair climbed frantically over the body of his employee and tugged at the seat of his trousers to pull him away from his objective. Hans, who was having some difficulty reaching the object, looked around in consternation. But the professor was not to be dissuaded. He seized the opportunity of Hans's momentary lapse to wedge himself forcibly between the chauffeur and the back tire. There, as a crowd began to gather, he wriggled under the car while Hans fought equally forcefully to hold his position and perform his duty. Being the larger and stronger, he eventually won. Despite the puffings, the pantings, the squirmings, and the undignified scrabbling of the professor, Hans reached the box first.

With as much dignity as he could muster he then withdrew from under the car and stood up while the professor followed suit. Hans's face was a model of outraged dignity. When the professor had extricated himself and stood erect with a smudge of grease on his button nose and his spectacles awry, Hans drew himself up to his full height and with a gesture that spoke louder than a thousand words, presented the box to the professor with cold dignity. There was a delighted laugh from the onlookers. The professor took the box without a word, jammed it into his pocket, and, his face red with effort, glared up at Hans like a bantam cock ready for battle. Hans said nothing. He stared straight out into space a good foot above the professor's head, and when, with a snort, the professor turned and marched with ludicrous disdain up the stairs to the waiting room, Hans sighed, got the suitcase, and followed him in.

The next few minutes prior to the departure of the plane constitute a period which airline officials, emigration authorities, and baggage personnel are not likely to forget. Professor Klaus Bochner may well have been the world's most eminent scientist, but trying to get him through the red tape of departure and safely on board an airplane was a job that taxed the abilities and nerves of the heartiest and most experienced employees.

Fortunately, he had been given a seat by himself where he disturbed only the two passengers behind and ahead of him with unexpected *sotto voce* mutterings and rattlings of note paper throughout not only the afternoon but the entire night. The steward insists that he did not sleep at all, refused to eat, and acted in an extremely eccentric manner. Each time someone passed down the aisle the professor would push something into his pocket and sit bolt upright in his seat, staring straight ahead as if he were frozen, until the interruption had passed, at which point he would whisk whatever it was he was concealing out of his pocket again and return to his muttering.

Many sleepless hours later the professor arrived at Idlewild Airport, where with unexpected guile he eluded not only his official reception committee but a horde of reporters and photographers who were on hand to meet him. He disappeared with disconcerting thoroughness into the vast neon jungle of New York.

7

"People of Earth, this is *not* a commercial. May I repeat for those of you who may not have understood, this is not a commercial." Beneath the crop of silver curls the penetrating blue eyes twinkled in gentle amusement as the Alien voice continued. "We have taken the liberty of interrupting your program to make an announcement. I am not of your planet. I come from another world outside the limits of your solar system. I am speaking to you now from a space ship which in thirty seconds will appear in the sky above you. I repeat, I am speaking to you from a space ship which will appear in the sky above you within thirty seconds. I shall wait, if you care to verify this fact."

Five hundred million windows banged upward with a crash that sounded around the world. Traffic ground to a standstill as drivers reacted to the message from their radios. On ocean liners, cabins emptied like magic as passengers fought their way to the open deck. In movies, people were trampled as audiences turned into frantic mobs racing for the exit. There were few who could resist the impulse to verify what the screens, the radios, the television sets, and, in primitive parts of the world, a mysterious voice from the sky had told them. Two billion pairs of eyes strained at the heavens.

And then, suddenly, with a speed that defied belief, something plummeted from the farthest reaches of the stratosphere beyond the range of human sight into the realm of visibility. The atmosphere above the world rolled and crashed in terrible earth-shaking thunder as the roiled air, rent by the ships' passage, rushed back into place. The star ships of the Aliens hung motionless in the sky. Vast, pulsating disks of ice-blue luminescence in the darkness and shimmering circles of silver incandescence in the light, they waited while humanity viewed them in fear and open-mouthed wonder. Then, as quickly as they had come, they flashed upward and vanished into space while the earth reeled again to the echoing thunder of their passage.

The world scrambled back to its television and radio sets for the rest of the message.

The benign and imposing countenance on the screens waited until the last echoes of the ships' departure had died, and then spoke again: "Now that you have seen my ships in your skies, I hope that you will believe what I am about to tell you. Approximately thirty hours ago, five people from the planet Earth were our guests aboard one of the star ships which you have just seen. To them was imparted information of highly unusual nature. The names and addresses of these people are as follows: Jonathan Clark, Pasadena, California; Evelyn Wingate, Hampstead, England; Professor Klaus Bochner, who arrived early this morning in New York; Sergeant Ivan Godofsky, Soviet garrison at Vladivostok; and Su Tan of the province of Tsinghai, China, near the village of Ho Chin. That is all."

The face of the Alien disappeared. All over the world there was a period of thirty seconds before radio, television, and motion pictures were able to continue their interrupted programs. What happened during and after that terrible thirty seconds is a matter of history. The chronicle of mad, heroic, pathetic, and inspiring reactions to the broadcast is legion. People died of shock, plunged to their deaths from towers, walked into the paths of trains, threw themselves into the sea, knelt in the street in prayer, screamed that Armageddon was at hand. But what happened to the people who had been aboard the Alien star ship for the fateful and world-shattering interview is less well known.

In London, neighbors, police, government officials, and reporters descended like ravenous locusts on the apartment of Eve Wingate. She was not to be found, nor could anyone give any information as to where she had gone. She was, at that precise moment, winging her way through the skies over America somewhere between New York and Los Angeles under the name of Jean Meadows.

In New York the search for Professor Bochner which had begun immediately after his disappearance was intensified a thousandfold but with no results. He was safely hidden away with his little black box, oblivious to the cries of the world.

In China, a military convoy was forming to make the trip to the home of Su Tan, near the village of Ho Chin, ignorant of the fact that the Chinese girl that they sought had been far beyond human reach for more than thirty hours.

Jonathan Clark and Ivan Godofsky, however, found themselves in much more vulnerable situations.

8

Jonathan Clark sat at his desk in the editorial offices of the Los Angeles *Telegram* and found it impossible to keep his mind on the copy in front of him. Pressing against his left hip was the hard outline of a small black box. He was literally *sitting* on the greatest story in newspaper history, and there wasn't one damned thing he could do about it! He cursed softly and vehemently to himself, recalling the moment a little more than twenty-four hours earlier when he had first heard the voice speaking out of the shadows, almost at his elbow. If it hadn't been for his possession of the box on his return to the apartment, he would have been convinced he had had an hallucination. Even then it had taken the transatlantic call from Eve to convince him that it had actually happened.

He took out his wallet and scanned the list of plane arrivals he had made out. Making allowances for the differences in time, the earliest she could arrive would be two o'clock that afternoon. He had decided it would be simpler to meet half-a-dozen flights at the airport than sit at home in his stifling apartment waiting for her to telephone that she had landed. She didn't have his address, so it was unlikely she would try to cable. And the Sky Bar would be a pleasant place to spend the afternoon. He could watch most of the arrivals from the windows without having to move.

Abruptly, the orderly confusion of the office oppressed him. He picked up his hat, took the elevator to the ground floor, and walked across the street to Max's Bar and Grill.

He ordered a cup of coffee. The time was ten forty-five A.M. and there was a panel show on the TV set. Jonathan was following it abstractedly when the program was interrupted by a massive leonine head and a voice said, "People of Earth, this is not a commercial. . . ."

Jonathan was one of the few people who did not rush into the open to look for the space ship. He knew it would be there. He also anticipated that its appearance would be the forerunner of more headaches for humanity, but even he was not prepared for the subsequent announcement. It left him momentarily stunned. The enormity of the Alien treachery as he saw it, the fiendishly shrewd manner in which they had stuck to the letter of their promise not to exert any external influence on the holders of the black boxes and yet had managed to loose upon them, in one devastating step, every internal pressure which could be imagined, filled him with unreasoning anger. He felt that he and the other four captives aboard the space ship had been brutally betrayed. What good would their pact do them now with the entire world at their heels like a pack of wild hounds? In almost the same reflection, he realized that he could no longer return to his office or his apartment. He couldn't even chance getting his car out of the parking lot. He was suddenly, unexpectedly, and completely on his own.

At the mention of Jonathan's name the bartender, who had known him for years, swung around, his mouth hanging slackly open. Before the man could find his voice, Jonathan bolted for the door. As he plunged into the crowd on the streets he heard the bartender shouting his name and, throwing a swift glance over his shoulder, saw a crowd gathering at the entrance he had just left. He pulled his hat well down over his eyes and kept going. Apparently, no one was trying to catch him, but, in this neighborhood, any one of a hundred people might recognize him. Moreover, the difficulties of getting out of the neighborhood seemed enormous. Traffic was at a standstill. No buses were moving and, second by second, doorways of office buildings were pouring floods of people into the street. Despite the fact that the Alien had explained that he had not come from this universe, Jonathan heard the word "Martians" on every side.

He moved steadily away from the vicinity of his office building, his mind battered by the impact of what he had just heard. How can we keep it from them now, he thought. How? Up to now his responsibility for the guardianship of the bomb had been almost hypothetical. No one knew he had it and since he had no intention of using it or even of bringing the attention of anyone to the fact of its existence, there had been no real problem. Now everything was changed. If he gave himself up, there was little doubt in his mind that sooner or later they would discover that he possessed the capsules. They couldn't torture him, of course, as they might do to that Russian.

My God, the Russian! The thought struck him like a blow. He recalled only too vividly the methods the Russians were known to use on people who tried to withhold information they wanted. Didn't that put a whole new complexion on the matter? If Godofsky could be forced to reveal the secret he had sworn to keep, shouldn't he, Jonathan, as a loyal citizen turn his own knowledge over to the U.S. government? But that was exactly what the Alien expected. What was it he had said? The probability that the earth would destroy itself was nearly 100 per cent, and there was a better than 50 per cent possibility that it would be destroyed by the weapon he held in his pocket within twenty-seven days. He had been tempted to scoff at the figures when he heard them; now he wasn't so sure.

In the distance, thunder rolled ominously. The sky was dark and threatening. Rain in Los Angeles in July! It seemed impossible. It never rained in the summer. Never! Perhaps the passage of the Alien ships had set up a reaction in the atmosphere. Whatever the reason, the darkening sky and the distant rumblings of the heavens seemed gloomy omens for the future. He realized he must have been walking for some time, for the street he was on was unfamiliar to him. He glanced at his watch. Almost forty minutes had passed since he left the bar. He couldn't keep walking forever. He had to make some kind of a plan. He stepped into a doorway and fumbled in his pocket for a package of cigarettes, lit one, and tried to marshal his thoughts. It was obvious that within a few minutes he was going to be the subject of the biggest man hunt in the history of the United States, if indeed the hunt had not already begun. But he had to stay free until he had decided what to do. He had to have time to think.

He put his hand in his hip pocket, drew out his wallet, and

counted the bills. Thirty-seven dollars. He felt in his trouser pocket and found eighteen cents in change. Thirty-seven dollars and eighteen cents, and half a package of cigarettes. The outlook was not exactly promising. He had no home to return to, no friends who could be trusted to keep a secret of such momentous importance; to top it all off, it looked as if it were going to rain and he didn't have a raincoat. He couldn't wander around in a downpour without a coat; it would attract too much attention; and he couldn't go into any of the customary places to avoid walking around in the rain. He began to realize what it must feel like to be a criminal, except that he couldn't think like a criminal and he didn't know what a criminal knew.

There was one place where he might be safe; but how to get to it? That was the problem. He needed money and he needed a car; but if he wanted to remain free, it was much too dangerous to try to get either.

Suddenly he remembered Eve! In the name of heaven, how could he have forgotten? She was on her way to Los Angeles! She would be arriving in two or three hours! The chances were a hundred to one she'd be caught the moment she stepped off the plane. But supposing by some miracle she wasn't? He couldn't leave her alone in a strange country. It was a big risk, but he'd *have* to be at the airport when she arrived. But he couldn't wait around looking like Jonathan Clark. He'd have to change his appearance, and quickly. Halfway down the street was a drugstore. There was a sign in the window: "We Carry Theatrical Make-up." Jonathan threw his cigarette into the gutter and stepped out of the doorway. From here on in, it was in the lap of the gods!

9

At the time when the Alien appeared on television screens and radios throughout the world, it was four o'clock in the morning in Vladivostok. Sergeant Ivan Godofsky was billeted in a private home fifteen minutes' walk from the installations which he guarded. On this particular morning he was due on duty at five and had arisen at three in order to have time to write his regular letters to his mother and to Gerda, the girl he one day hoped to be able to marry. He had made it a habit to write twice a week and usually the task was not difficult. He always said that he was well and happy and hoped that they were the same and that he hoped that he would be allowed to return to Stalingrad as soon as his tour of duty was finished. Once a month he included a postal money order for as much money as he could spare. But this morning his pencil would not work. The stamped and addressed envelopes lay on the table beside him. The two postal money orders (the big one for his mother and the smaller one for Gerda) were ready and waiting, but he could not get started. Everything he tried to say seemed curiously empty and stupid. After the miraculous things that had happened to him, all of the customary words had lost their meaning. He wanted painfully to tell his mother and Gerda about his experiences and yet he knew he did not dare. All the letters were censored and, even if they weren't, he couldn't risk telling anyone about the existence of the capsules. Not even his mother.

He took the box from his pocket and weighed it in his hand, trying to imagine his mother's face if she could hear the story of how he had gotten it. He could see her now, sitting very erect in a straight chair, snow-white hair caught back under a dark shawl. She would watch him out of those wise, gentle eyes, deep-set in their network of wrinkles, and her hands, never still for a second, would be busy with the knitting needles or the paring knife. She would listen quietly, nodding now and then but saying nothing–not even making an exclamation. Then, when he had finished, she would fix him with a stern look and she would bob her head up and down and say, "Ivanovitch, you are a very great liar!" And he would protest as he always did when she caught him in some childhood untruth. Only this time it would be true. Gerda might believe, but then, it had to be admitted, Gerda believed everything. He chewed on the end of his pencil, trying to think of a new way to say all the old familiar things. A small portion of his mind was following the musical program on the radio tuned to the all-night station. It was a second or two before he realized the music had stopped in mid-note. He glanced over at the radio. It was still on, but the program had been cut off. He started to rise from his stool to see what was wrong when the voice came through: "People of Earth, this is not a commercial. . . ."

When it was over, Ivan sat stone still on his stool and realized that for him, at least, the end was near. Strangely, he was not very frightened. He had only a peculiar feeling of emptiness and futility.

He stood up slowly and walked over to the window. What should he do? What was there to do? He knew that, once he had been found, there would be little hope of concealing the information he had or the existence of the black box. And yet he wanted to keep this information to himself. He wanted to, desperately. He had made a pact with four other people, and he wanted to keep that pact, not only because he did not want to break faith with them but because he, too, wanted the world to stay at peace. He was sure that if he was forced to reveal his knowledge, he could also be forced to launch the capsule.

And there was another problem. The newspapers and the radio had been telling him for years that the Americans were war mongers; that only the great patience and alertness of the Soviet diplomats and the peaceful desires of the Union of Soviet Socialist Republics had prevented another war. Was it true? No one seemed to know for sure. Everyone was a little confused. There had been that time after the death of Stalin when the whisper of peace had run through the land like the wind through a field of grain. Heads had nodded to the talk of disarmament and something called peaceful coexistence. The leaders of America, England, and France had met with Russia in Switzerland and there had been an exchange of atomic information for peaceful uses. Russian farmers had gone to America and American farmers had come to study in Russia. There had been a kind of promise in the future and for a while even the little people had begun to prosper. Then there had been the campaign to discredit Stalin—the reduction of armaments —the shorter hours of work.

And then, out of nowhere, had come the Great Leader. In one bloody night he had stepped from relative obscurity in the secret police into the footsteps of Stalin. He had railed bitterly against the ones he had overthrown, had accused them of selling out their homeland to the West, of crucifying the great Stalin for their own paltry ends, of delivering up their allies on the altar of appeasement. He had wept tears of rage when he spoke to the people for the first time, producing the proofs of the treachery of the Triumvirate; Russia had not supported her Chinese allies when the Americans had driven them back from Formosa (which certainly belonged to the Communist mainland). She had given up Austria; she had courted the traitor, Tito, made concessions in Berlin. Harkening to the lying voices of the West, she had forgotten her glorious destiny. The Iron Curtain had thundered into place; all the old fears of the imperialist West had returned. And who was to say the Great Leader was not right? All the things he said were true. Life had not been so pleasant since his coming and, as in the days of Stalin, one had to walk carefully and be scrupulous about his loyalties. But, again, who was to say that the Great Leader did not find this supervision necessary?

Everyone knew that in a good army discipline had to be enforced, and these, if you could believe the newspapers and the radio, were dangerous times. Under Stalin, Russia had become a great nation. Under the Triumvirate, she had lost much and achieved nothing, except a deluded sense of well-being. Now she was again making her might felt throughout the world. And yet, in spite of everything, there was a vague sense of uneasiness throughout Russia, a whispered conviction that perhaps everything was not quite as it should be. The point was that, if everything he had been taught were true, he had no right to withhold from his government the information he possessed. He owed his country and his people the protection of the bomb. What if he disposed of the bomb or refused to use it, and then America began making demands for Russian territory? Without bombs of her own, Russia would have no recourse but to give in.

On the other hand, if everything he had heard and read were not true, or was only partly true, or if the American kept to his side of the bargain, then he, Ivan, might be wrong in delivering himself up to the leaders of his country. What was it the Alien had said? It was always the leaders that caused the war and not the people! And in that moment five thousand miles from California, Ivan Godofsky reached the same decision as Jonathan Clark. This was a question that he alone could decide and he had to have time to think. There was only one way to get that time. He had to disappear. How long it would be before they ran him to earth he didn't know, but at least he had to try. Swiftly he crossed to the room's tiny closet, took out his only civilian suit and began to rip off his uniform. Meanwhile, in an area of four square blocks around his house, a cordon of police and soldiers was forming rapidly. The streets which a few moments before had been a bedlam of noise and confusion as people poured out of their houses to get a glimpse of the shimmering disks in the sky, were now falling silent. Four blocks down the street an enormous black limousine slipped silently through the cordon. Seated inside the car was Comrade Nikolai Raskovich, the most powerful party official in Eastern Russia. His eyes were cold and his face was set in a mask of anger. This impudent Russian soldier had had information which might be of incalculable value to his government for a period of more than thirty hours and he had said nothing. The car glided to a stop in front of Ivan's house. From every window, rooftop, and doorway of the street, white tense faces watched Raskovich get out of his car and enter the house preceded by his bodyguards.

In his room Ivan donned his threadbare overcoat and started for the door. He never reached it. It was not locked and it opened from the outside. Framed in its portal was a man whose face Ivan had seen on a thousand posters around Vladivostok. The face wore a broad convincing smile and Comrade Raskovich's hand was outstretched. He advanced into the room. "Comrade Godofsky," he said warmly, and one of his three henchmen closed the door behind him.

Several hundreds of miles away in the province of Tsinghai, China, near the village of Ho Chin, a column of military trucks was churning wildly down the rain-soaked road and into the courtyard of the gutted farmhouse which had been the earthly home of Su Tan. Fifteen minutes later, it drove slowly back on the same road by which it had come. In the hand of the officer in the leading truck there was a tiny black box which he had been unable to open but through whose transparent cover he could see three mounds of light gray ashes. In the back of the truck, partly covered by a filthy blanket, lay the lifeless body of Su Tan.

Seven thousand miles away in an outlying section of Brooklyn, New York, in a small unoccupied fish store, whose windows he had sealed against prying eyes with sheets of brown wrapping paper, Professor Klaus Bochner, oblivious to the madness which was engulfing the world, was beginning to feel slightly lightheaded. He couldn't for the life of him understand these feelings of faintness which were coming over him more and more frequently. Once he had actually fallen asleep over his work table for what he took to be two or three hours. He drank a glass of water and returned to the second-hand microscope beneath whose lenses rested one of the golden capsules from the black box.

There was every reason for the professor's lightheadedness. He had not eaten for about fifty-two hours. He was not accustomed to eating breakfast and, on the morning of the luncheon at Heidelberg, he had somehow managed to miss even his usual cup of coffee. He had arrived, as was his custom, late at the luncheon because he had refused to let Hans, the chauffeur, into his laboratory till he had finished a discussion with a junior colleague about some obscure scientific theory. As a result, he had nothing but half a glass of champagne at the reception and subsequently had existed in a state of such sustained excitement that he had refused food on the plane and later had forgotten to eat. It was typical of him now not to be conscious of the reasons for this feeling of faintness and to be annoyed at the frailness of his body for failing him at such a crucial moment.

Despite his irritation, he could no longer ignore the weakness that was sweeping over him. He steadied himself against the battered table upon which the microscope was resting and the effort to fight back the faintness bathed his body in cold perspiration. Finally he realized that he could no longer go on. With tremulous fingers he replaced the capsule in its box, closed the lid, and put it into his pocket. He made up his mind that a breath of fresh air might help. He opened the door, inhaled deeply, and collapsed on the threshold. Within ten minutes he was in an ambulance on the way to the hospital where his case was diagnosed as simple malnutrition.

10

Eve Wingate left the London airport at twelve midnight on July 18. Her flight was delayed by strong headwinds so that she arrived in New York just in time to get into the city and cash the check Harry Bellows had given her and return to the airport to make her California connection. There was no opportunity to wire Jonathan (on the chance that the telegraph company might reach him by checking the Pasadena directory), and so Eve had to content herself with the thought that she would phone him from the airport when she arrived.

Two hours out from New York she fell into an uneasy slumber to be awakened by the sound of the cabin loud-speaker announcing that they were flying over Kansas City. She looked dutifully out of her window at the ugly blotch of the rail-laced metropolis against the lush green of the surrounding countryside, then leaned back in her chair and closed her eyes. She began to doze off again, her senses lulled by the muffled drone of the motors. Suddenly her eardrums were shattered by a piercing scream. She sat bolt upright, her nerves starting wildly.

Outside the plane, a great shimmering disk was plunging out of the heavens directly toward them. She caught her breath in horror, tensing her body against the shock of collision. And still the thing came on. There seemed no power on earth capable of staying that terrifying mass of plummeting steel. Over the screams in the cabin there was a sound like distant thunder. She felt the helpless, insane terror of the trapped animal. The thing grew until it blotted out most of the sky. Now —now—now—this instant it would hit! And suddenly it was over. The disk had stopped! Incredibly, miraculously, it hung motionless in the midday sky, so close she felt she could reach out and touch it—poised impossibly between heaven and earth, with no sign of jets or engines to defy the pull of gravity against its enormous bulk. Behind her in the cabin, a woman was sobbing brokenly and Eve could feel the pounding of her own heart. Her fingers were dead white and painful, so fiercely had she been clutching the arms of the chair. She did her best to relax. She knew now what the thing was—the Alien star ship. She watched it with a sinking expectancy—an intuition of impending disaster. Was this to be another ultimatum? As abruptly as it had stopped, the great disk thundered into life and almost immediately began to recede. Within seconds, it had completely disappeared from view. She sank back in her seat exhausted and shaken. The pilot came out of the cockpit and the hubbub in the cabin, except for the sobbing woman, ceased. He looked almost green, though his voice was reasonably steady as he spoke.

"Ladies and gentlemen, what you have just seen was allegedly a ship from outer space. Just before and after its appearance, a voice interrupted our radio receptions to identify five people from earth who were taken aboard one of these ships thirty hours ago and given some kind of information. Then the broadcast ceased. I won't try to explain this phenomenon because I don't know how, but I want you to know we are in no danger and we will land in Los Angeles on schedule. Thank you." He retired to the cockpit.

As the import of the pilot's announcement took hold, Eve felt her blood turning to ice in her veins. In the brief fact of that announcement, the Aliens had destroyed every hope she had entertained for herself, for Jonathan, for all of them who had been aboard the space ship. In one brutal stroke, they had subverted the plan on which she had pinned so much faith—the hope of finding the other four and persuading them to dispose of their capsules as she had disposed of hers. There would be no chance now to reach Professor Bochner, Su Tan, Godofsky, or even Jonathan himself. Within a few minutes, all of them would either be in custody or fugitives with the whole world in pursuit. She blessed the inspiration which had prompted her to buy her ticket under the name of Jean Meadows. She had done so in case Harry tried to trace her. It wouldn't help much in the long run, of course, because she had had to give her real name and present her passport at Immigration, but it would give her at least temporary protection from discovery. She knew she was listed on the passenger manifest as Jean Meadows because the stewardess had checked her off before the flight began. But what about Jonathan, whom she was flying to see? She was momentarily safe, but Jonathan did not have the protection of a skybound airplane or a false name. The possibilities that she would even get to see him now seemed very remote. She could imagine the hordes of reporters, the officials, the politicians and curiosity seekers who would be surrounding him within the next few hours. She wondered with a sudden start of fear what her own position was. Perhaps it had not been so wise to travel under an assumed name; in the light of the unexpected betrayal from space, her departure would look like flight. It might give rise to all sorts of complications. And her parents–good God!–what a shock this would be to them!

Then she remembered Harry and the fact that he had seen the box containing the capsules before she had thrown it into the sea. She knew that in the light of this broadcast that fact, too, could have grave repercussions. She spent the rest of the seemingly interminable flight in a state of unbearable anxiety.

When she descended from the plane in Los Angeles she had already given up hope that Jonathan would meet her. But she was not prepared for the hysteria which greeted her on her arrival. Crowds were mobbing the airport; the place was in chaos. As she fought her way to the exit, a newsboy thrust a paper in front of her eyes. "Read all about it," he croaked hoarsely. "Space men visit earth." There before her was a full page picture of Jonathan Clark. Oh God, she thought, it's much worse than I imagined. Beneath the picture on the front page was the caption, "Jonathan Clark Flees Police Dragnet." She crumpled the paper with trembling hands. What could she do now? She was alone in a city where she didn't know a living soul. Within a few hours they were bound to trace her and she wanted desperately to talk to Jonathan before submitting to any official inquiry. There was only one good thing about it: caught up in this hysterical mob she had somehow avoided Customs and Immigration. Well, there was nothing to be gained by standing there feeling sorry for herself. She began again her struggle for the exit. At every step she was pushed, cursed, and jostled. An insane cacophony of screams, threats, and wild snatches of conversation assaulted her senses.

"It's an invasion, I tell you. An invasion! It's the end of the world!"

"For Crissakes, stop sniveling. If we die, we die!"

"Kneel and pray, brothers, kneel and pray!"

"Sure they was brain-washed–what else would they be doin' to 'em up there."

A well-dressed woman grabbed Eve's arm, her voice hysterical. "You were on that plane, weren't you, lady! You must have a return ticket–I'll pay you anything." Eve shook her head and struggled out of reach.

"What kind of a government have we got. They should have *known!*"

"Do you know you can't even buy flight insurance? It's disgraceful!"

"The day of the Lord is at hand! Pray, brother, pray! Thine eyes have seen the Glory!"

"Henry, Henry! Over here! Rose's got the baby."

"Buy lead mines, Carter, lead mines. Sell everything else we've got, understand!"

"I don't care if they're Martians or Egyptians. They ain't from earth and what ain't from earth is dangerous!"

"Maybe they'll brain-wash everybody!"

Suddenly Eve found herself blocked by a tall figure anchored like black granite in the midst of the swirling confusion. She looked up into a wild bony face out of which two red-rimmed eyes glared at her, while the booming sepulchral voice roared down upon her head, "Kneel and pray, sister, kneel and pray. Put your trust in the Lord." She ducked under his outstretched arms while the voice thundered after her, "Beware lest thy sins discover thee. The day of retribution is at hand!"

Suddenly a pair of strong hands seized her from behind and she was pulled around into a crushing embrace. A familiar voice said,

"Don't say anything. Don't say anything at all. I thought you'd never get here."

Sheer relief flooded through Eve like wine. She found herself clutching Jonathan fiercely, almost hysterically, letting the strong circle of his arms reassure her. Completely forgotten was her resolution to greet him with cool ladylike formality. "Oh, Jonathan! I thought I'd lost you for good."

The scent of her hair and the warm softness of her as she clung to him did alarming things to his pulses. Reluctantly he released her, his voice a little unsteady. "You damned near did lose me," he said. "I've met three planes at this airport in the last hour only to find out that you might have been rerouted to Burbank."

She stepped back to look at him. "My God, Jonathan, what happened to you?"

He glanced around almost furtively. "Will you stop using that name," he whispered. "It's become poison in the last few hours. Call me Joe, call me Mike–call me anything."

"But the hair! And where on earth did you get that mustache?"

He glared at her. "I'm disguised."

Eve didn't know whether to laugh or cry. Here he stood, all six foot plus of him, in the midst of what could very easily be the prelude to global catastrophe, blandly confident that he had concealed himself behind a wisp of false hair and a bad henna rinse. After everything else, it was almost too much. She fought for control. She had an awful conviction that if she began to laugh now she would never be able to stop.

"Come on," Jonathan said. "Let's get out of here." He took her hand and began shouldering his way through the crowd to the exit.

Fighting to stay close to him as he plowed through the crush, Eve was suddenly struck by the thought that he had taken a grave risk in waiting for her. He must have known, in spite of his disguise, that only luck and the unprecedented droves of the people at the airport had saved him from discovery. Remembering her own situation a few minutes earlier when she stepped off the aircraft, alone, friendless, and soon to be hunted, she felt a warm glow of gratitude toward Jonathan.

Outside they somehow–miraculously enough–found a taxicab.

"Where to?" the driver asked.

"Just drive," Jonathan said. "I'll think of something."

"What about my luggage?" Eve exclaimed.

"Leave it where it is. We've got no place to take it."

"But how did you happen to meet me?" she said. "I couldn't send you a telegram."

"If you had, both of us would be in the hands of the law by now," he whispered, glancing at the driver. "I'll bet you half of America is camped in my apartment at Pasadena."

"What are we going to do?" Eve exclaimed *sotto voce*.

"I haven't the slightest idea. Since eleven o'clock this morning I've been living like a hunted animal."

"Jonathan, those people back there at the airport–it was a madhouse–like they'd all gone crazy. Is it all like this?"

"No, not all, but it's not pretty anywhere."

"It scares me."

"It would scare anybody," he said ruefully. "But there doesn't seem to be much we can do about it."

"What happened?" she asked.

He told her the sequence of events up to the moment of their meeting. Sensing the tension in her, he concentrated on the lighter aspects of it and even made something of a production out of the mustache and the henna rinse. Despite her ragged nerves, Eve actually found herself laughing once or twice before it was finished. There was something very reassuring about this big, almost ugly man and his bantering acceptance of adverse fortune.

"Well, I must say that, at least, you're a man with initiative."

He grinned. "It's supposedly a characteristic of rude Americans."

She made a little *moue* at him. "I told you I was sorry about that." The *moue* was adorable. Without the slightest warning, Jonathan leaned over and kissed her. It was more than a platonic kiss. It left Eve a little breathless.

"Would you mind telling me the reason for that?"

"Let's say it's a kind of apology."

"It seems to me, Jonathan Clark, that you are taking an awful lot for granted. You're also taking advantage of the dramatic nature of this situation. You wouldn't like more complications?"

Jonathan's face split into an even wider grin. The mustache looked ridiculous in this position with patches of spirit gum showing through the crepe hair. "This kind of complication," he said, "I like."

Eve held him firmly away from her. "Now, look, let's be serious. What are we going to do? We can't keep driving around in this cab forever."

"No, we can't. For one thing, I can't afford it. I had thirty-seven dollars and eighteen cents at noon. I've got twenty-six left. At this rate, I'll be lucky if I last a day and a half."

"But haven't you anyone you can turn to? There must be someone you can trust."

"Not with something as big as this."

"What about your parents?"

"I haven't any."

"I'm sorry."

"Thanks, but you needn't be. I was only four when they died. I don't remember either of them. What about you?"

She sighed despondently, "I have parents all right. They're on a Mediterranean cruise. It's their first holiday in years and I'm sick with worry about them. After this announcement from space they'll be at their wits' end. What are they going to think when they cable my flat and find I'm not there?"

"You didn't tell them you were leaving?"

"I didn't tell anyone. As far as my parents were concerned, I thought I'd save them a bit of worry by not telling them about my flight here until after I'd arrived. Now, thanks to that awful broadcast, I don't dare try to get near a cable or telephone office."

"You can write them."

"Yes, but who knows how long it will take them to get back to England, now that everything's in such a mess." She turned to Jonathan. "I suppose that sounds callous, doesn't it? I'm worrying about my folks having to interrupt their vacation when the whole world is in danger."

"Don't talk nonsense. Nobody can think emotionally in terms of global catastrophe. The concept is too big to grasp. Everybody thinks first of themselves and the people they love. It's like the newspaper business. You print a story of two million people dying of famine in India and nobody gets very excited about it. But find a little girl trapped in a well, and you've got a story that will make headlines anywhere in the world. Suffering is an individual thing. It can only be appreciated in terms of the individual."

She looked at Jonathan appraisingly for the first time. He was a strange paradox, this man. The words themselves had an undertone of cynicism and yet his voice had been kind and sympathetic, and his eyes as they returned her gaze were warm and understanding. The big rough-hewn nose and the wide mouth gave his face in this moment a very definite appeal and there was a vaguely disquieting electricity in his physical presence. She knew from her first meeting with him that he could be brutally caustic when he chose and a few moments ago when he should have been wholly preoccupied with the problem of what to do, he had been cavalierly . . . Well, one thing was certain. This man was not cut to a pattern as most of the men she had known. She realized he was speaking.

"I beg your pardon?"

"I said, 'A penny for your thoughts.' "

"I'm sorry. I was thinking how little we know about each other."

"Does it matter?"

"I suppose not. The question of the moment seems to be, where do we go from here?"

"Exactly. If I had enough money, there might be one way out of this. I've got a cabin in the mountains which nobody knows about."

Eve raised an eyebrow. "A cabin in the mountains?"

To her amazement, he began to blush. "Oh, now look, Eve. . . ."

She laughed delightedly at his confusion, the last vestiges of immediate anxiety sliding from her. "Having just had my lipstick smeared four minutes after meeting you, I can imagine what delightful little revels you are planning in the mountains."

"Damn it, Eve, that's unfair. I . . ."

"You what?"

"Supposing I promise to be good?"

"Why promise? You said we had no way of getting there."

"I could try to steal a car."

She regarded him speculatively for a few moments, then clicked open her purse and handed him a manila envelope.

"What's this?"

"I have a feeling, Jonathan, that your blushes and your insouciance are a snare and a delusion, but there's enough money in that envelope to buy an automobile."

Jonathan stared at her and then opened the envelope. He whistled softly. "You're not only pretty; you're loaded."

"I'm sure you *meant* that as a compliment."

Jonathan chuckled. "Then you'll come?"

She looked at him and smiled ambiguously.

"It seems I have no choice."

11

Professor Klaus Bochner sat propped up by three huge feather pillows in a private room. He had on a white hospital gown which had the effect of making him look more like a Rubens cherub than ever and he was contentedly sipping an American malted milk. He was enjoying it thoroughly. It was his third in the last three quarters of an hour. As a matter of fact, had it not been for the serious nature of his newly acquired knowledge, Professor Bochner would have been having the time of his life.

There were five people in his room. One of them was the Vice President of the United States of America. Another was the head of the Federal Bureau of Investigation. The third was a man whom Professor Bochner knew by reputation—America's most prominent atomic physicist. The fourth was a blond nurse. And the fifth was a stenographer.

Since the news of the professor's arrival in the hospital, there had been a constant procession of dignitaries of steadily increasing importance of which these were the latest, but, Professor Bochner suspected, not the last. Each of the dignitaries had questioned him tactfully and, for the most part, thoroughly. Their inquiries had elicited exactly nothing—nothing that is, of any practical value. The professor had explained his trip to the space ship in great detail. He had described the chamber in which he had awakened as a visual representation of pure mathematics, which, he was at some length to explain, was therefore an expression of pure beauty. He had waxed eloquent about the regal poise and bearing of his Alien host; he had recounted with juvenile enthusiasm the scientific marvels he had encountered during the episode, had speculated upon the possible necessity for revision of the present theories about the time and space continuum in view of his and his companions' instantaneous departure from and return to the earth, and had been responsible for several humorous reports which reporters firmly expected would go down in history. The professor had been describing Eve Wingate and had concluded his description with an appreciative comment on Eve's figure in a bathing suit. A reporter had remarked that he thought the professor was interested solely in the curvature of space and the professor had answered with artful celerity, "*And* what it curves around, young man, *and* what it curves around!" And had chuckled mischievously at his own daring.

Up to this point in his life, the professor had invariably been ill at ease in the presence of anything but an equation or a scientific theory. He had an abnormal fear of crowds and special receptions. For this reason he had, heretofore, avoided the public gaze whenever possible.

But the present situation was somewhat different. The people who were visiting him now were not here because he was a world-famed scientist, but because he had been one of the five citizens of the world to have been in actual contact with the Aliens. This put him, as he saw it, for the first time since his early youth, on a level of social relationship which had nothing to do with his contributions to science or to the world in general. It made him just another citizen and the experience was peculiarly satisfying. And so he had held forth for hours on every possible topic with regard to the space ship and its Alien pilot but had politely, firmly, and consistently refused to divulge one word of information about what had been said to him aboard that space ship, or to clarify the significance of the black box containing the three capsules which had been found in his jacket pocket and which the Vice President was now holding in his hand.

"But," said the Vice President, "can't you see, Professor, that we have no way of knowing whether or not the information you are withholding may not be jeopardizing the security of the United States."

The professor took another sip of his malted milk. "That is right," he said. "You haven't."

The Vice President sighed and tried again in a more conciliatory tone. "Will you not at least," he said, "give us some idea of the import of the Alien's message to you? As a citizen of the world," he added, sententiously.

The professor smiled benignly. "But you don't seem to understand, Mr. Vice President," he said, "that it is as a citizen of the world that I withhold this information."

The Vice President was getting nowhere. He turned to the atomic physicist, who had previously examined the black box. "Can you not, Karl," the Vice President said, "give me any indication of what this box contains?"

The physicist, whose full name was Karl Neuhaus, arose from the chair by the window, where he had been sitting ever since he had entered the room. He came over and stood beside the Vice President. He was a tall man, very erect for his fifty-one years, and he carried the distinction of America's foremost atomic physicist with a fine nonchalance. He had an angular frame and a bony but likable face in which a pair of keen blue eyes twinkled with a constant suggestion of ironic amusement. They had been twinkling rather more than usual during this interview between the Vice President and the professor. He was already convinced that there was nothing that he or any of his colleagues could do to open the baffling black box, and he had become aware–long before the Vice President–that the good professor had not the slightest intention of clearing up the mystery of its nature. What made the situation doubly interesting was that he was also convinced that the professor knew a great deal more about the box than he cared to reveal.

He answered the Vice President's question as succinctly as he could. "No, sir. We have given the box every test we can think of without success. The box gives forth no radiation of any kind. None of our instruments, except the common scale, reacts to it in any way whatsoever and even here the results are baffling. Its density indicates that it ought to be about ten times as heavy as it is, but that's all. We've tried fire, acid, radium, diamond cutters, acetylene torches, atomic bombardment . . . everything. It can't even be scratched, let alone opened. Naturally, we haven't the remotest idea of its purpose or functioning. We will keep on trying, but my personal opinion is that we will get nowhere." He glanced wryly at the professor. "What is your opinion, Professor?"

Professor Bochner smiled back. He had heard almost as much about Neuhaus as Neuhaus had heard about him, and he had liked him on sight. "I can only agree with you, Dr. Neuhaus," he said. "I am sure that, if you have been unsuccessful in opening the box, there is no physical force at our disposal which would be more effective than those you have already tried."

The Vice President sighed audibly. "Well, gentlemen, I suppose there is nothing further to be done." He bowed slightly in the professor's direction. "Thank you, Professor. I shall tell the President everything you have told me." The tone implied that the "everything" was not very much.

The professor smiled. "Good-by, Mr. Vice President."

As the Vice President and the stenographer left, Karl Neuhaus came around the bed and took the professor's hand. "It's been a great pleasure meeting you, Professor," he said. "I hope when all this has settled down we will have a chance to talk together. I'd like your opinion on several ideas which I have been turning over lately."

The professor returned the handshake warmly. "And I, Doctor, would like your opinion on almost everything."

Neuhaus smiled. "Then it's agreed." His eyes twinkled. "My best wishes for a rapid recovery." He released the professor's hand and started for the door. He was about to leave when he turned back and surveyed the professor with a slight smile. "You did say, didn't you, Professor, that there was no *physical* force which could open the box?"

The professor smiled back. "I believe I did," he said mischievously. "But, mind you, Doctor, it's only my opinion."

Dr. Neuhaus closed the door quietly.

12

Ivan walked down the deep-piled carpets of the Kremlin behind the Great Leader's personal secretary. It was just six and a half hours since Comrade Raskovich had forestalled his attempt to escape, but he would not have relived those six hours for anything in the world. First, there had been the harrowing and hollow attempts to explain his reason for leaving his quarters in civilian clothes; then a terrifying session during which he had doggedly refused to reveal to Raskovich what had happened aboard the space ship; the frantic but successful effort to transfer the black box back to the pocket of his military uniform without being observed; and finally a supersonic flight to Moscow with every nightmare mile charged with the realization of the interview to which he was now proceeding. His heart was beating so violently he felt sure the secretary must hear it. The corridor seemed endless and the silence was almost tangible. Finally the secretary paused before a pair of massive teakwood doors and turned to Ivan. His impassive face betrayed not the slightest flicker of emotion.

"You will wait here," he said.

Ivan found himself unable to say anything. He was forced to nod his acknowledgment. The secretary opened one of the vast doors and disappeared behind it. Ivan thought for a moment he was going to faint. He held himself stiffly erect and tried desperately to think of nothing. He began counting slowly to himself. At sixty-seven he lost himself and had to begin over again. The minutes ticked by in endless succession. The palms of his hands were clammy with perspiration. And still nothing happened. The silence remained unbroken. An eternity later, somewhere in the distance, a clock struck the half hour. Then the silence rushed back. The whole thing was becoming a nightmare. His head felt hot and his mouth dry. He knew that, unless something happened soon, he would shout, or cry, or do something he would regret for the rest of his life. And in that precise moment when he felt he could not resist one second more, the door opened and the secretary appeared. "The Great Leader will see you," he said.

For the first second, Ivan's muscles refused to obey him. Then, trancelike, he found himself moving through the door and into the private sanctum of the Great Leader. The door swung noiselessly shut behind him.

He was in the most enormous room he had ever seen in his life, but there was no time to examine it. Directly opposite him and at least a mile away, it seemed to Ivan, there was a large glass-topped desk. Behind this sat the Leader. Ivan's first impression was one of shock. *The Leader was small!* Even in the specially constructed chair intended to make him look as big as possible, he was tiny, and the proportions of the room made him look even smaller. His posters had given Ivan the impression that he was at least six feet and heavy. The discovery that he was considerably shorter than this startled him and increased his nervousness.

"Come forward," the Leader commanded, and Ivan began moving like an automaton across the abyss of space which separated him from the desk. At closer range he was able to see the details of the Leader's face. The eyes were small, dark, and icy, sunk in deep wells of puffy flesh, and they stared at Ivan with what seemed to be a frightening malevolence. The nose was short and broad and the cheeks were red-veined and unhealthy looking. Beneath the jawbones the flesh hung in flabby jowls. The mouth and chin were its only relieving characteristics. The chin, despite the folds of surrounding flesh, showed vestiges of strength and the mouth was cleanly chiseled. It was not a nice face but it was an arresting one, full of pride and cunning and knowledge of power. It continued to regard him silently and Ivan, with a guilty start, found himself comparing it to the clear piercing eyes, the tumbling silver curls, the taut skin, and the sculptured perfection of the face of the Alien.

"So you are Ivan Godofsky?" The harsh staccato voice startled Ivan out of his preoccupation. He nodded, standing stiffly at attention. "Comrade Raskovich has sent me a report that you refused to tell him anything." The satiric tone seemed to demand a reply, but for Ivan it was a futile struggle. His tongue refused to respond to the frantic commands from his brain. Strangely, the Leader did not seem to mind. He sat staring at Ivan dispassionately as if he were examining some unique insect under a microscope. "I congratulate you," he said unexpectedly. "It would have been very foolish of you to tell your story to anyone but me." A thin film of sweat beaded Ivan's forehead. The Leader noticed it. He smiled thinly and leaned back in his chair. "You are afraid of me."

This time Ivan managed to find his voice. "No, sir." The tremulous voice betrayed the lie.

"Good," said the Leader softly. "I should hate to think that any comrade of our great nation was afraid of me. It is my wish that every citizen of this great country regard me as a friend and a brother. You will talk to me on that basis."

"Yes, sir."

"I'm glad that we understand one another. Now to the facts. I have been told that the people from space gave you some information."

Ivan felt the last vestige of his courage oozing out of him. "Yes, sir," he said.

The Leader regarded him coldly for a full ten seconds then leaned back in his chair. "I'm waiting," he said.

Ivan Godofsky took a deep breath.

13

A few minutes before Sergeant Godofsky was faced with his great decision in the Kremlin, the world was stunned by a story which broke on the front page of a popular London newspaper under the by-line of Peter Brighton. It is a story that stands today as one of the grossest abuses of freedom of the press in the annals of newspaper history. The fact that it was 90 per cent pure speculation based upon the relatively few facts which Peter Brighton had gleaned in an interview with Harry Ward-Bellows, escaped the public entirely in the beginning. Brighton, a reporter for the newspaper, had been in Torquay during the time of the Alien broadcast and had met Eve Wingate and Harry Ward-Bellows at a cocktail party a few evenings earlier. After the broadcast he had gone directly to Eve's apartment and, not finding her there, he had proceeded to Harry's address where, after hours of waiting, he had intercepted Bellows when he returned home.

Harry, who had had an engagement with Eve that evening, was in a state of nerves. He had been on the way to her apartment when he had heard the broadcast listing Eve as one of the five people who had been interviewed by the Aliens, and he had immediately linked the revelation with her strange behavior of the previous day. He had been unable to get his car through the frantic throngs in the streets and had made his way on foot to Eve's apartment, only to find that she had disappeared and that no one had the slightest idea where she had gone. Frenzied trips to their mutual friends had availed him nothing and he had arrived home about midnight to find Brighton waiting. With a little careful encouragement by Brighton, he had poured out the whole story of the telephone call, the check, the motorboat, and the black box containing the three gold capsules which Eve had hurled into the sea.

Brighton wrote the story, highly embellished by his own imagination, and it appeared on the London streets the following morning. It provoked a nationwide and very nearly world-wide panic. Briefly, his story made the same assumption on Eve's disappearance as the population of the United States had made on the flight of Jonathan Clark. Since she had disappeared, she must have something to hide. She was, in other words, guilty.

Guilty of what, Brighton had been careful not to say, but he implied a great deal. He pointed out that the appearance of the space ships themselves, the facility with which the Aliens interrupted radio and television programs throughout the world and even managed in some incredible fashion to have the figure of their leader appear on motion picture screens throughout the nation, indicated a level of science away and beyond anything that we could approach. This being true, he continued, who could tell what had happened to the five citizens of earth aboard the ship. Had they, in some fashion, been made the dupes of the Aliens? And what of the ominous black box containing the three golden capsules which Eve had flung into the ocean? Why had she taken the trouble to go to a specific spot off the south coast of England to dispose of the box? Brighton pointed out that it was disposed of in a manner in which one might sow a mine. If her interest had merely been to get rid of the box, why go to so much trouble? Why not merely throw it into the sea from the cliffs of Torquay? He was not prepared to say that the box in actuality was a mine and had been deliberately planted in an area which the Aliens had decreed, but the implication was certainly there. And where was she now? Was her request for American money proof that she had joined Jonathan Clark–the story of his flight was already known–or was it (and Mr. Brighton liked this idea) just a ruse to make people think she had left the country? And what about the others who were on the space ship–did they have black boxes too?

The front page of the paper carrying the story bore a remarkable resemblance to the extra which appeared on the Los Angeles streets. It took half an hour for the British government to get its policy of restraints into action, but in that half hour pandemonium reigned.

Even the normally staid and controlled English commentators were carried away by the rising flood of hysteria. Within minutes of the appearance of the story on the streets of London, radio and television programs were interrupted by hasty and ill-conceived recapitulations.

It is inconceivable that Brighton could have written the story he did without foreseeing, at least in some measure, the panic it would generate. There was just enough probability therein to fray the nerves of a world already teetering on the brink of chaos. Only the promptest action by Her Majesty's government, aided by the *Times,* the *Daily Telegraph,* and other responsible London publications, averted complete catastrophe. Within three quarters of an hour after the story's appearance, the Prime Minister spoke on radio and television, condemning the story as sensationalism of the worst kind and pleading for restraint and discipline from the people. The papers carried the text from his speech and editorials culled from a special release from Central Intelligence damned the Brighton story as unverified, premature, and criminally dangerous.

Peter Brighton was arrested, publication of his newspaper was suspended, and an uneasy peace reigned throughout Britain, as the people waited anxiously for the true story to be revealed. The real tragedy was, of course, that though the story was quelled and order restored, the seeds of fear had been sown. Until some definite word was forthcoming to replace Brighton's explanation of the strange behavior of Eve Wingate and the significance of the black box, the fear was to represent a steadily increasing danger to the security of the world.

14

The used-car lots were jammed. Los Angeleans were taking no chances on being trapped in the city in an old automobile, should there be an invasion. In front of Jonathan and Eve, a mechanic rubbed the white-washed $2,000 sign off the windshield of a late model Buick and wrote $2,500.

Jonathan grabbed Eve's hand. "Come on," he said. "Ten minutes more and we won't be able to afford a car."

He ducked under the railing behind which the Buick was resting. He took the mechanic by the shoulders as he was starting for the next car. It was an Oldsmobile convertible priced at $2,200. "Look," he said sharply, "is this car in good shape?"

He pointed to the Oldsmobile. The mechanic wiped the chalk from his fingers. "There ain't a better car on the lot, Mac," he said laconically.

Jonathan knew nothing about cars, but this one certainly looked new. Besides, the mechanic was more likely to be honest about it than the dealer.

"I'll take it," he said to the mechanic. "Call the boss."

"I'll have to change the price first," the mechanic said. "I just got orders that everything goes up five hundred bucks."

"Look," Jonathan said, "when I got here, this car was priced at $2,200. Go get the boss."

The mechanic hesitated, shrugged, and looked into the lot. "O.K.," he said, "it's no skin off my nose." He stalked off.

They waited for some time before the boss got himself away from the horde of customers. They were all looking, but so far the buying was cautious. The boss finally arrived at their side. He had on a bright Hawaiian sport shirt on which a button was missing over the bulging paunch. His face was beefy, mottled, and beaded with perspiration, but he was in high spirits. Business in the next few hours was going to be sensational. He rubbed his hands together expectantly.

"Now then," he said heartily, "what can we do for you? Want something clean and classy? You've come to the right place. Honest John has a car for every budget. And believe me," he added in a dramatic whisper, "with them Martians in the skies, you never know when you are going to need a good car. No sir," he said, "you never know."

"I'll take this Oldsmobile," Jonathan said.

"Fine," said the dealer, "fine! You've got yourself a good car. There ain't a better car on the lot. It's got all the accessories: radio, air conditioner, swivel seats—the works."

Jonathan nodded. He began counting out hundred dollar bills from the wallet Eve had given him.

The dealer watched avidly. "You understand, of course," he said, "that this car is $2,700."

Jonathan stopped counting and turned his head slowly to stare at the figure $2,200 written on the car's windshield. The dealer followed the glance. "Ah, yes," he said, "I see the boy hasn't had time to correct the price. Since yesterday, all cars have been upped $500."

"You mean," said Jonathan coldly, "since you saw there was going to be a demand for cars."

The dealer's voice changed, and his voice took on a nasty edge. "Look, Bud, you want the car or don't you? If you want it, it's $2,700. If you don't, there's lots of people who will be ready to buy it in the next twenty-four hours."

Jonathan was a big man. His shoulders were very broad, and he had hands that looked on occasion as large as basketballs. He reached out with one of these hands, grabbed a fistful of the dealer's sweaty sport shirt, and jerked him toward him. The dealer grunted in surprise, and an edge of fear showed in his eyes.

"Look, Honest John," said Jonathan softly, "the sign on this car says $2,200. I'm not going to tell you that there is a law against profiteering, but I want that car, and I want it for the price that's marked on it." With one hand, he spun the fat man around and shoved him violently against the Buick on the opposite side. The man's head snapped back and hit the steel top with a distinct thud.

Jonathan handed the wallet to Eve to free his hands. He flexed them silently. "Now," he said, "do I get that car, or don't I?"

The dealer's jaw was hanging slackly. "O.K., O.K." he said, running his tongue over his lips nervously. "So maybe I made a mistake."

"So maybe you did. Now, you're going to get me the owner's certificate and the bill of sale, and I'm going to be right beside you when you get them." He extended his hand without taking his eyes off the dealer, and Eve put two thousand two hundred dollars in it. "Wait here," he said to Eve. "I'll be back in a second."

He looked at the dealer. "Let's go," he said curtly. The dealer went. With alacrity.

Jonathan returned in ten minutes with the keys and the documents. Eve was already seated in the car. "Ever since we met," she said, "I've been trying to think what it is you do for a living."

"And now you know?"

"Certainly. You're a gangster!"

Jonathan chuckled, then eased the car out of its berth and into the street. He made a quick stop for gas, then threaded his way north on Vermont and turned into the Hollywood freeway. Both of them fell silent as they noted the increasingly heavy traffic. Their tension mounted when they reached the Harbor cloverleaf and bore off into the Pasadena speedway, for here the cars were jammed bumper to bumper in all the outbound lanes. A few minutes later, they came to a dead halt. For half an hour thereafter, seething with impatience, they eased forward a foot at a time. It was impossible to tell the reason for the delay until it was too late to do anything about it. After thirty minutes of inching along, Jonathan glanced ahead. There was a roadblock! Just ten cars ahead state troopers and local police were stopping each car and questioning its occupants. There was no way out. The jam was four cars wide and who could tell how many cars deep. There was no turning around or backing up. There was nowhere to go but forward.

Eve saw the block at almost the same moment as Jonathan. "Jonathan–" she began.

"I see it," he interrupted, "and there's not a damn thing we can do about it! How stupid can a guy be?" he added bitterly. "Naturally, they'd be checking all exits from the city. Why didn't I think of it before!"

"Why didn't I?" she moaned. "I guess neither of us has the criminal mind–no foresight. What are we going to do?"

"Just sit here and get caught, I guess," he said disconsolately. "If they ask me for my driver's license, we've had it."

"Maybe if I drove," Eve said. "They aren't looking for a woman."

"And what if they ask you for identification? Once they see 'Eve Wingate,' it's all up with us. Your name's as well known as mine."

"They may not ask for identification from a woman. Besides, the name on my passport is Mary Evelyn Wingate." She took the passport out of her purse. "If this were England," she said, "and they were looking for me, we'd never get away with it. But since they don't know I'm in the country, it just might work."

The cars inched forward. "Change places with me quickly," she begged. Jonathan held himself up against the wheel while she slid beneath him, and then he scrambled awkwardly over into the opposite seat.

"Have you got a pen?" she said. He fished in his breast pocket, and pulled out a fountain pen.

"What are you going to do?"

"Look," she said quickly. "If we were to change the 'g' in my name to an 'f' and make the 'e' into a 't,' it would read 'Mary Evelyn Winfatt.' We might get away with it."

"It's no good," he said. "It won't work."

"Why?"

Another car sped through the barrier and they moved forward. He held up his fountain pen. "Green ink."

"You're a big help," she said. "Look in my purse." There were now only four cars ahead of them before the barrier. He found the pen and uncapped it. "Hurry up!"

"I can't."

"Why?"

"Because," he said miserably, "my hand is shaking."

She wrenched the passport and pen out of his hand. "My hero," she said scathingly. She made two quick corrections in the book. "Here, blow on it."

"But your name is *printed* here on the next page. What are we going to do about that?"

"I'll hold my finger over it and hope he doesn't turn the page. I don't really expect we'll get away with it but we'll try. Put it back in my purse."

He did as she requested. "Listen," he whispered, "I admire your courage. But what are you going to do with *me!* Put me in the glove compartment? I'm the one they're looking for." There was only one car ahead of them.

"I don't know. I'll try to think of something." The last car pulled clear of the barrier. "Here goes." She put the car into gear. "Anyway it was nice while it lasted." The car moved forward the last few feet and came to a stop. A trooper approached from the side of the road.

"I'm drunk," Jonathan said in a flash of last moment inspiration, and turned his back. The trooper reached the side of the car. He was sandy-haired and very boyish. Eve thought maybe there was a chance. She gave him a dazzling smile.

"I thought we'd never get here," she pouted prettily. "Isn't it always the way? Every time you're in a hurry, something like this happens."

The young trooper's eyes widened as he took in Eve's face and figure; he grinned a little self-consciously. The frank and approving stare with which Eve was examining him made him somewhat uneasy. "I'm sorry, miss," he said, "but we've got orders to check all cars."

"Oh," Eve bubbled, "I'll just bet you're looking for the man who was aboard the space ship?" The trooper nodded. "You mean to say you haven't caught him yet? I thought you Americans always got your man."

"That's the Royal Canadian Mounted Police," the trooper said. "You've got your countries mixed. May I see your identification?"

"I've only got my passport. I arrived this afternoon to find that the world has gone mad over these space people. Everything's such a mess," she continued, fumbling in her purse. "Can you imagine–I flew all the way from England to meet this monster." She gestured disgustedly toward Jonathan. "My fiancé," she said, as she held out her passport for his inspection, her finger over the last name of the printed portion.

The trooper barely glanced at the passport, then peered at Jonathan's motionless figure. "What's the matter with him?"

"He's drunk. He was drunk when I arrived and he's been drunk ever since." She shook Jonathan forcefully. "David," she said. "David! For heaven's sake, wake up. The police want to talk to you."

"Tell them to come back in the morning," he muttered thickly.

"You see?" Eve said appealingly to the trooper. "He's impossible." She shook Jonathan again. "David! David!"

The cars behind were beginning to honk their horns impatiently. The trooper shifted uneasily and Eve pressed her advantage.

"What can I do, officer?"

"Can't you just get his wallet out of his pocket, ma'am?"

"But officer, he's *sitting* on it!" She held her breath.

Again the trooper hesitated. Finally he scratched his head. "I guess it's all right, ma'am, but at least pull him around so I can have a look at him."

"Gladly," she said, resisting an overpowering impulse to stop this nerve-racking game and blurt out the whole truth. She wrenched Jonathan around and slapped him sharply on the cheek. Jonathan's eyelids fluttered once, weakly, then his head fell forward on his chest. The trooper was now looking at the top of Jonathan's head. Between Eve's body as she turned to grasp Jonathan, the slap, and the falling forward of Jonathan's head the trooper had nothing but the briefest glimpse. He retained the impression of a slack-jowled face, a mustache, and red hair.

Eve pushed Jonathan away from her. "It's hopeless," she said. "I'm afraid, if you want his identification papers, you'll have to lift him out of the car. I can't budge him."

The cars behind were blaring. From the side of the road a voice said, "All right, Johnson, she's pretty, but let's not be all day!"

The trooper blushed. "Drive on, miss," he said.

For five minutes Eve drove steadily while neither she nor Jonathan, who had remained frozen in his original position, said a word. Then she pulled over to the side of the road and stopped the car. She took her hands off the wheel and two shiny spots of moisture remained on the hard rubber where they had rested. She expelled a long deep breath. "Whew!" she said.

Jonathan raised himself slowly from his recumbent position. Along his face were four red weals. "You did not," he said accusingly, "have to hit me so hard!"

Eve lit a cigarette and blew the smoke out of the window without looking at him. "I had to make it look good," she said.

He rubbed his cheek reflectively. "Why is it that, every time you have an idea, I get hurt? The last time it was a machine gun in my stomach."

"My hand is shaking," she mimicked scornfully. He took the cigarette from her and blew a perfect smoke ring.

"Try to remember that it is not shaking any longer and, unless you behave yourself in the future, I shall know where to apply it."

She wrinkled her nose at him disdainfully, put the car in gear, and pulled back onto the highway. Jonathan threw the cigarette out of the window and switched on the radio. There was a brief humming and then a voice came through:

". . . and all citizens are asked to be on the lookout for this man wanted for questioning by the federal government. He is thought to be in possession of valuable information. I repeat, do not try to apprehend Clark; he may be armed and there is reason to believe he is dangerous. If you have any information as to his whereabouts, you are requested to phone your local police station immediately.

"On the national scene, last reports from New York indicate that world-renowned scientist Professor Klaus Bochner, who arrived at New York airport this morning, is still missing, and the hunt for him going on throughout the eastern United States is so far without success. There is an unconfirmed report from London that the English girl, Eve Wingate, has also disappeared, leading to speculation that all five citizens of earth may be acting under orders from the space men to avoid capture. All defense units are being mobilized throughout the nation, but government releases urge all citizens to act with calmness and discipline. Local police throughout the nation have been requested to take prompt and firm action against profiteers in an attempt to halt inflation, which has already begun in some parts of the nation. The Stock Exchange this afternoon took the steepest plunge it has taken since the crash of '29. We have received no news of the Russian soldier and the Chinese girl who were aboard the saucer. All news sources from Moscow and Peiping have apparently been plugged. . . ."

Jonathan reached over, switched off the radio, and grinned at Eve. "You hear that–I may be dangerous. How does it feel to be a fugitive's moll?"

She glanced at him a little impatiently. "Don't you ever take anything seriously?"

"Meaning?"

She compressed her lips. "I'm sorry, I shouldn't have said that."

"Why shouldn't you? If you have something to say, say it." His voice was faintly amused and she felt herself becoming angry.

"All right, I will. The whole world is in danger from those frightful bombs. Everybody is panic-stricken. We're being hunted like animals, and you act as if the whole thing were some sort of parlor game."

"And you don't think it's quite 'cricket' to be flippant when the world's in a mess, is that it?"

"Something like that."

"I see." There was silence for a minute, but she felt his eyes on her as she watched the road. Finally he said quietly, "Look, Eve. It's been less than forty-eight hours since this whole thing started. You saw what it was like back there at the airport, and the used-car lots. If I'm any judge, it's going to get worse . . . a hell of a lot worse. There's almost a whole month ahead of us before we're going to be able to breathe freely again. If you start out by carrying your responsibility like a martyr, you're going to be in bad shape before it's over."

"Then you advocate a kind of protracted hilarity as an antidote."

"Hell, no. I only meant that if something has a funny side and you're in the habit of seeing the funny side of a situation, then for the love of Mike, see it! Don't kid yourself you have to act like the chief mourner at a funeral because it seems like the correct social behavior for the occasion."

She looked at him again. "Did anyone ever tell you you were something of a paradox?"

"No, why?"

"You are, you know. What do you do for a living when you're not threatening car dealers?"

"I'm a reporter."

"Do you like it?"

"Uh-huh."

"What else?"

"You mean, case history?"

"If you like."

"O.K. I work for the Los Angeles *Telegram*. I earn a hundred and nine dollars and four cents a week after taxes and I never have a nickel. I own a '62 Chevrolet convertible, two good suits, a collection of damn good jazz, and an original Toulouse-Lautrec. I drink a little, smoke a lot, and am nuts about all kinds of sports. I'm thirty-seven, unmarried, unengaged, and an absolute pushover for well-constructed girls of twenty-six with auburn hair and green eyes."

"Twenty-eight, but thank you for the compliment."

"What about you?"

She steered the car deftly around a truck and then said, "I should have thought that you would have had me neatly pigeonholed by now."

"If you want the truth, I had you pegged as the poor little rich girl type. You know, the Riviera, the Derby, the social whirl–terribly rich and terribly bored. Now, I'm not so sure."

"Why?"

"I don't know. You've got something that doesn't quite fit that pattern."

"What gave you your first impression?"

"I'm not sure of that, either. I lost my temper on the space ship because I thought you were a spoiled brat who wasn't up to handling responsibility. Was I a long way off?"

"Not so far. My parents aren't rich, but they're quite well-to-do now. After the war it wasn't so easy. They scrimped and saved to send me to the best schools. I've met all the very best people and found very few I really liked."

"Why?"

"It's hard to explain, really. They're all gay and charming, but all the girls look like they had the same mother and you have to look at the men when they talk or you can't tell them apart. Do you know what I mean?"

He laughed. "I think so."

"Everybody always says the correct thing at the correct time. The conversation is generally clever, often brilliant, and inevitably trivial. After a while you begin to wonder if there's a point."

"So what did you do about it?"

"I took a secretarial course and went to work as a private secretary to a cinema producer."

"And?"

"Well, I'm afraid I spent more time defending my virtue than I did taking dictation. After ten days I gave it up. I went swimming and a three-eyed gargoyle with green hair beckoned me lovingly. The rest, you know."

"Miss Wingate, I'm beginning to like you tremendously."

"Do you always kiss first and decide afterward?"

"I was carried away by the situation."

"That's not very flattering."

"It's not very true. Hey, there's a drive-in! Let's eat!"

"Do you think it's safe?"

"As safe as driving. Besides, it's a long way to the cabin and I'm starving. The longer we wait, the more dangerous it will be."

"All right, but all this is beginning to wear on my nerves."

Jonathan frowned. "Take it easy. It's only the beginning!"

15

In Moscow, Sergeant Ivan Godofsky felt the blood draining away from his face as the impact of the Leader's question struck him. What could he say? He had been asked point blank by the Great Leader to reveal the information which he had sworn to keep secret and because of which he had made the fruitless attempt to escape from his room in Vladivostok. He felt the outline of the black box in his pocket pressing against the inside of his wrist as he stood at attention. A flash of inspiration lanced through him. Perhaps a solution of his immediate predicament lay here. Hadn't the figure on the dais said that there was no power on earth capable of opening the box? If he could trust the truth of that statement, he could give the box to the Leader and gain a temporary respite in which to marshal his thoughts. He had to do something quickly because he realized with simple shrewdness that the present situation was too much for him to handle. His nerves were frayed to such an extent that if he didn't get out of here quickly he would soon be pouring out the whole story.

He took a deep breath. He would have to lie. But to lie to the Leader could mean death, and Ivan did not want to die. He suffered his own particular and lonely martyrdom in those few seconds. He opened his mouth only to find that his tongue was paralyzed, glued to his palate.

The Leader recognized the symptoms. He had seen them before.

The boy was frightened to death. It had not yet occurred to him that the boy would have the backbone to lie. He simply assumed that Ivan was laboring under the same fear stimulus that affected 90 per cent of those he confronted in personal interviews. He waited expectantly, patiently. Always, he derived a certain cruel satisfaction in these incidents. They brought home to him even more powerfully than the cheers of the masses or the tramp of the booted feet of his troopers the extent of his power, the absolute and final authority which he exercised over every one of his people. He pulled his mind away from these reflections as he saw that the boy had found his tongue.

"Sir," said Ivan unevenly, "it wasn't really anything definite."

"What wasn't definite?" the Leader said.

"The–the information."

The Leader raised an eyebrow and pursed his lips reflectively. "No?"

"No," said Ivan, praying that he would be clever enough not to give away more than was necessary. "But they gave me this." He withdrew the small black box. His fingers were trembling as he handed it across the desk to the Leader.

The Leader leaned forward and took the box from the outstretched fingers. "Ah," he said, and began to examine the box intently. He looked through the transparent cover at the three ovoid golden capsules. They meant nothing to him. He turned the box over and scrutinized it carefully, looking for a way to open it. He could find none. There was no line of demarcation except in color between the black base and the transparent top. It might have been one solid piece of plastic. It was incredibly light. The dictator had no idea of what the box was made of, but it looked as though it ought to weigh a great deal more than it did. He turned it over until he was once more looking through the transparent top. In the subdued light of the chamber, the capsules glittered coldly. "Very interesting," he said. "What are the capsules for?"

Ivan's heart was in his throat again, but he committed himself bravely. "I don't know, sir."

The Leader's head snapped up and anger smoldered in the tiny eyes. "You don't know!"

"Not exactly. They gave us these boxes."

"All of you?" The tone made Ivan quail. His "yes" was almost inaudible.

"They gave you this," the Leader continued, "and they didn't tell you what it was for?"

"Not exactly."

"Well, what *exactly* did they tell you?"

Ivan took a deep breath. Here it was again. He saw that lying was bound to entail one crisis after another. "They said," he replied, his mind working furiously, "that it contained a secret of great power, but, to free the power, the box would have to be opened."

The eyes of the Leader seemed to bore inside Ivan's head. "And they didn't tell you," he said suspiciously, "anything else?"

Ivan swallowed painfully. "No, sir. Except . . ."

"Except what?"

"Except that without me, whatever was in the box would be useless."

The Leader mentally examined this statement for some seconds before he spoke. Then he said, "I see. And they didn't tell you how to open the box?"

"No, sir."

The Leader continued to look at him steadily, then pushed himself back in his chair and stared at Ivan from beneath half-lidded eyes. Was it possible, he thought, that the boy was lying? He couldn't bring himself to believe it. He was obviously frightened out of his wits, and the story he told was just fantastic enough to be true. If so, the Aliens were pitting the nations of the world against each other in a race to discover the secret they had given to people on earth. Perhaps it was some kind of a test. The boy had said each one of the participants had been given a box. And who had them? The Americans, damn them, had one; and if that capitalist toady, Bochner, had reached America, they probably had another, unless his agents could get to Bochner first. It was dangerous to touch him in America, but perhaps it was worth trying. They might be playing this game for control of the world. He snapped the switch on his desk and spoke again at some length into the hidden microphone in a low tense voice, the name "Bochner" appearing several times. Almost immediately after he clicked off the switch on his desk, the door to the left of the room opened. A man entered, crossed the carpet swiftly, bowed, removed the black box from the desk, bowed again, and left as swiftly and silently as he had entered.

The dictator turned his attention to Ivan again. "Well," he said, "if the box contains anything of importance, you can be sure that our great Russian scientists will be the first to find it."

The Leader's confidence shook Ivan's belief in the wisdom of what he had done, particularly since it was impossible for the boy to know what a wise decision he had made in surrendering the box. During Ivan's interview with the Leader, Peter Brighton's story about Eve Wingate's disposal of her capsules had broken on the London streets. Only the Leader's strict orders that he was not to be disturbed in his interview with Ivan under any circumstances prevented his learning of the existence of the box seconds before Ivan disclosed it. When the Leader did hear the story, his assurance that the soldier had told him the truth was to be bolstered, at least temporarily. Having set in motion the forces which he was sure would deliver the box's secret to him within a short time, he settled himself to hear the complete story of Ivan's visit aboard the ship from outer space.

Ivan told him the story in detail, being careful to explain everything exactly as it had happened and in its proper sequence, eliminating only those portions concerning the pact of secrecy he had made with the other four prisoners, and the revelations about the purpose and potential of the boxes. At every point he tried desperately to check against saying anything which might later trip him up. Here again he was to be later protected by Professor Bochner's disclosures which were to appear in the American press. Considering the fact that he was not an accomplished liar, he did very well.

16

In New York, Professor Bochner switched off his radio and slumped back into the hospital bed, his normally cherubic face lined with concern. It had never occurred to him that the coming of the Alien might not represent to the rest of the world what it did to Klaus Bochner. The news reports of a steady increase in outbreaks of panic and violence both shocked and bewildered him. The public had no knowledge of the dangerous charge that the Alien had made to the five individuals aboard the space ship. Consequently they should have seen only the ultimate miracle–that Earth, at last, was in contact with intelligence from the stars; that they were within reach of tapping undreamed reservoirs of knowledge. It seemed to the professor that this revelation should have been greeted with awe and wonder and delight. Instead, the market was collapsing, banks were being drained of their reserves of capital, a violent inflation was in progress. The entire world was in a grip of hysteria heretofore unknown. The whole thing was inconceivable.

To the professor, the advent of the Alien had been an ultimate peak in a life devoted to the search for knowledge. This fact had blinded him to other aspects of the problem which Jonathan, as a newspaperman, had seen immediately.

The news about Jonathan himself was particularly unsettling. Commentators were shouting that he could be armed and might be dangerous, and there were already several rewards for information as to his whereabouts. The only happy aspect seemed to be the fact that Eve had probably found him. Less than four hours after the Alien broadcast, thanks to her transatlantic call to Jonathan, Scotland Yard knew she had been aboard the midnight Clipper to New York. The F.B.I. had traced her as far as Los Angeles. And then the news had been released to the press. Latest reports indicated that both of them were still at large. The knowledge filled Professor Bochner with a vicarious elation. He chuckled to himself, remembering the sparks they had drawn from each other on their first meeting.

His mind was carried back to a picture of himself and a girl on the shore of a lake near the small university town where he had studied. Strange, he no longer remembered her face, but he recalled that she had been devastatingly beautiful, and that she had been wearing a large picture hat that was fashionable at the time, and a pale taffeta dress that rustled enchantingly in the afternoon breeze. What had happened to that budding romance, he wondered. He recalled vaguely some argument about a masked ball she had wanted him to attend and the lecture on astrophysics which he had thought too important to miss. He supposed, with a sigh of regret, that the lecture on astrophysics had won out, because there remained no recollection of the girl from that moment on. She had been replaced by equations and light years. And only the rustle of pink taffeta and the picture hat remained to bridge the years between.

He sighed again and sank back into his pillows, closing his eyes. He had been questioned almost unceasingly since eight o'clock the previous night and he was close to exhaustion. Almost before the nurse had adjusted the pillows and cranked the hospital bed into a prone position, the professor slept. She smiled fondly at him. In the eight hours of her shift, she had developed a deep affection for this kind and brilliant little man who had undergone such a remarkable experience. She smoothed an invisible wrinkle out of his already neat pillow and tucked the sheet around him, then crossed to the easy chair by the window. Within a few moments, she too was asleep.

At about the same moment that the professor's eyes closed on the pillow, a black Cadillac was threading its way through the streets of New York. At its wheel was a big stone-faced man in a chauffeur's uniform. In the back were two distinguished-looking individuals bearing on their knees small black bags which are the mark of the physician. The taller of the two was quite handsome, with an aquiline face, iron-gray hair, and a trimmed gray mustache. The other was less prepossessing in appearance. He was short, with a small pale face, and he wore gold-rimmed spectacles over large protruding eyes. The eyes and the spectacles gave him a serious and somewhat scholarly appearance. The taller man was Feodor Bracovich, the most valuable and astute Russian agent in the Americas.

At the moment he was distinctly unhappy. He was performing, or was about to perform, what he considered to be the most dangerous and foolhardy commission of his life. It was a mission which he felt had little chance of success and which, whether it was successful or not, seemed certain to curtail forever his usefulness in America, and perhaps in the world. But the order had come directly from the Leader himself, and it had been for immediate action. Should he be apprehended, he would be publicly disowned and condemned by his countrymen. In other words, he was expendable. He didn't like being expendable. He was a brave man, but he was extremely nervous. He was a believer in carefully laid plans. It was his experience that only the most perfectly conceived and precisely executed plans had a reasonable chance of success in his business, and on this particular occasion he had had no time to conceive anything but what appeared to be ridiculously inadequate strategy to get to the internationally celebrated Professor Bochner, who he had already learned was closely guarded. He was in search of a small black box containing three gold capsules, and his instructions had left no doubt in his mind that the box and its contents were a great deal more valuable to the Kremlin than was the life of Feodor Bracovich.

Well, he had done what he could. The car in which he was riding bore the license plates of a distinguished doctor who, at that very moment, was asleep in his own bed unaware that not only his license plates but all his personal medical identification papers were in the possession of one Feodor Bracovich. In addition to the car plates and the identification, Feodor had in his breast pocket a letter giving him permission to visit and examine Professor Klaus Bochner at will. The letter bore an amazingly accurate facsimile of the Great Seal of the United States on State Department stationery. Feodor only hoped it would be enough.

The car drew up at the gates of the hospital, where a police cordon was stationed. The head of the detail glanced at the medical license plate and moved up to the car. A federal agent, leaning against the gate in shadow, jotted the license number down on a pad and walked casually up the steps into the hospital. The captain of the police detail looked through the car's window, saw the two occupants and the doctor's bags on their knees, and said, "What is your business, Doctor?"

The doctor spoke, and his voice betrayed none of the tension that he felt. "I've been ordered to give Professor Bochner a thorough examination prior to his removal from the hospital in the morning."

The police captain scratched his head. "Strange," he said, "we've got orders that no one was to see the professor till further notice."

The agent smiled just a trifle condescendingly, and produced from his breast pocket a letter which he handed to the captain. "I think, Captain," he said, "that this will supersede any previous orders."

The captain read the letter carefully. It was certainly permission for the doctor to enter. On the letter was the Great Seal of the United States, and it was signed by the Secretary of State. Had the captain been familiar with the Secretary's signature, it would have made absolutely no difference. The signature was a nearly perfect forgery.

"May I see your identification?" he asked the doctor. Bracovich produced the identification of Dr. James Muir. The captain scanned it carefully and handed it back.

"Go ahead," he said. The car drove through the gates and stopped outside the door of the hospital. The doctor and his associate stepped out of the car and hurried up the hospital steps. The nurse on duty was impressed with the taller doctor's distinguished appearance. In any case, security was not the nurse's concern. She gave them the number of Professor Bochner's room. The doctor smiled and thanked the nurse. He crossed the lobby and entered the waiting elevator.

A minute later a federal agent rushed out of the telephone in the lobby, sprinted down the steps of the hospital and over to the cordon at the gate. He grabbed the captain by the arm. "Who was in that car?"

"Dr. James Muir," said the captain. "He had a letter from the Secretary of State."

"Dr. Muir is at home! I just talked to him. Come on!" He turned and ran toward the hospital, followed by the captain and one of the men. He had his gun out of his holster before he got back to the steps. He didn't wait for the elevator. He took the stairs three at a time.

Inside the hospital room of Professor Bochner, the policeman who had been on guard outside the door lay in a heap, on the floor. The man with the gold-rimmed spectacles was standing over the nurse, who had awakened to find a revolver resting against her forehead. "Just be quiet, my dear," the little man was saying in cultured tones, "and you will be unhurt."

The room was already a shambles. The bedding had been torn off the professor's body, the drawers were emptied, the contents of the closet were thrown on the floor. The erstwhile Dr. Muir stood over the professor, holding a second gun and his voice betrayed the tension under which he labored.

"Now, for the last time, Professor," he said. "Where is that box?"

The professor looked into the little black hole in the muzzle of the revolver. "But how can I make you believe," he said nervously, twisting his head around to take in the little man who was confronting the nurse, "that I haven't got the box. You must believe me, they . . . they took it away from me."

Bracovitch glanced at the man with the spectacles. "You think it's the truth?"

The smaller man nodded. "We didn't really expect they'd let him keep it."

Bracovitch took a deep breath and raised the revolver, centering the silencer of the muzzle on the professor's chest.

The professor looked at the gun. "I don't think you quite understand," he said gravely. "If I die, the box will be useless."

Bracovitch nodded. "Exactly, Professor." His fingers began to tighten on the trigger.

The nurse screamed. The little man hit the girl across the side of the head with the muzzle of his gun. It was close to the last movement he ever made.

The door smashed open and the little man spun halfway around before a bullet caught him full in the chest. Bracovitch's shot went wild as the professor kicked his gun arm, and the next four shots drove the Russian's body all the way back to the wall before he crumpled.

The F.B.I. man rushed to the professor's bedside. "Are you all right, Professor?" he said.

The professor nodded. "Yes, yes of course. Look after her."

The agent crossed to the unconscious nurse and made a quick examination. "She'll be all right, Professor."

The professor looked down at the body of Bracovitch and then back to the F.B.I. agent. "Who were they?" he asked uncertainly.

The federal agent holstered his gun. "I can make a pretty good guess," he said grimly, "but I'll bet a year's pay we'll never be able to prove it."

17

Jonathan was asleep when Eve stopped the car at the turnoff he had marked on the map. Patches of spirit gum stuck to his upper lip where he had removed the mustache, and a lock of hair had fallen across his forehead. On a sudden impulse, she leaned over and brushed it back into place. He smiled, his eyes still closed. "Am I dreaming," he said, "or did I just feel a cool hand on my fevered brow?"

"You were dreaming," she said. "Now wake up and listen. We have, as the novels would put it, reached an impasse."

Jonathan did not open his eyes. "What kind of an impasse?" he murmured.

She blew out a mist of smoke from the cigarette she was lighting. "There are two roads. The car doesn't know which one to take."

"Tell it to try the one on the right."

She glanced out. "That's not a road," she said. "It's a goat track."

Jonathan stretched and sighed. "I can see the time has come for a touch of the master's hand."

He got out of the car and came around to the driver's seat as Eve slid across to make room. She had scarcely released the wheel when exhaustion hit her like a physical blow. Her arms were numb and she felt almost giddy with fatigue. She slumped back in the seat as Jonathan eased the car slowly onto the trail. Eve was right; it could scarcely be dignified by the name of road. In various spots, miniature landslides had poured debris and small boulders on its surface over which the car lurched perilously in low gear. In other sections, giant holes had been eroded by the spring rains and had dried into bone-jarring crevices. Some of the pine branches brushed the top of the car as it slid under them. It was difficult going and Eve found herself once more strung taut when Jonathan finally came to a stop at a point where the road ended. Here the mountain and trees had been hacked away, making a level area large enough to accommodate two cars. There was no sign of habitation.

"Where's the cabin?" she said, her voice riding up with fatigue. Jonathan caught the note and put an arm around her shoulder.

"We have to walk a little bit," he said gently. "Can you make it?"

"I'll try."

He took her hand and led her to where there was a break in the face of the cliff. They started up a boulder-strewn path. When they had covered about thirty yards, she tugged at his hand. "Jonathan," she said breathlessly, "I don't want to be difficult, but these shoes were not made for climbing mountains."

She pointed to her high heels. Jonathan helped her down to a seat on one of the rocks. "I'm sorry. I didn't think about the heels."

She smiled at him, a little ruefully. "I'll be all right. Just give me a minute. I can't seem to catch my breath."

"It's the altitude. You get used to it after a while. Cigarette?"

"Thanks."

He lit two and handed one to her. She took the cigarette and held it while she caught her breath and gazed around her. The sun had almost set and in the cleft up which they were climbing the shadows of the giant firs were dark and heavy. Jonathan shifted his weight and a stone slid out from beneath his foot and rattled down the path. In the silence the noise it made was unnaturally loud. The world seemed very far away and again she had that queer sensation that none of this was really happening. She couldn't be sitting on top of a mountain in the state of California, calmly smoking a cigarette with a man she had known less than forty-eight hours. She just couldn't!

"Crazy, isn't it?"

She looked up, startled. "Are you telepathic, too?"

"No. Just observant. I wish you could have seen the look on your face. You looked like a small boy I once saw, trying to figure out how the magician got rabbits out of a hat."

She smiled wanly. "Are you real?"

"Uh-huh."

"I still don't believe it. I never believed the rabbits either." She took one brief pull on her cigarette and then dropped it.

Jonathan ground it out under his heel along with his own. "Ready?"

"I think so."

He leaned down and picked her up.

"Put me down. I can make it by myself."

"Stop squirming. It deprives you of dignity."

She subsided.

"That's better." He picked his way carefully up the incline for another fifty yards. When he had almost reached the crest of the path, he stopped. "Now," he said, "close your eyes."

She did as she was bidden. Jonathan stepped over the crest of the hill and stood on a small open mesa, almost at the very top of the mountain. Opposite him a path climbed off it into the trees and twenty feet to his left, nestled at the base of the cliff which sheered up perhaps a hundred feet, was the cabin. He carried Eve across the intervening distance, paused a moment, noting that the lock had been broken again, then kicked open the rough door and set her down. "Okay, open," he said.

She opened her eyes and gazed around in astonishment. "Jonathan, it's wonderful. How did you get all these things up here?" Her glance took in the couch, the books, the albums of records, the skins of mountain lions decorating the walls, the massive andirons in the fireplace.

"I didn't," he said. "It's being loaned to me by a friend of mine. He's a writer who's doing a book on Africa. He won't be back for another ten months. The whole thing was his idea, and I may add, was done with his money–even to the electric generator which pumps the water up for the shower and runs the lights. All I did was help him a little when he built it."

"How long has he been gone?"

"Four or five months."

"What about the people who know you've got the use of the cabin?"

"Nobody knows I use it. As a matter of fact, nobody except myself even knows where it is. The only two people who have ever been here are George and I."

"Not even one or two girl friends? It looks like a lovely place for a quiet week end."

"I'm a misogynist, remember?"

"So I noticed in the taxicab." She crossed the room and dropped into one of the armchairs. "Well, I suppose, since nobody knows you've got it, we should be safe."

"We should be. Even if the police discover we ran that roadblock, they don't know where we've gone. We might be on our way to New York or Mexico for all they know."

Eve sighed. "It just seems too easy, that's all. Suppose they decide to search the mountains?"

"Suppose they do? There's nothing to connect me with this cabin. We might be anywhere. They'd need two full divisions to comb all the hills between here and Arizona, and if they found us then it would be sheer blind luck. George likes to get away from it all. There's not another human being for fifty miles as far as I know. He and I cut that last ten miles of road ourselves."

She held up her hand. "All right. I believe you! I don't know George but I can well believe you had something to do with that last ten miles of road."

Jonathan grinned. "You're pretty damned saucy for a girl who's fifty miles away from help."

She made a *moue* at him. "Go start that generator or whatever it is while I freshen up a bit."

Jonathan grinned and went out.

He returned to find the phonograph playing Debussy and Eve stirring a pale liquid in a fruit jar. "I found the cache," she said. She poured into a water glass.

He sipped it and looked at her wonderingly. "Where did you learn to make such a good martini?"

"It's easy. I couldn't find the vermouth."

He laughed. "Are you hungry?"

She shook her head. "That snack at the drive-in filled me up. No, all I want is a bed. I'm exhausted."

Jonathan looked over at the twin bunks at the far wall. "The sleeping accommodations aren't exactly the Ritz."

"They'll do." She began unbuttoning her jacket. "Suppose you take your drink outside and watch the moon rise."

"I'd much rather stay here."

"Out!"

Jonathan smiled and left the room.

He returned to find her snuggled up in the lower berth. The auburn hair made a bronze halo on the pillow and the long lean lines of her body were outlined beneath the rough blanket. Jonathan looked at her appreciatively. She opened one eye.

"The top bunk," she said, "is for misogynists."

18

Ivan Godofsky lay on a bed in a pleasant room in the Kremlin. Since the Soviet officials had not yet made up their minds whether he was to be a villain or a hero, they had compromised by making him comfortable as far as his quarters were concerned, and keeping him in a state of virtual imprisonment. He had not slept in the twenty-four hours since he arose in Vladivostok prior to the Alien broadcast, and for the last fourteen he had undergone a merciless interrogation. Throughout the questioning, he thought he had managed to keep his story straight. He had concentrated, as in his interview with the Leader, on telling the truth down to the most trivial detail about what had happened, and had eliminated only the parts of the Alien's speech dealing with the significance of the black box and his pact with the four foreigners. After fourteen hours, unable to glean anything further, they had permitted him to get some rest.

Despite the fact that his eyes were bloodshot with fatigue and his body leaden with weariness, he had found it impossible to sleep. His brain swung in endless gyrations around the pivot of his lie. So far, he had been able to make it stand, but how long could he continue? He knew that his questioning was not over, that at this very moment the interrogators were comparing their notes and impressions, fitting the incidents together, trying to find a flaw.

It seemed to Ivan that his greatest hope lay in the fact that the experience was so extraordinary. He sensed during the interview, that the interrogators, despite their air of confidence, were up against something for which they had no precedent. The answers they received to most of their questions were answers that strained the limits of the most versatile imagination. An insane idea kept occurring to him; perhaps the interview as he conceived it had not really taken place at all. Perhaps the whole thing had been an hallucination induced by the Aliens and he had not really left the earth. And yet, his possession of the black box and his physical contact with the other four people were concrete proofs that drove his mind into a mire of confusions and self-contradictions.

He wondered what would happen if the Leader's scientists could not open the box. He was no longer capable, after so many hours of interrogation and lack of sleep, of feeling the immediate and paralyzing fear which had characterized his earlier state. His ragged nerves refused to accept further excitation and had defended themselves by driving his body into a state of numbed acceptance. He lay back on the bed and closed his eyes. The sensation was painful, almost as if the insides of his eyelids were coated with sand. An overwhelming lassitude crept over his limbs and he fell, finally, into an uneasy slumber.

In another part of the Kremlin, a violent scene was being enacted. The Great Leader was having a tantrum. His face was suffused with blood, the eyes staring out of their fleshy sockets, and tiny white flecks of foam showed at the corners of his mouth. He pounded his desk in a manner that, under any other circumstances and coming from any other person, would have been ludicrous. Coming from the Leader, it was terrifying. These tantrums, which were in themselves almost a kind of epilepsy, generally presaged even more dreadful periods of deadly calm in which men had a habit of disappearing, never to be heard from again. The men standing before the Leader were the most noted scientists in Russia. They had not been able to open the box.

Since they had entered his presence, they had not been permitted to say a word. They had heard that other boxes existed in America and England. They could only believe, from the violence of the Leader's outburst, that the Americans had somehow solved the riddle of the box. Exactly the opposite was true and the Leader knew it. He had intended only to create a minor scene, to frighten the scientists into more intense endeavors, but somehow the affected anger had become real. Somewhere in the back of his mind, the thought fought its way to the surface that his rages were becoming more frequent and consistently more difficult to control. With an obvious effort he brought his tirade to a halt and sank back into the chair, his face beaded with perspiration. He drew out a handkerchief and mopped his forehead. When he spoke it was with a voice that was still trembling from his earlier release of violence. "Perhaps you can give me an explanation of your failure to carry out my orders."

There was silence from the group. Uneasily the eyes of seven of the eight men began to turn in the direction of a small, emaciated man with a hooked nose and a receding chin who wore a pair of thick glasses. The little man, whose appearance had been marked during the interview by a lesser degree of terror than his compatriots said quietly, "Sir, our failure to open the box is as embarrassing to us as it is annoying to you. We have given this object"—he raised his hand to show the box in question—"every test available to modern science. We have been unable either to open it or even to mar its surface. Our strongest microscopes reveal no division of structure between the transparent top and the black base of the object. It gives off no radiations. Electronic bombardment is useless. The electrons not only refuse to pass through this material; they are actually, in some manner unknown to us, reflected from it. It is a marvel of scientific ingenuity." The scientist finished on a note of awe which seemed to indicate that he had almost forgotten the presence of the Leader.

The Leader looked at them malevolently but found himself at a loss. Further anger, it seemed, would avail him nothing. Finally, he said, coldly, "Are you telling me that you cannot open the box?"

The little scientist pursed his lips. "No," he said dispassionately, "but, as I have told you, we have given it every test we can think of. We have been working at this steadily for thirteen hours and have discovered nothing except that the box does not react to any known electronic, chemical, or physical agent. I can offer you no guarantee" —the little man was cautious here because it was just within the barest possibility that the Americans might have succeeded in opening the box—"that we will ever be able to open the box. I can only say that, if it can be opened, eventually we will succeed, but it will take time."

"But we haven't got time," the Leader screamed. "What if the American warmongers get it open before us?"

The scientists heaved an inward sigh of relief. At least the Americans, too, were at a standstill. The little scientist, with the discovery that he had not, so far, been beaten to his objective, felt a bit more secure. "I must also point out to you, sir, that if we do succeed in opening the box, we have still to determine the function of its contents. If they present the same problems as their container, it may be years before we can know, for sure, their significance."

"Years!" the Leader said.

"I merely said it *might* be years. It is also possible that we might open the box and find the significance of its contents tomorrow or next week."

The Leader said nothing. He chewed the edge of his tongue nervously while his right hand opened and closed the communication switch at the right hand of his desk. In the ensuing silence, the clicking had a strangely oppressive effect on everyone's nerves.

One of the other scientists ventured a question. "May we ask," he said tremulously, "if the soldier Godofsky has been able to shed any light on the subject?"

The Leader riveted his eyes upon the speaker. "Get out, all of you, and don't come back until you have opened that box."

The scientists turned and made for the door with a haste that was more in the nature of a rout than of a dismissal. When the door had been shut, the Leader took out his handkerchief and mopped his brow again. He flipped the communication switch open. "Get Gregor in here." Thirty seconds later, Gregor, chief of the Leader's intelligence corps, who had supervised the interrogation of Ivan, hurried into the room and approached the desk silently.

"Well?" snapped the Leader.

The intelligence man shook his head in negation. "Nothing, sir. His story agrees in every detail with the one you recorded in your original interview with him and also with the reports we received from Comrade Raskovich in Vladivostok."

"Raskovich is a fool," the Leader said. He pointed a stubby finger at Gregor. "You're a fool. I'm surrounded by fools! The boy is lying. He must know more than he is telling. You are supposed to be intelligent. Do you believe for one moment that these Aliens gave this soldier a box which couldn't be opened without telling him what it contained? Do you suppose that they came all the way from outer space to this planet for nothing? Do you suppose they went to the trouble to make a broadcast to earth telling us that they had given these five people some very unusual information, if it weren't true? *Do you?*"

"No, sir. I do not."

The positiveness of the intelligence chief's reply caught the Leader off guard. He checked the phrase on the tip of his tongue and looked at the agent. "Ah," he said in a different tone. "Then you believe the boy is lying."

"No," said the agent, "I don't think he's lying. I think he's telling the truth. But I don't think," he added, as the Leader opened his mouth for a second explosion, "that he is telling *all* of the truth."

The Leader dropped the hand which he had leveled in Gregor's direction, and the beginnings of a smile came over his face. He walked slowly around the desk and sat down. "Now," he said, with a vicious note of satisfaction in his voice, "now we are beginning to get somewhere. I hope you have an explanation as to why you didn't continue the interrogation when you suspected this."

Gregor hesitated briefly. "I felt I should confer with you first. There's a delicate point to be considered here. The boy insists that, without him, whatever is in the box will become useless. He *may* be telling the truth. We know, for instance, that the box of the dead Chinese girl contained only powder. It may once have contained capsules like Godofsky's. If so, we must move carefully. The motivation for the boy's concealment may be so deep-seated that it's possible even torture or death may not get it out of him."

"You mean to tell me," the Leader rasped, "that the combined abilities of my entire interrogation staff can't get the truth out of one ignorant soldier?"

"If a man is strong enough, the truth takes time. Complete destruction of the human will is a slow process. I understand that in this situation our time is limited, and an attempt to speed up the customary approach would be very dangerous. So might force."

"You have a solution?"

"I think so. I've checked the boy's record. He is a good soldier and a good citizen. It might be wise to try a bit of simple psychology first."

The Leader scowled impatiently. "You talk too much, Gregor. Get to the point. What is your plan?"

"I think we could assume on the basis of the story from England that the box contains some sort of weapon. If we are right, it shouldn't be too difficult to persuade Godofsky that America is threatening us. I suspect, if he thought his country was in danger, he might give us the whole story."

"And how do you propose to persuade him of this?"

"The usual way. A few specially prepared newspaper headlines—a radio broadcast written for his benefit."

The Leader eyed Gregor coldly. "What about narcosynthesis?"

"There have been occasions when it didn't work. I prefer to use it when we've got him to the point where he's almost ready to break. If he still hesitates, we'll try to push him over the line with the serum. We'll hit him with everything after another fifteen or twenty hours of questioning. I don't think it can fail."

The Leader sat silently twisting a pencil on the blotter. Finally he looked up. "It had better not!" he said finally.

Gregor went out.

19

"But, damn it, Eve, why couldn't you have been more careful!"

"I know, I know. Say what you will. I deserve it. All I can say is, it was an accident. I was overwrought."

"But couldn't you have found some place else to put it?"

"You saw my bathing suit. Where else *could* I have put it?"

"You're *sure* he saw the capsules?"

"How could he help it? He had the box in his hand when I came out of the call office."

"Did he ask you about the phone call?"

"Yes."

"What did you say?"

"I said I couldn't tell him anything." Her voice broke on the last words.

"For the love of Mike, don't start crying."

"I'm *not* crying."

"When you came back in the boat, was he waiting?"

"Yes."

"Then what happened?"

"He drove me back to my flat, wrote out the check, and left. I phoned the airport and booked a seat."

"Under a false name?"

"Yes."

"That's great!" Jonathan paced the room like a caged tiger. "If this doesn't blow the roof off, I don't know what will. Why in heaven's name did you have to go miles out to sea to dispose of the damned thing? Why didn't you just bury it in the sand before you returned to your friends?"

"I started to, then I changed my mind. How did I know I was going to lose it? How did I know the Aliens were going to make that broadcast? If it hadn't been for that, everything would be all right."

"So you didn't know about the broadcast. Great. But you didn't have to act like the devil was on your tail when you came back to the beach. No wonder Bellows was suspicious."

"I told you I was upset."

"So, in typical female fashion, you thought with your emotions instead of your head. Let's face it, Miss Wingate, you blew it. High, wide, and handsome!!"

"All right! It's all very well for you to stand there and pass judgment. The Aliens plumped you back down in a nice safe flat, where you were all alone with plenty of time to think. I ended up on a beach in broad daylight with no place to hide the bomb and a group of friends who might be looking for me any minute."

"I still say you didn't have to act like Mrs. Siddons."

"You, I suppose, would have carried it off with cool confidence as you did at the roadblock."

"At least, I wouldn't have panicked."

"How do you know what you'd have done in my situation? Damn you, I wish I hadn't told you anything!"

"Sure you do. You'd expected me to tell you you'd done a fine, brave, intelligent thing, and you're all burned up because I told you that, regardless of the circumstances, you'd made a damned big mistake."

There was enough truth in it to hurt. She had wanted to be reassured, and, try as she would, she couldn't help herself. The tears came. They were too much for Jonathan.

"Look, Eve, I'm sorry. Don't cry. I'm . . . I'm . . ."

"You take your big paws off me–you–you . . . *American!*"

"I said I was sorry."

"I heard you. Leave me alone–go back and mend your old wireless."

"I've done all I can. I even changed the tubes, but it just won't work. The light goes on but nothing happens."

Eve got up from the couch, rubbing her fists into her eyes. She crossed to the radio, banged it hard twice. The second time it began to hum and a voice came through. She looked at Jonathan, her lower lip trembling. "Superman!" she said scathingly.

". . . the attempt on Professor Bochner's life was made at four o'clock this morning by two unidentified men carrying documents bearing the forged signature of the Secretary of State."

Eve threw Jonathan a look of shocked surprise and both leaned forward intently.

"Both men were killed in a violent gun battle with an agent of the F.B.I. Latest reports from the hospital indicate that the professor is unharmed and resting comfortably.

"For those of you who have not heard the early morning announcements: Professor Bochner was picked up on a Brooklyn street yesterday afternoon and taken to a hospital. He was suffering from malnutrition. Subsequent investigations disclosed that the professor had not eaten for about fifty-two hours. He had been preoccupied with a mysterious black box which, next to his attempted assassination, has been the most exciting news story since the broadcast from space." Jonathan glanced at Eve in acute discomfort.

"The box was found in the pocket of his jacket when he was admitted to the hospital. He had apparently been attempting a scientific analysis of it in a makeshift laboratory in an empty Brooklyn fish store which he rented yesterday morning. The box is now in the hands of the federal government. Indications are that it may be a replica of the one which Eve Wingate is believed to have hurled into the sea off the vacation resort of Torquay, England, before her dramatic flight to America for her alleged meeting with Jonathan Clark.

"The reward for information as to the whereabouts of Miss Wingate and Mr. Clark has been increased to one hundred thousand dollars.

"Here's a special bulletin. Thirty-nine cities in the United States are now under martial law and outbreaks of panic are spiraling. The government requests all citizens to remain calm and to exercise restraint and discipline. There is absolutely no reason to believe this country or any country in the world is in danger of invasion from—"

The radio stopped. Eve got up hurriedly and pounded it again. Nothing happened. Jonathan crossed from his chair and brought his fist down on it. The whole apparatus shuddered alarmingly, but there was no further sound. There was a heavy silence during which he fingered his ear uneasily, not quite able to meet Eve's eyes.

"Look, Eve, I'm—" His words were cut off by the slamming of the cabin door. "Eve!" By the time he had reached the door she was gone. She must have taken the path off the left of the mesa at the foot of the cliff. Jonathan picked up a small branch and broke it angrily in his fingers. He was feeling like the world's prize idiot. He had made that colossal fuss about Eve's carelessness with the capsules and now it turned out the authorities not only knew of their existence but even had a set of them in their possession. Damn! Why couldn't he have kept his big mouth shut? She was right, of course. Who was he to pass judgment on her actions? But then how could he know the professor would go and lose his box of capsules so soon. Now who was making innocence a defense! She had asked him how she could know she was going to lose the box, how she could know the Aliens were going to make that broadcast. The point was, she couldn't, and he had acted like a perfect heel. He had made her cry–a fine reassuring gesture. He flung the stick away, furious with himself, then noted with a start that in less than an hour it would be dark. Abruptly he felt frightened. If Eve strayed far from the cabin, she could easily get lost in these heavily wooded ravines.

Furthermore, there was the matter of that broken lock. He had not mentioned it to Eve, but this was the second lock which someone had forced on the door of the cabin. Neither time was anything of much value taken. On both occasions it had been some food, a few picture magazines, and a couple of bottles of liquor. Things a man might want if he lived up here and seldom went down to the valley. But the manner in which they had been stolen indicated a strange kind of personality. Oftentimes things were taken from isolated cabins but more often than not the owner would find a note of apology or a few bills to cover the loss. This was something different. Furthermore, last night Jonathan could have sworn he heard someone outside the cabin, but when he had gone out to look the clearing had been empty.

The thought drove him into action. He began to run toward the woods. Perhaps it was the train of thought that prompted him to caution: he ran through the trees as silently as he could, forcing himself to deny an impulse to shout Eve's name. After a few minutes with no sign of her his anxiety mounted. He plunged on, his breathing becoming harsher with the effort of running on the uneven ground. He made little noise because the thick carpet of pine needles muffled his footsteps, but they were dry and slippery and several times he lost his footing and sprawled headlong. He was just arising from one of these falls when he heard a male voice say, "Don't talk!" It was said in a half whisper and Jonathan's hackles rose. It was followed after a second by another voice, considerably louder, which said, "I didn't hear anything." The sound froze Jonathan where he was. It was Eve's voice and it was frightened. The first voice came again in a hoarse falsetto, "I told you not to talk, lady. I heard somethin'. I got good ears. Maybe it's your fellah come lookin' for yuh!"

There was the sound of a twig breaking; then, "Now you just stay real quiet." The voice came from Jonathan's right and a little ahead. He rose slowly, easing off into the deeper brush and began to circle cautiously. He cursed himself under his breath. He hadn't even brought a gun and there were half a dozen in the cabin. For a split second he debated going back and immediately discarded the idea. He might never find them again and there was something unnatural in the voice which had spoken to Eve–something that made his pulse pound in alarm. The shadows of dusk were beginning to creep in. At least this was a stroke of luck. For the purposes of approaching unobserved the time couldn't be better. Suddenly he saw them. In a small clearing to his left now Eve stood, white and tense in front of a fallen log.

The man had his back to Jonathan. He was big and heavy. He had on miner's boots and filthy red underwear, the top of which was visible above tattered overalls supported by grimy suspenders. He was holding a deer rifle at his hip, carefully watching the bush to his left. Jonathan rose from the crouch and started forward a step at a time flicking his glance down to watch for branches and twigs that might betray him. He froze as the man moved and began to speak.

"I guess I musta made a mistake, lady, but I sure thought I heard somethin'. Too bad. It would have saved some trouble if he'd come lookin' for you. This way we'll have to go and find him. You can go in front just so he don't start shootin'. Shootin' sure makes me nervous!"

Eve had seen him now and hadn't batted an eyelid. She was asking the man something to hold his attention. Jonathan's palms were sweating and his heart pounding. The man was only a few feet away. It seemed incredible he could get so close and not be heard.

Then unexpectedly the man tensed. Jonathan sensed rather than saw it. Instinct told him the man was going to turn. It was now or never. He launched himself. He was a split second too late. The man spun. Jonathan was in mid-air. He had no chance to duck. The rifle barrel coming up smashed against his forearm with agonizing force. The muzzle struck his left temple. He felt the hot blood flush over his eyes and face and then he was on the ground only half-conscious. Dimly he saw the man coming at him, shouting hoarsely. It was his year in the South Pacific that saved him then. With every atom of his strength he lashed out with his feet. One of his heels made brutal contact with a kneecap. He heard the sickening crunch of bone. The man went down screaming and groveling in agony. Then Eve had him in her arms. Her voice was far away. "Jonathan–Jonathan!"

His tongue was thick. "Get the gun."

She left him for a second. There was a loud noise, and then she came back. He was propped up on an elbow. He couldn't see out of his right eye and he knew he was covered with blood. He heard Eve crying his name again, "Jonathan, Jonathan. Oh, my darling!" He fought his way up out of a sea of mist.

"I'm all right–I think. He got my arm, but this head cut can't be too bad or I'd be out now."

"Thank God!"

"Is he finished?"

She was tying her scarf around his head. "Yes, I think he fainted. I never heard a man scream like that."

He grunted. His arm hurt like hell. He had a feeling it was broken. "There isn't much that hurts like a smashed kneecap. Help me up."

"Are you sure it's all right?"

"Help me up!"

She aided him to his feet. He swayed, fighting back a wave of faintness. "Come on. Let's go." They started back down the trail, Eve's little figure propping his big one. "Where's the gun?"

"I smashed it on a rock."

"Good girl." He was breathing heavily.

"What about him?"

"He'll keep till I can get this fixed up and a shot of liquor. He isn't going anywhere; that's for sure." He staggered and almost fell. Eve gasped as the full weight of his body sagged against her.

"Are you going to be able to make it?" Her voice was anxious but steadier now. Out of his one good eye he could see that she, too, was covered with blood. She had what it took, this girl! Most women would have gone to pieces by now. Unexpectedly he made a painful sound something like a chuckle.

She looked up from his arm which she had draped over her shoulders. "What in the name of God are you laughing at?"

"You were mad enough to bite my head off back at the cabin. There in the clearing you called me darling."

Eve looked up, half exasperated, half terrified. He looked so awful. She tried to hide her fear. "Come on, you big idiot," she said chokingly. "I haven't time to stand here and listen to your jokes!"

20

Ivan was sitting on a hard, straight-backed, wooden chair in the exact center of a perfectly bare room. There was absolutely no way he could relax in this position and, after twenty-two hours of questioning, there was not a muscle in his body that was not an individual thorn of agony. Over his head a single unshielded bulb bathed him with harsh pitiless light. Beyond its orbit, in a circle around his chair, his inquisitors sat in almost total darkness, visible only as vague shadows to his aching contracted pupils. Their questions shot at him from every point of the compass and he had long since given up turning his head to try to address his replies in the direction of the voices. Every so often one of the interrogators would lean forward to say something and for an instant a pale waxen face would stare at him out of the background of darkness like a hideous disembodied ghost. Somewhere in the room there was a bucket of ice water used to revive him when he showed signs of slipping out of his chair. But twice they had not been quick enough. Twice he had fallen forward to the floor and been set back in position with the utmost courtesy. The seven interrogators had apologized to him each time, but had pointed out that, for the good of his country, he must continue to cooperate. The most trivial detail, they said, seemingly unimportant to him, might be of overwhelming value.

To Ivan, the apologies and the questions no longer meant anything. His body was drunk with fatigue, his mind sliding into a miasma in which he found it difficult to separate the real from the imaginary. A hundred times he had been on the point of revealing the whole truth and a hundred times something had prevented him from speaking. He no longer feared death or imprisonment. His body and his mind no longer cared. Death might be a welcome release.

Suddenly the door at the end of the room banged open. Gregor stood on the threshold, his figure lighted by the glare of the adjoining office, his face working with fury, his eyes glaring at Ivan's helpless figure in the chair. In the sharp silence he strode across the room, the heels of his shoes smashing against the bare pavement of the floor at each step. In front of Ivan's chair, he raised his hand and lashed Ivan across both cheeks. The boy's eyes flew open in shock.

"You liar!" Gregor stormed. "You filthy, traitorous, scheming liar!"

They had found out! The thought stabbed Ivan's consciousness like a knife. Gregor leaned down and grabbed him by his jacket.

"You filthy traitor!" he screamed. "It's a weapon! It's a weapon! And you pretended you didn't know." He spat directly into Ivan's face and flung him back into the chair.

Terror seared the boy like a hot iron. Before he could say anything, Gregor ripped a newspaper out of his side pocket and held it in front of Ivan's eyes. "Read it. Read it! And then tell us you don't know anything about the box."

Ivan tried to read. The print swam before his eyes. A hideous black envelope, a cowl of strange and viscous ugliness began to close in on him and through its gathering darkness the huge letters came into focus: AMERICA REVEALS BOX FROM SPACE IS WEAPON!

But Gregor was not finished. He hurled the newspaper into Ivan's lap and strode to the radio which he had placed there during one of the boy's brief absences from the room. He snapped it on.

"The dupe of the American warmongers, Jonathan Clark, has divulged that the black box he possesses is a weapon more deadly than any yet devised on earth. Its possession, capitalist warmongers are screaming, makes them the undisputed leaders of the world. The Great Leader has declared a state of emergency throughout the Union of Soviet Socialist Republics and has decreed general mobilization for the defense of our homeland. Effigies of the cowardly traitor, Ivan Godofsky, are being burned in the streets. Godofsky, who has refused his Russian comrades access to knowledge which might protect us against the threats of the English and American capitalists, will go down in history as the greatest traitor that Russia has ever known."

Gregor clicked off the radio. He turned and stared at Ivan. In his pocket his fingers touched the outlines of the hypodermic needle primed with truth serum. He felt confident he had won. The boy was broken. It was obvious even before the broadcast. Then as he watched a strange thing happened.

Ivan placed his two hands together so that the heels of the palms were touching and the ten fingers spread out fanwise. Then he raised them slowly and put them against his face, so that his thumbs touched the lobes of his ears and the nails ran into the hairline of his scalp. He held them there.

Gregor felt that the moment had come. He crossed the room to Ivan's side. "I see," he said in a soft understanding voice, "that we have made a mistake. You wanted only to protect the world from the horrors of war. This we can all understand. But now the moment has come when your country and your people are at stake. We know that you will not want to stand by and watch your party and your comrades destroyed by a weapon against which we can have no defense. Will you tell us now?" he said.

He waited. There was no sound from the figure on the chair. "Ivan," he said again. "Believe me, we are your friends. I am sorry I struck you. You must forgive me. You must tell us the truth."

Still the figure on the chair remained motionless and silent. Gregor bent down and pulled the hands away from the face gently, and then he froze.

The hands that he had pulled away from Ivan's face remained precisely in the position he had released them. The eyes that stared back into his were blank and uncomprehending. The mouth hung slightly open, a trickle of saliva running out of one corner. With a trembling hand, Gregor reached up and closed the mouth. It remained closed. Gregor knew what it was. Waxy flexibility, the psychologists called it. He felt a great empty hole developing in the pit of his stomach. It would be some time before Ivan made any kind of intelligent sound.

21

Jonathan awakened in the cabin the next morning to the fragrant aroma of brewing coffee. He lay for a long while, motionless, gazing up at the bunk above him, while the events of the previous night came back to him. He had a fairly clear and very unpleasant memory of the trip back to the cabin with Eve doing her best to support him while he fought off wave after wave of pain and faintness. They had been a long time getting back. It had been pitch black by the time they reached the mesa. After that everything was hazy. He remembered drinking quite a lot and being sick–talking–God knows what he had said. It must have been a nightmare for Eve. He turned his head to look at her. The movement caused him less discomfort than he expected, but the cabin was empty.

He glanced at his arm. It was swollen to half again its normal size and looked like a muddy rainbow. Also, it ached like fury, but he could move it, so perhaps it wasn't broken after all. He put the other hand up to his eye. It was swathed in bandages. He must look a mess. He heard the cabin door open. Eve came in. She looked fresh-scrubbed and vibrant. She smiled at him.

"Well, so you finally came to?"

He scowled. "What in the name of heaven are you so happy about this morning?"

"You."

"I'm a mess."

"You are not. Your arm isn't broken and I fixed your head."

"How?"

"I put stitches in it."

"What?"

"I said I put stitches in it."

"With what? How many?"

"Fishing leader. Seven. It's not neat, but it'll do."

"But you can't go around putting stitches in people–you have to be a doctor."

"Don't be so stuffy. What was I going to do? Let you bleed to death?"

"There is something very strange about all this."

"Is there?"

"Yes. First of all, I ought to have a terrible hangover, and I don't."

"Of course you don't. I couldn't stop you from drinking–you had to have something. But after I found the morphine I made you sick."

"Deliberately?"

"Certainly. You can't mix morphine and alcohol, and anyway you'd have really been ill if you'd gone to bed full of gin with seven stitches in your head."

He touched the bandage gingerly. "What happened to our friend?"

Eve poured a steaming cup of coffee from the percolator and brought it over to him. "He's alive, but he's in quite a lot of pain."

"How do you know?"

"I was out to see him this morning. The morphine is wearing off."

"Morphine again. Where did you get all this morphine?"

"I found it in the medicine chest."

"When?"

"Last night."

Jonathan started spilling his coffee. "You went back there in the dark last night after what happened?"

"What else could I do? I couldn't let him be there in agony all night long."

"Why not? He deserved it."

"Not really. I found the morphine, so I took it to him along with a couple of blankets. Since I didn't feel up to bringing him home too, it was the best I could do."

"But you're crazy. He might have killed you."

"I don't think so. I was terrified actually, but it wasn't so bad. He was awfully grateful. He's not all there you know."

"You mean he's a looney?"

"Sort of. He's very childish really."

"Childish!"

"You frightened him. I don't mean he isn't dangerous, but I don't think he's vicious. He was so terrified when you came up behind him, I think he really might have killed you if you hadn't disabled him."

"What did he want?"

"He's been hanging about the cabin ever since we arrived. He heard the broadcast offering a hundred thousand dollars for our capture."

"He doesn't sound so stupid to me."

"Wait till you hear what he was going to buy with the money he got for turning us in."

"What?"

"A music box, a trombone, and a green silk handkerchief."

"Good God. What's he doing up here?"

"He prospects a little and steals your liquor."

"I know."

"You've seen him before?"

"No, but the lock has been broken on the cabin twice and some stuff has been taken. Never very much–I guess it all fits. How did it all happen?"

"Very undramatically. I ran out in a huff and stormed off into the bush."

"I could hardly forget that part."

"Well, I came to the clearing and sat down to wait."

"For what?"

"For you to come after me."

"You knew I'd come?"

"Of course I knew, you idiot."

"Just what made you so sure?"

"If you don't know the answer to that, I doubt that an explanation from me would help. Anyway, since I knew you'd come, when I heard footsteps I turned my back. Just a little. You deserved it."

"I agree. Go on."

"Well you can imagine my surprise when I raised my eyes and saw a pair of legs beside me that definitely didn't belong to you. I jumped up and found this great hulking man with a gun. He said, 'You're real pretty.' But he said it like a little boy. I knew then that he wasn't all there and I got thoroughly frightened. I started to back away and he told me to sit down."

"God!"

"As soon as I realized what it was he wanted I kept him talking. I hoped you'd hear our voices."

"I did, but I still don't know how you were so damn sure I'd follow you."

"Jonathan, don't be dense."

He looked at her, tugging at his ear lobe; then he said, "There's something very peculiar going on here."

She stared back innocently, "What do you mean?"

"After what you went through last night you're too damned happy this morning! What are you up to?"

"Shame on you. Is that any way to talk to your future wife?"

"My *what?*"

"Jonathan, please don't keep saying *what* like that. It makes you sound idiotic."

Jonathan's one good eye regarded her balefully. "Suppose you tell me exactly what happened last night."

"Don't you remember?"

"Not enough, that's for sure."

"Well, first of all you told me that you loved me—deeply and passionately and purely."

"I don't believe it. I never said that to any woman, particularly the purely part."

"You did to this one, darling. Several times and very fervently."

"God! What else?"

"You told me how lovely I was, how intelligent, how courageous, how much you admired me—how sorry you were about making such a fuss about the capsules. You asked me to marry you and swore you'd kill yourself if I refused."

Jonathan groaned. "Got around to just about everything, didn't I?"

"You did indeed. It was quite thrilling!"

"I was drunk."

"Of course you were. That's what made me believe you."

"Is this on the level?"

"What do you think?"

"Kiss me." She leaned over and pecked him on the cheek. "Unh-unh. That doesn't convince me a bit. Kiss me like a future wife." She hesitated, then she smiled.

"Jonathan, it's all right. I was only teasing you."

"Then I didn't propose?"

"Yes, you did. But you were awfully drunk." She touched his lips gently with her fingers. "I couldn't resist the temptation to scare you a little. Actually, you were terribly sweet and very brave about the stitches."

"Kiss me."

"Jonathan . . ."

"Kiss me."

She leaned forward. Her lips touched his almost tentatively, brushed gently, caressingly. Oblivious to the pain in his arm, he half turned and drew her to him. She put up her hands and held his face between them. Suddenly he crushed her against him almost brutally. Her arms went around his neck, her body yielding to him. He buried his face in her hair. He said, "Damn, damn, damn!" When he pulled away to look at her, her eyes were moist. He said, "Damn it, can't you say anything?" His voice was husky.

She said, "Can't you say anything but 'damn'?"

He swallowed. "I love you–you know that."

"Yes."

"There may not be much time."

"Don't talk about it."

"You haven't said you love me."

"Do I have to?"

"You'd better."

"I love you."

"When did you know?"

"When you made me cry."

"Does that make sense?"

"To a woman it does."

"How?"

"I found out I didn't dislike you even when you were furious with me."

He brushed the hair back from her temples and stared. "I guess it makes as much sense as the rest of this."

"When did you?"

"When did I what?"

"Decide you loved me?"

He grinned. "It started when I saw you in that bathing suit."

"I paid a lot of money for that suit. It shows you can't beat good merchandise."

"I wouldn't have looked at it twice in a store window."

"You're terribly physical."

"Lady, so are you in that bathing suit."

"What about the inner me?"

"That came by degrees."

"Which do you like the best?"

"I can't decide."

"I'm glad."

He kissed her again, then released her.

She said, "Jonathan, we've got a problem."

"The music-box man?"

"We can't leave him out there forever. That knee needs attention."

"We'll have to go down then."

"I'm afraid so."

"Are you sorry?"

"Not really. These last few days, with things going from bad to worse down there, I've felt a bit strange sitting up here safe and secure, even though it seemed the right thing to do."

"Yes. If we came in of our own free will, even if we refused to say anything, it might help allay some of the panic."

"Do you feel well enough to get up?"

"I think so." He pushed himself erect. He glanced down suddenly, realizing he was in pajamas, and looked up at Eve.

She blushed. "Well, I couldn't very well put you to bed swimming in your own blood!"

"You have an answer for everything, haven't you?"

She shrugged expressively. "I wish I thought I was the first woman to put you to bed." She jumped as he lunged for her and then groaned, holding his head. "It serves you right! I'll meet you outside when you're dressed–that is, if you can get dressed alone." She raised one eyebrow archly.

Jonathan threw the pillow at her.

Later they stood outside the cabin at the edge of the mesa overlooking the valley. Directly in front of them the mountain fell away in an almost sheer drop. From where they were standing they could not even see the base of the incline. Against the far horizon, a low line of hills blocked the view, and behind them huge masses of foaming white cumulus cloud mushroomed into the bright blue sky. The hills themselves were painted a faint purple with the haze of distance. Off to the right and above them, snow-capped peaks of the High Sierras nuzzled the heavens.

Eve crumpled a piece of shale between her fingers and let the dust float down to the ground. "It's beautiful," she said.

Jonathan nodded. "It's a little frightening to wonder who it's going to belong to thirty days from now."

"Can it really happen or is it just a bad dream?"

"It can happen. When the Aliens first gave us the boxes and we all made the pact, I thought the whole thing was preposterous. It didn't seem so very difficult for five people to keep a secret for twenty-seven days. Well, I'm finding out differently. Within a week the secret is almost as good as out."

"How do you mean?"

"Those men that attacked Professor Bochner. Doesn't it seem strange to you that the broadcast we heard said so little about that incident?"

"Not particularly. After all, they didn't succeed. They're dead, the professor is unharmed, and the box is in the hands of the government. The incident is over, that's all."

"Perhaps you're right. What worries me is how the dead men knew the box was important."

"Good Lord, I never thought of that."

"Whoever they were, they must have had a pretty good idea of what was in that box to take such a risk."

"And that means," Eve said anxiously, "that somebody talked."

"Possibly," said Jonathan.

"Ivan!"

"Not necessarily. It might have been the Chinese girl. It could even have been the professor, or it may be that nobody talked. It may be that somebody put all the facts together and came up with an answer that fitted. My guess is that someone had a strong suspicion of their nature, so strong a suspicion that they were willing to go to almost any lengths to get control of the boxes. The only good thing is they can't know *all* the secret or they wouldn't have threatened the professor's life because without him the box is useless. All I can say is, if Ivan talked, I for one don't think he can be blamed too much."

"Nor I," Eve said thoughtfully. "But if he has, it puts a whole new complexion on our situation, doesn't it? If the Russian government knows what the boxes contain, and our governments don't, it could mean war."

Jonathan crossed to a nearby tree stump and sat down. "It could. There are three bombs in Russia, or at least in communist hands, and three in America. We're scared to death of the Russians and they're scared to death of us. Until the governments know what the information is we have, they'll never stop trying to break us."

"I feel sorry for Ivan. I'm sure he was sincere when he made the pact with us."

"Maybe he was, but, after that broadcast, I wouldn't give a plugged nickel for his chances of keeping quiet. Before, we might have taken his word. Now I don't think we have any guarantee. The only solution as I see it is to hang on to the capsules till the twenty-seven days are over. In the meantime, we'll go in and hope our presence helps a little."

She bit her lip. "Has it occurred to you," she said, "that if we go down there, they may separate us?"

Jonathan looked at her and grinned. "Has it occurred to you that at the present moment, no separation is necessary?"

She crossed to him slowly. She took his face in her hands. She said, "It's nice to find a problem I can solve." She kissed him.

After a few seconds, he said, with his mouth against her ear, "It would be just my luck to have the world end right now."

"I told you before, don't say it. Don't even think it." She was silent for a moment, and then when she spoke, her voice was so soft he could barely hear her. "Jonathan, there's one morphine tablet left. We could give it to the music man. Would it be too terribly cruel?"

He tightened the pressure of his arm around her. "I'll make it up to him," he said huskily. "I'll buy him a whole case of music boxes."

22

Gregor tore his eyes away from the blank face of Godofsky and took one step backward away from the chair. His mind was racing. His eyes took in the seven stone-faced interrogators, who by now must know what Gregor knew: that Ivan for the moment was a lost cause. He wondered how long he could keep the news from the Leader. Once the Leader discovered the truth about the interrogation, he was finished. He had been an intelligence chief too long not to know the kind of finish it would be. He had a few hours, perhaps. There was one advantage in holding the position he did. None of the interrogators would dare reveal to the Leader what had happened. Until Gregor himself was purged, their lives were as much in his hands as his was in those of the Leader.

He straightened up and looked at them coldly. "There will be no mention of Godofsky's reaction to this experience until I have had a chance to talk personally to the Leader. You will take him to the Villa immediately."

The Villa was a private hospital which Gregor maintained for his own use. It was staffed with some of Russia's most skillful doctors and scientists. Gregor used it as a last resort in cases where normal questioning procedure proved useless. All that was known to medical science about truth drugs and narcosynthesis was applied to patients in an effort to make them produce results. It was also an excellent place of concealment for those whom Gregor and the Leader wished to keep out of sight.

Gregor hurried out of the room, left the Kremlin, and got into his car. If only he could keep this hushed up until midnight, perhaps he had a chance. By tomorrow morning nothing on earth could save him. He drove back to his house dangerously fast. His wife met him in the hallway, her face white and strained. She had seen him turn the big car into the driveway, and his presence at home at this time of day indicated something serious had happened.

Gregor put his arms around her and held her tightly. She felt the tautness of his body and tried to restrain her anxiety. "What is it?" she asked. "What's happened?"

"There's no time to explain," he said. "I want you to pack two suitcases, one for yourself and one for me. Pack only what you need. And hurry."

"It's come, then?"

"Yes. I haven't time to explain. Just do as you're told. Don't answer the telephone and don't go out. If anyone comes, tell the servants to say you're not in and that I'm at the Kremlin. I'll be back as soon as I can."

He kissed her on the cheek and left. Tanya Gregor stood motionless where he had left her. Somehow, she had known that some day this had to happen. She had no knowledge of just what had taken place, but for a long time she had been afraid. Her husband knew too much, had too much power, and was always a potential danger to the Party. Her mind rushed over the list of names of those she had known who had disappeared from sight. Sooner or later, it had had to happen to Gregor. In a way she was almost glad. At last the waiting, the intolerable expectancy, the gnawing terror were at an end. Within the next few hours it would all be over, one way or the other.

In the meantime, Gregor was hurtling down the road toward the Villa. He parked the car at the front steps and hurried inside. At the desk he threw a curt syllable at the male receptionist. "Where?"

The receptionist stood up. "Thirty-seven, sir."

Gregor strode down the hall and entered the room. Three doctors were grouped around Ivan. Gregor watched as one of the doctors closed Ivan's fingers into a fist and withdrew his hand. The fist remained closed. The doctor nodded his head and glanced at Gregor.

"Shock," Gregor said curtly, trying to appear at ease. "We pushed him too far. How long will it be before you can get him out of it?"

The chief doctor shook his head. "It's difficult to say. We are a long way ahead of the treatments of five years ago, and Dr. Kolinsky here did some research on cases like this last year, but I can't be certain."

"Don't evade the question," Gregor said harshly. "Give me a minimum time at least."

The doctor drew a deep breath. "Well, it's almost impossible to give you a minimum, but if he responds well—perhaps four or five days. If he doesn't, it might be six weeks, two months—a year. There's no way of knowing."

"There's no possible chance of his coming out of it before, say, tomorrow morning," Gregor said.

"I shouldn't think so," the doctor said, and raised his eyes to his colleagues for confirmation.

"In my opinion, Doctor," said one, "four days is cutting it much too fine."

The second doctor nodded assent. "It will be a miracle if we can get him out of this in that length of time. There have been isolated cases of a patient recovering by himself within a matter of a few days, but the chances are negligible and don't depend on therapy."

Gregor's worst fears were realized, but he still had to play his part. "Very well," he said. "But you understand that this soldier's complete and rapid recovery is of the utmost importance to the Leader and to the Party. I don't think I have to warn you, gentlemen, that, if his recovery is delayed, you will have to answer to the Leader himself." Turning on his heel, he marched out of the room. In the outer office he made a brief call to the private airport reserved for high Party officials. It was dangerous but less so than driving there in person. He could only hope the call was not being monitored.

Back at the house he said nothing until he and his wife were alone in the bedroom. "Are you ready?"

She pointed to the two suitcases on the bed. "Do the servants suspect anything?"

"No," she said, "why should they?"

"No reason except that we can't take any chances." He drew a cigarette from a platinum case and lit it. His every movement betrayed the tension that was in him.

She laid a hand on his arm. "Where are we going . . . . England?"

He didn't look at her. "The less you know, the better. We're going on a trip, that's all."

"I'm glad," she said after a while. "I don't care what happens, I'm glad."

"There's something else," Gregor said. "I want you to cut down a pair of my trousers to fit you and shorten the sleeves of one of my overcoats. You've got an hour. Can you do it?"

She nodded. "Yes, I can do it." She crossed and sat at her dressing table. He moved toward her. He slid his fingers beneath the blond hair that fell to her shoulders.

"There's another thing," he said softly. "You'll have to cut your hair."

She looked at him in the mirror and her voice was husky as she spoke. "It doesn't matter."

He smiled briefly, crossed to the window, pulled back the curtain, and looked out. Across the street a sleek limousine was drawing to the curb. Gregor turned slowly away from the window. His face was ashen. As he met his wife's eyes, she gave a little broken cry. In his hand, the cigarette held too close to the end was burning his fingers, but he did not notice.

23

Eve steered the car around the last turn of the mountain into the long straight sweep into the valley, and glanced at Jonathan. "How's our friend?"

Jonathan looked into the back seat and grinned. "He's sleeping with an idiotic smile on his face. He's never had it so good! All that morphine!"

"Do you think he'd forgive us if he knew?"

"I think he'd go back and do it all over again, if you smile at him the way you did when we brought him to the car. You ought to be ashamed."

"My conscience hurt me. Besides, he really is very sweet."

"He's your slave for life I'm afraid."

"Poor thing. How could he live up there all alone?"

"Who knows? There are more things on heaven and earth, Horatio . . ."

"Will there be a hospital in this town?"

"Probably. There'll at least be a doctor."

"How is your arm?"

"All right. It throbs a little."

"Maybe we should have given you the morphine."

He grinned. "I preferred the substitute."

"Don't be lewd."

"O.K., I'll forget it ever happened."

"I'll kill you."

He laughed, "How do you feel?"

"Scared."

"So do I. Never mind, it'll soon be over. There's the town limit just ahead and if I'm not mistaken that building there on the outskirts will be the hospital."

Eve slowed the car as they approached and then pulled into the graveled drive. A man in a white smock came out on the porch. "Mornin'!"

Jonathan stuck his head out of the window, "Good morning."

The man took in the bandage. "Accident?"

"A minor one."

"Walk?"

"Sure, but——"

"Come on in."

"It's not for me. We've got someone in the back."

"Oh. That's different." He came down the steps leisurely nodding to Eve. "Mornin', miss."

"Good morning. He's there."

The man nodded and looked in the window. He made a clicking sound with his tongue. "John Doe."

"John Doe?"

"We call him that. Nobody knows where he came from. Lives up there." He pointed to the mountain.

"You know him?"

"Yep. He's been in a couple of times. Broke both arms once. Damned if I know how. Seen a man break one arm lots a times–two almost never."

"But how did he get down here?" Eve said.

"Rode his mule."

"All that way? With both arms broken? How did he ever do it? How did he get on the mule's back?"

"Same question we asked. Never got no answer. Strong as a horse but nothin' much up here." He tapped his forehead significantly. "What's wrong with him this time?"

"Smashed kneecap."

"How'd it happen?"

Jonathan decided there was no point in lying. It was bound to come out some time. "I did it."

The man glanced at Jonathan's head bandages and the sling on his right arm. "Looks like the odds was about even. After the reward, I suppose?"

Jonathan's mouth fell open in surprise. "You . . . you know who we are?"

"Couldn't hardly miss it. Everybody in the country's lookin' for you."

"Then you know there's a reward?"

"Yep. A hundred thousand–tax free."

"You–uh–you could be making a mistake."

"Not a chance. Your pictures are on that danged TV every half hour." He reeled off a detailed description of them both with laconic accuracy.

Jonathan swiveled to look at Eve in amazement, then turned back. "Well, it looks like you've got yourself a reward."

"Me? Hell no! What'd I do with all that money? Just get me into trouble. You figurin' on going back up the mountain?"

Jonathan swallowed. It took all kinds of people. "No. We–uh–we just wanted to drop John Doe off and then we thought we'd look for the sheriff."

The man looked down the road and then spat reflectively on the graveled drive. "Guess you musta heard the broadcast."

"What broadcast?"

"President talked on TV this mornin'–asked you two to give yourselves up. Said there wasn't no charge against you. Asked everybody to give you all the help they could gettin' to Washington."

Jonathan had the conviction it was one of the longest speeches the man had ever made. He smiled, shaking his head. "We didn't hear it, but I'm glad he made it. It'll make things a little less difficult."

The man nodded. "Better get this one inside."

They managed to get John Doe out of the car and into the hospital. Even with the three of them lifting together, it was no easy job. They put him down on a couch in the office. The man examined the knee. Jonathan watched the long fingers moving gently over the swollen tissue. "Are you the doctor?"

"Nope. Chief cook and bottle washer. Doctor'll be back in a few minutes. This is a job for him. Needs an X-ray. Let me see that head of yours." Jonathan sat and the man unwrapped the bandages, carefully sponging away the dried blood. When he saw the wound his face cracked in what might possibly have been the suggestion of a smile. He looked at Eve speculatively. "You been practicin' without a license?"

Eve blushed. "Is it . . . is it all right?"

The man scratched his head. "Well, it ain't too neat, lady, but it sure is thorough. It'll heal O.K. if you don't mind a bit o' puckerin' in the scar."

Jonathan grinned, "It'll be a souvenir."

The man grunted and rewrapped the head with a neat bandage. "Arm's O.K., too. Bad contusion. Nothing broken. You'll live."

Jonathan held out his good hand. "Thanks. It's been a real pleasure, Mr. —?"

The man took the hand. "Jenks," he said, "but everybody calls me Pete."

Jonathan squeezed the hand warmly. "It's been a real pleasure, Pete."

"Mutual. Incidentally, you'll see the sheriff's office about a mile down the road on your left. 'By, miss."

"Good-by, Pete." She turned to Jonathan and whispered in his ear. Jonathan smiled and turned back.

"Pete, would you do us a big favor?"

"Sure, if I can."

"Is there a music store in this town?"

"Yep."

"They got music boxes?" He realized with an inward smile how easy it was to fall into Pete's habit of cryptic monosyllables.

"Uh-huh."

Eve took out some bills. "We'd like you to buy every music box in the store, and a trombone. And a green silk handkerchief," she added quickly.

Pete nodded. "For John Doe?"

"How did you guess?" Jonathan asked.

"We keep harmonicas for him here. He won't leave the hospital till he gets one."

Eve whispered to Jonathan, who grinned and then turned to Jenks. "Will that be enough money?"

"Plenty."

"Keep what's over for yourself."

The man shook his head. "I'll send it to you in Washington—care of the President. Write me a letter on that White House stationery. I can give it to my niece."

Jonathan felt a warm glow. "I sure will, Pete. I sure as hell will."

He took Eve's arm and started down the steps. They got into the car and then Jenks came over to them. "None of my business, but what is all this for?"

Jonathan looked at Eve. Her eyes sparkled and then she leaned out of the window. "Let's just say it's sort of an unofficial wedding present!"

The car drove off. Jenks stood in the driveway scratching his head.

The speed with which things happened after their departure from the hospital left Eve with a permanent memory of American efficiency. Within thirty-seven minutes of their arrival at the sheriff's office a state police caravan had rushed them to the airport, provided them with an F.B.I. escort, and bundled them aboard a jet bomber with priority clearances for Washington. As a result she was now, only five hours later, looking down at the lights of the nation's capital as the plane began losing altitude for a landing.

One of the copilots came out of the cockpit into the cabin. "Fasten your safety belts," he said, "we'll be landing very shortly." He bent over the nearest of the two men seated opposite Eve and Jonathan and whispered at some length in his ear. The man nodded several times and, when the copilot had returned to the cockpit, he fastened his belt and looked across at Jonathan.

"It seems," he said, "that our efforts to make this a private party have failed. The papers are on the streets of Washington announcing your arrival. There are more people at the airport than there were for Lindbergh, so I want you to do exactly what I tell you. I will get off the plane first and I want both of you to stay close behind me. My friend here will bring up the rear. We will follow our escort through the crowd to the waiting automobiles. We'll have a police escort to the White House."

"I understand," said Jonathan.

The man hesitated, then spoke again. "Look, I don't suppose it's necessary to tell you this, since you gave yourselves up of your own free will, but this would be a bad time to change your minds."

Eve looked surprised. "What do you mean?"

The man shrugged. There was dislike in his voice. "I said the remark was probably unnecessary, but, if you had decided to make a break for it, the obvious time would be in that crowd when we land. I wouldn't advise it."

Something in the tone of his voice made Jonathan look up sharply. "What the hell are you getting at?"

"Crowds have a funny psychology," he said, "and this crowd nobody can figure." Anything else was cut off by the whine of the jets as the plane touched ground.

It screamed down the runway, losing speed, and gradually came to a stop, guided by an army sergeant on the runway. The four passengers unbuckled their safety belts and stood up. The copilot hurried through the plane to open the door. A blinding glare of klieg lights stabbed into the gloom of the cabin. The two agents walked ahead and stepped out onto the steps as they were shoved into place. Jonathan and Eve followed.

The empty runway was bathed in harsh pitiless light and beyond the light the horizon appeared jet black to their eyes. Behind the fences of the airport and to the farthest extent of vision there was a solid mass of people. It had spilled through the gates and offices of the airport and was being restrained by cordons of police, soldiers, and rope barriers. For a moment Jonathan was aware only of a sense of cold horror without understanding the reason, and then suddenly he caught it. A mass of humanity such as this should have emitted some sound, some indication of life, but there was nothing. Only black ominous silence. A silence which carried to the four people on the steps tangible waves of hostility which struck them with the force of a blow.

Somehow the mob was like an enormous black panther—quiet, menacing, deadly. Five seconds after Jonathan and Eve emerged from the plane, there was a sudden simultaneous forward surge from the mass as if it were a single entity. The dike of soldiers wavered, fell back, swayed, and held. But during the brief instant when it appeared the barrier might be breached, Jonathan felt a cold sweat break out on his palms. Had the movement come with any kind of a vocal sound —a roar or a shout—it might perhaps have been bearable. But that instinctive and almost irresistible advance in absolute silence was more harrowing than anything he had ever known. He felt that one scream, one tiny break in the bulwark of police could unleash a violence which defied imagination.

He took Eve's arm and shakily descended the few steps to the ground. As their feet touched the asphalt, they were surrounded by a platoon of police. The whole situation had an awful sense of unreality. Like figures in an ominous ballet, they moved across the concrete toward the exit. No one spoke. Jonathan felt the tense movement of Eve's body as she walked beside him, was conscious of the fright in her as she gripped his arm.

As they advanced, the crowd became a face, and the face had a million eyes, and the million eyes became one giant orb which followed every step of their progress with a pale dangerous scrutiny. They passed the barrier at the entrance to the airport and the eye followed them. They made their way to the waiting automobile and the eye followed them. Through the streets of Washington on the way to the White House, the eye followed them. And the sounds of the traffic and the garish winking of the neon signs failed to have any effect on the tangible, curious, and awesome silence which pervaded the city.

When they arrived at the White House, they were ushered immediately into an elaborate study. A distinguished man with snow-white hair rose to greet them, extending his hand. "My name is Ingram. The President will be down in a moment. He asked me to speak to you first."

Jonathan responded to the introduction with a voice that was a little shaky and reached for the package of cigarettes which had been given to him on the plane. "Do you mind if we smoke, sir?"

"Please do."

Jonathan offered one to Eve, and as he lit her cigarette and his own, "You'll forgive me," he said, "but our arrival was a little nerve wracking."

Ingram frowned. "There was no trouble?"

Jonathan blew out a cloud of smoke and swallowed, shaking his head, "No, sir, there was no trouble. I don't know how I can explain it. It was just . . . just . . . frightening."

Ingram nodded soberly. "I think I know what you mean. It's the silence. The tension is unbearable. You can't escape it anywhere in Washington. I doubt if you can escape it anywhere in the world. After the panic and hysteria of these past few days, it's like the vacuum in the heart of a cyclone. We are all keyed to the breaking point waiting for the second onslaught." He put his hands behind his back, paced halfway across the room, and turned to face them. He regarded them fixedly for so long that both Eve and Jonathan began to feel uncomfortable. "Has it occurred to you," he said finally, "to ask yourselves what this silence means?"

"I don't think I quite understand, sir," Jonathan said.

"You should," he said gravely. "You're responsible for it. I'm very much afraid that, unless you two are more cooperative than Professor Bochner, this silence we are speaking of may very soon be broken —and I hate to think of the situation we are going to have on our hands if that happens."

Jonathan opened his mouth to speak and Ingram raised his hand. "Before you say anything, let me finish. I am sure this has not been easy for you. I know that you didn't ask for these responsibilities. I'm sure you believe you had just reasons for your disappearance and for your refusal to speak, but—it's just possible that—you have been so preoccupied with your own problems you have missed the fact there is another side to this whole situation—a side that may even be more difficult than your own.

"I want you now to try to see that other aspect. A few days ago, the world was confronted with a situation for which there is no parallel in history. In our skies there appeared the star ships of another race; on our airways there was the voice of an alien intelligence, an intelligence, it seems, that far surpasses our own. We have been fed on science fiction, invasions from space, and monsters from Mars for two generations and we're frightened. Fear is a dangerous poison and it feeds on ignorance. Until we know what the Alien's intentions are, we're going to go on being afraid. In all the world there are only four people who can give us the answers we want."

At the looks of sharp surprise from the two, Ingram explained. "Yes, four. It is not common knowledge, but the Chinese girl is dead." He rode over Eve's gasp of horror. "Come here." He crossed to the window and pulled back the curtains. Jonathan and Eve walked up to him slowly. He nodded his head toward the outside. Jonathan and Eve looked. Beyond the fence which had been erected around the White House were the people. They stood in the darkness and in the glow of the street lamps, massed in a black sea of silence.

"There are the people," Ingram said. "Forget yourselves for a moment. Think how they must feel. On a more personal level, think how you would feel if you were the father of a family and did not know whether there would be any future for that family or not. Think how you would feel about two people who could answer the question about that future and who could not be found. Is it any wonder that they are waiting? Is it any wonder that there was silence when you got off the plane? Is it any wonder that silence was charged with hostility?"

He let the drape fall slowly back into place and went over to the desk. He didn't sit; he stood leaning slightly forward, his knuckles resting on its varnished surface, looking at Jonathan and Eve. Neither of them had turned. They stood staring at the curtain which had fallen back into place a few inches in front of their eyes. Then Eve stretched out her hand and drew it back so that she could see outside once more. Jonathan turned and came back into the room. He looked haggard and drawn.

He sat down in his chair and buried his face in his hands. He did not look at Eve, nor she at him. Ingram waited while the world outside crept into the space bounded by the four walls of the study and filled it, till there seemed to be no room for anything else. Finally, Jonathan raised his head. His eyes met Ingram's.

"Supposing," he said hoarsely, "supposing that the only way I can keep faith with those people is to say nothing?"

24

The execution of Joseph Gregor for crimes against the State took place on the morning of July 24, only six days after the first Alien contact with the people of Earth. Later, on July 29, the Great Leader received an urgent phone call from the Villa informing him that Ivan was in a position to talk.

In exactly eleven minutes he was marching into the hospital room where the boy was propped up in bed. Ivan looked much thinner and exceedingly pale. The drastic treatment to which he had been subjected to speed up the time of his recovery had brought his overtaxed body to the brink of death more than once. He was still far from well. It was doubtful if he would ever be completely well again. The human body can absorb only so much without being permanently affected. But Ivan's physical well-being for the rest of his natural life was expendable. The doctors had been told they were to make him well enough to talk. They had done just that and considered themselves more than fortunate to have succeeded.

The head physician spoke quietly into the Leader's ear. "He can answer any question you put to him, but he has just recovered. His condition might still be described as dangerous. If his life and sanity are important to the Party, you must be very gentle. Once a shock of this nature has been induced, it is ten times easier to produce a similar effect. If he is upset again, he will go back into shock and we cannot guarantee his recovery."

The Leader nodded his understanding. He crossed to Ivan's bedside and sat down on the chair.

"Comrade Godofsky," he began warmly, "I want you to know how happy we all are that you have recovered from your ordeal. I have declared a national holiday in honor of your return to health. I want to assure you that the Russian people no longer believe you to be a traitor."

Ivan managed a wan smile of relief.

"Now then, I do not wish to ask too much of you on the first day of your recovery, but our great nation is being threatened from within and without. There have been uprisings in many of our major cities because the capitalist nations have already demanded our withdrawal from Germany and Poland. Since we have no defense, we have been forced to begin evacuation. Russian prestige is crumbling throughout the world. The great courage and spirit of our people are being humbled before the imperialistic warmongers of the West. They threaten us with total destruction if we do not accede to their demands. You, and only you, can save your country and your people."

From the other side of the bed, the chief physician's lips were pulled into a thin hard line, his face set with anxiety. He had never expected the boy to be exposed to this kind of pressure, no matter how gently it was done. He noted the traces of strain etching themselves into Ivan's face, the beginnings of withdrawal in the boy's reaction. He shook his head again warningly at the Leader. But the Leader was not to be dissuaded. The same instinct which had won him so many political victories told him that the great gamble must be made now, or perhaps the opportunity would be lost forever.

"We know that your father and brothers gave their lives in the defense of their country at Stalingrad. We know that you can do no less."

His father! Abruptly the face of the gnarled wiry little man leapt into Ivan's mind. He had died defending his country against German invaders. What would he have thought as his blood seeped into the mud before Stalingrad if in the moment of death he had known that his son would one day hesitate to use a power which might save his country from another aggressor? And his brothers who had called the Russian artillery down on their own heads because the Germans had overrun their positions? They, too, had died in the defense of this land. Would he ever have a moment's peace if he allowed everything they fought for to be destroyed? There could only be one answer. He raised his eyes. They were all looking at him, waiting. In a low, barely audible voice he began to speak. He recanted laboriously the whole of his experiences aboard the space ship; the significance and power of the black box; the area of its destruction; the methods of launching; the manner in which the box could be opened. He told everything in its entirety without omission, even to the pact with the other five people.

When Ivan had finished, there was no sound in the room. The Leader nodded understandingly. Looking at him it was hard to believe that he was not a man humbled and saddened by the enormity of his responsibility. Ivan looked and believed that he had not delivered the information into hands that would wield it unwisely. The Leader laid his fingers gently on Ivan's arm. "For these revelations," he said, "all of your Russian comrades are grateful. There is only one more thing you must do. You are ill. If you should have a relapse, Russia would be left to the mercy of her enemies." He put his hand into his pocket and withdrew the black box. "You must open the box."

The physician on the opposite side of the bed held his breath. It didn't seem possible that the boy could stand any more, and yet he knew he dare not intervene.

For a second Ivan hesitated, then he stretched out a thin pale hand and took the box with trembling fingers. He held it in his palm and stared at it, then slowly he raised his head and moved his eyes from face to face around the room in pathetic entreaty. The faces gazed back at him, intense, impassive, expectant, frightened, but in none was there a look that would aid him in his decision. His eyes came to rest on the face of the Leader.

Inwardly the Leader was seething with uncertainty. He realized the extent of the gamble he was making; he knew that here was the crucial moment. If the boy refused now, it was almost a certainty he would never be persuaded to open the box. With an effort he held his face in a mask of benign understanding.

Ivan pulled his eyes away from the Leader's face and looked again at the box. "Couldn't I," he whispered, and the poignant appeal in the tone was like the voice of a child crying in the dark, "couldn't I wait?"

By the tone of Ivan's voice the Leader knew he had won. "You may do as you wish," he said with gentleness. "I don't know if even I would have the courage to open this box if I were in your position. I can only ask you to remember again the plight of your comrades and to do what you think is right."

Ivan raised the box to his eyes which were flooding with tears. He looked at it for a long time. Suddenly the box was open. There was an involuntary gasp of astonishment from everyone. The three golden capsules lay in their bed of white foam, glittering strangely. It seemed to every pair of eyes focused on them that the emanations of power could be felt as tangibly as the waves of heat from a blast furnace.

The Leader slowly held out his hand and took the box. He held it now in the palm of *his* hand. He looked down at its contents. He felt a surge of triumph such as he had never known, a sensation of power greater than he could have believed possible. He held in his hand, to do with as he wished, a force more potent, more terrible than the world had ever foreseen. *In the palm of his hand!*

He stood up. He had forgotten Ivan. He had forgotten those around him. He had forgotten everything except that he was now, as of this particular earth-shaking moment, the most powerful man in the history of the world.

He walked slowly out of the room.

25

The unbearable tension held for three days after Jonathan and Eve's interview with the President. During these three days, the government, hoping to prevent a panic, issued cautious and ambiguous bulletins that "some progress was being made" in the interrogation of Eve and Jonathan. But when, on the morning of the fourth day, it became apparent to the public that they had either refused to speak or that the government refused to reveal what they had said, the dam broke.

It began with a group of rabble-rousers and ne'er-do-wells from the outskirts of Washington. They marched through the streets, carrying placards lettered: GIVE US THE TRUTH!–HANG THE TRAITORS!–MAKE THEM TALK!–DOWN WITH THE MARTIAN DUPES! By the time they reached the White House, they were five thousand strong. The troops and police were called out, and, before the demonstration was quelled, one policeman had been killed and a dozen rioters seriously injured.

The incident touched off similar uprisings throughout the nation. Within a few hours, half of the United States was under martial law as incidents of looting, rioting, and panic spiraled into national catastrophe. The repercussions, of course, were inevitable. Industry ground to a standstill, ships ceased to be unloaded, transportation facilities broke down. Within two days, large portions of the nation were rapidly approaching famine. Epidemics of disease broke out as public utilities went untended. The demagogues and the rabble-rousers, the criminals and the fanatics took over.

The majority of intelligent and disciplined citizens who preached patience and understanding had their voices drowned in the welter of violence. Those of them who formed organizations to combat looting and crime found themselves waging pitched battles against the forces of disorder. It was the most serious crisis in the history of the nation.

In Washington, where the first demonstration had begun, visiting dignitaries were escorted through the streets in armored cars with a strong military guard and it was not uncommon for those parties to engage in several skirmishes with rioters before reaching their destinations.

The White House itself was in a state of siege. Ugly electrically charged fences grew out of the turf at the edge of the grounds, and machine gun emplacements blossomed on the lawn. Behind the high voltage wire, details of soldiers carrying weapons loaded with live ammunition stared coldly through the barriers at the restless mobs.

Inside the White House, Jonathan, Eve and Professor Bochner were being held under heavy guard. They had finally been permitted to meet together. None of them had had much sleep in the days since their encounter with the Aliens. But on Jonathan, because he was thin and rangy to begin with, the ravages of tension and sleepless nights had left their most obvious mark. His cheeks were sunken and his gestures were abrupt and ill-coordinated. The professor had lost all of his engaging brightness of manner and the rosy childlike blush which had characterized his physical being. Of the three, Eve had fared the best, at least to outward appearances. She comforted Jonathan as well as she could, soothing him when possible, sympathizing when she could not. She spent days and nights listening to his protestations of anger against the Aliens, who, he insisted, had broken their word, and she did her best to pull him out of the recurrent periods of depression.

She was watching him now as he paced the floor, his voice rasping in hard-edged bitterness. "We can't just sit here and do nothing. I agree that to tell the truth might make things worse. But it will be another three weeks almost before the expiration of the twenty-seven days. At the end of that time, the world will have been set back a thousand years. It's possible that our economy might never recover.

Already we've got disease, the beginnings of starvation, the nearly total destruction of police forces; we can't go on like this. Let's tell the people *something*. Let's tell them that the boxes are a gift from the Aliens, that they contain a power for a great good, but that we must find the secret of how to open the boxes before they can be utilized."

The professor shook his head. His accent had become much thicker during the last few days, as it always did when he was under tension. "Jonathan, you want to do good, but it is wrong."

"Why is it wrong?" Jonathan demanded angrily.

"Because you are just making words. You know yourself that it won't work, that no one would believe it. If these boxes were a gift of good, we would have announced it immediately. None of us would have run away. And if the box had contained a beneficial power, Eve would not have thrown hers into the sea. They have guessed what the boxes really contain, and that is why they are afraid."

"Then what do we do? Just sit here and let the world destroy itself? This way, the Aliens will be able to take over whether we use the bomb or not."

The professor smiled softly. "You exaggerate, Jonathan. The world cannot wipe itself out, even with disease and famine, in three more weeks, no matter how hard it tries."

"It can come pretty close," Jonathan said bitterly. He paced to the table, picked up a cigarette, and snapped the lighter. "All of this talk about their high morality and not giving the bombs to the governments! What the hell difference does it make? They might just as well have given it to the Kremlin as to make that announcement."

"I don't think you are being fair to the Aliens," the professor said.

"Fair!" Jonathan exclaimed.

"Give him a chance," Eve said, crossing to Jonathan.

Jonathan ground out his cigarette. "I'm sorry, Klaus. Go ahead."

"I have thought about it a good deal," the professor said gently, "and I think they have not been unfair. They stuck to the letter of their agreement. They said they would not invade us and they have not. They said they would give the weapon to five people chosen at random, which they did. They said that they personally would not exert any pressure on the world from the outside to use that weapon, and they did not. They said that any pressure would come from the people of the world itself. If we had been astute, we should have foreseen their announcement in that remark. We must remember that they did not give us this energy as a whim. They are fighting for their lives, not only for their lives, but for their very existence as a race, as we are fighting for ours. And it seems to me they have fought honorably."

"But the announcement——" Jonathan began again.

"The announcement," the professor interrupted firmly, "was inevitable. As I said before, we were stupid not to foresee it. I say again, they are fighting for their lives. And it would be ridiculous for them to give the bomb to five individuals and let it go at that. The chances of the bomb being used under those circumstances would be a million to one. Even as they have executed this plan, they have taken a great gamble by expecting the bombs to be used, and they may yet lose that gamble. Considering that they could, if they had so wished, have sprinkled a few bombs around our planet and simply walked in, it seems to me they have been a great deal more than honorable. You must remember that they have been observing us for four hundred years. Has it occurred to you what an insignificant facet of our culture could be dignified by the term 'admirable' in those four centuries? Our history has been a manuscript of horror capped by the final exclamation points of Buchenwald and Hiroshima. The miracle is that, in this morass of criminal irresponsibility, we have still found time to build a few enduring monuments in the world of music, art, and science. Yet, in spite of our record, the Aliens have not tried to judge us. They have merely shoved into bold relief the choice which has faced us since Enrico Fermi made the first atomic pile."

Jonathan was still not convinced. "It seems to me, as far as we're concerned, it's not so much a choice as an ultimatum–shut up or die! –anyway who can figure a race as crazy as this! They want our planet but they won't take it. They seem to consider us lower than beasts, yet they won't kill us. They give us a weapon which they expect us to use, and somehow manage to give the impression they hope we won't. If they're so all-fired chock full of loving kindness, how come they just *happened* to have fifteen nice shiny superspecial human exterminators on hand to pass on to us?"

"Jonathan," the professor said, "you miss a significant point.

Don't you see how ridiculous their ultimatum would be if we were a morally and intellectually mature people?"

"What do you mean?"

The professor smiled sadly. "Try to imagine what would happen if we were *not* fundamentally a neurotic life form. The Aliens would have whisked us off into space and presented us with these bombs and we, on being returned to earth, would have marveled at the unique nature of the experience and promptly tossed the boxes into the nearest sewer, or, as in the case of Eve, into the nearest convenient ocean. When the announcement came, we would have explained what had happened. The entire world would have had a good laugh at the ridiculousness of the whole thing and gone back to work. We might perhaps, as a gesture of kindness, have invited the Aliens to share as much of our planet as we could conveniently spare, but that is all. Instead, we returned to earth, having sworn ourselves to secrecy. Why? *Because we were afraid*—afraid of the knowledge we possessed—afraid of the results if the truth ever got out, because we *knew* that we, the human race, could not be trusted to handle these bombs any more than an undisciplined child can be trusted with a high-powered rifle."

No one spoke. "All you say may be true, Professor," Eve said finally, "but it doesn't solve our problem. What can we do?"

"There must be some way out," Jonathan said. "There's got to be!"

The professor tugged at his right eyebrow. "If . . . if only they would let me work on the capsules."

Jonathan raised his head sharply. "You've got an idea?"

The professor bit his lower lip and took off his spectacles. "I don't know . . ." he began. "I don't pretend to know now how they work, but if I could only get at one of them, perhaps I could . . ."

"Could what?" Eve asked anxiously.

The professor sighed deeply and put the glasses back on his nose. "It doesn't matter. It's not really an idea of what to do. It's just a feeling that I know something which I can't seem to bring to the surface of my mind. Since there doesn't seem to be any hope of my getting the capsules, I suppose it's useless even to think about it."

Eve and Jonathan looked at each other disconsolately.

But, for the professor, *saying* it was useless to think about the capsules was not equivalent to putting the statement into practice. He couldn't tear his mind away from the certainty that he had forgotten something of vital importance. In the back of his mind a small elusive thought throbbed away, refusing to break through his consciousness. Somehow or other, he knew it was connected with the black box–and he knew he had been closer to it in the past hour than at any time since the Alien's arrival, but how or why he had been so close he could not tell.

26

In the large conference room of the Kremlin in Moscow, the Leader rose dramatically to his feet, at the head of the long polished teakwood table. Arranged on either side of it were his general staff, the important names in the highest Party echelon, the top brains in every department of government. The Leader surveyed them critically. In spite of the shortness of his figure, the fat jowls, and the tiny piglike eyes, there was inherent in him in that moment a kind of dynamic impressiveness. One saw the jut of purpose in his jaw, the glint of recklessness in the eyes. His ideas might be right or wrong but one knew instinctively that he was a man possessed of fanatic convictions as to the validity of those ideas and the implacable purpose to put them into force.

Grouped around him were men far superior in intellect. And yet, there was about him a consciousness of power which left no doubt that he and he alone was the leader. In front of him, on the otherwise naked surface of the table, was a tiny black box opened so that those nearest him could see within it the three repositories of unimaginable potency. The Leader let his eyes pass slowly from face to face, weighing in the instant of passage the ability, the loyalty, the daring of each. When he had completed his scrutiny, he seemed satisfied. He raised an arm and pointed a finger toward the box on the table.

"Here," he said, "is Russian domination of the world."

There was a murmur of shocked surprise. The Leader let the surprise sink in and, when the attention of everyone was focused on the box, he picked it up carefully.

"You all know what this is. It is the box given to Ivan Godofsky by the people from space. You will notice that the box is open and that its contents are intact. As of the moment that I entered this council chamber, it was the only unsealed box of its kind in the world. One, as you know, was destroyed when the Chinese girl killed herself. A second lies at the bottom of the ocean. Two more are in American hands, but their owners refuse not only to open them but also to divulge their significance. Comrade Godofsky, however, a true Russian patriot, has told us the secret of his box and, in opening it for us, has given us the world."

The edge of irony in the words "a true Russian patriot" did not escape the men around the table. They had all heard something of the methods which had been used to persuade the "true Russian patriot" to give up the secrets of the box. Nor had they missed the warning contained in Gregor's execution. Unlimited devotion to the Party was not enough. It must be coupled with a record of success in carrying out the Leader's commands.

The Leader tilted the box slightly down the length of the table so that each of the group could see the capsules. "Each one of these capsules," he continued, "has many thousands of times the power of the X-bomb. Each one of them has a circular area of absolute destruction with a diameter of three thousand miles. Within this area of destruction, there is no possible means of screening or protection which can prevent the instantaneous destruction of all human life. Furthermore, there is no residual radiation. The weapon is harmless to all types of life other than human and to any form of vegetation which exists on the earth. The weapon is designed solely to destroy human life. It was given to Comrade Godofsky by the Aliens, who hope we will use it to wipe ourselves out. Their morality," he said deprecatingly, "does not permit them to invade another planet, but they plan to occupy two thirds of this one, should that much of it be freed of human life.

"Comrades, I intend that we shall use this weapon to rule the world!" He paused dramatically, relishing the stunned expressions on the faces in front of him, giving the enormity of his words time to register before he went on.

"I repeat, I intend that we shall use this weapon to rule the world. I shall use it at such a time and in such a manner that our own security will not be greatly endangered. And I shall see to it that the Aliens never occupy this planet by confining the elimination of humanity to the elimination of life on the North American continent." He smiled coldly. "I see that you are dubious, Comrades. I will answer questions. General Zamki?"

The general arose in his place. He spoke, choosing his words carefully. "May we ask how you intend to proceed with this conquest of the world?"

"I intend to make public the news that we have opened the box, and I shall announce to the entire world the nature and power of its contents. I shall then drop some gentle hints to the American warmongers that they withdraw from Europe and Asia and remain like good children in their own playground."

The general looked nonplused. "And if they refuse?"

"I am prepared to destroy all life on the North American continent."

There was a second involuntary exclamation from the entire group. The general looked thunderstruck. "But this will mean war," he said, "a war which could finish us as well as them."

The Leader fixed the general with a cold malevolent stare. "You do not learn, do you, General?" his voice rose suddenly. "You–none of you learn. The lessons of history are wasted on you. Does nothing penetrate your thick heads from the lessons of Hitler and the Rhineland, Mussolini and Ethiopia, Japan and Manchuria, Munich and Czechoslovakia! Does one have to drive understanding into your heads like a wedge?

"The Americans are appeasers! They have always been appeasers. And so have the British. Do you think, for one second, that the American people will permit a war of attrition over a few far-flung bastions like Berlin and Formosa? Never. America cannot be provoked into a war–she has to be bombed into it. I refer you to Pearl Harbor. They have never begun a war and they will not begin one now. They will bluster and they will talk, they will threaten, they will make concessions, but when they are sure that we mean what we say, that we will launch the capsules unless they withdraw—they will withdraw to the American continent and they will leave the rest of the world to us.

"This is the first step. With American troops, experience, and money gone from Europe and Asia, there is nothing to stop us. The whole of Europe, of Asia, of Africa, of Australia, and of that stumbling-block England will become part of the U.S.S.R. You comrades may choose your posts in the new world order.

"The Americans will then tell themselves, because they always believe what they want to believe, that we have no further territorial ambitions, and they will still not launch their bombs against us because, in addition to their national reluctance to strike first and precipitate war, they will be afraid. All of their eggs will be in one basket; the basket, comrades, is the United States of America. With these three capsules, we can squash those eggs with one blow. They, on the other hand, cannot destroy the rest of the world with both of their boxes, even if they wish. And so, they will once more threaten and bluster, but they will not dare to use the weapon they have, because they are outnumbered—we hold three fourths of the world to their one fourth.

"And when we have consolidated the rest of the world, comrades, we shall launch these tiny capsules against North America unless the Americans realize that they too, whether they like it or not, are a Soviet colony. May I remind you—if we are forced to use this weapon to destroy, once and for all, the American people, we will not destroy, as we would with atomic missiles, their vast resources and industries. These will be ours for the taking. Do I make myself clear?"

The full impact of the Leader's words was making itself felt around the table. The men seated there had been schooled all their lives to the conviction that Russia would some day rule the world. They had lent themselves tirelessly and avidly to fomenting revolutions in countries outside the Russian sphere of influence; they had labored equally fanatically to build for Russia the greatest offensive power in the world, to the same end. They had listened to and propounded propaganda, hailing Russia and its form of government as the eventual Utopia for all peoples. They were all convinced that a war against the United States was inevitable.

But the sudden realization that absolute victory in this was actually within their grasp staggered their imaginations. And yet the most cautious among them saw that the plan had a strong possibility of success. Its only flaw lay in the reasoning that America had never yet begun a war and would not begin one now. The only way in which the plan seemed liable to fail was if the Americans decided to launch their missiles first. It was a grave risk, to be sure, but there was not one man there who truly believed the Americans would strike first. And if they would not attack, they must withdraw under the threat to their very existence, and, having once withdrawn, they were forever lost, for they were forever vulnerable.

For a period of five minutes, during which the Leader sat down and waited, no one said anything. Then one by one as the possibilities of the plan began to form in their minds, the commissars came out of their reflections and started to nod at one another. Little spates of excited conversation broke out here and there. Chairs were pushed back, as doubts were driven aside in the first flicker of rising enthusiasm. The macrocosmic greatness of the proposition stimulated their imaginations. They began to see themselves as undisputed rulers of the world. They began to see in their minds' eyes the prestige of the hated Americans crumbling away before the genius of the Russian attack.

The Leader watched, a triumphant smile turning the corners of his mouth. The voices in the council room grew louder. Discussions became more heated. By now everyone but the Leader was on his feet. A current of waxing enthusiasm flowed back and forth through the room carrying the men in it to an apex of ecstatic dedication. There was no longer any thought of failure. Before every pair of eyes the golden chalice of success assumed with every passing instant a more solid shape.

The Leader waited until the intoxication had reached its highest peak. Then he stood up and spoke.

"Comrades, are we agreed?" The chorus of assent was greater than the Leader had dared to hope for when he had laid his plans for the meeting. "Then, comrades, I suggest you return to your seats and we begin immediately to map out the strategy of our attack. You, General Zamki, will order a general mobilization of all Russian forces by land, sea, and air. Call up all reserves. You will be responsible for seeing that every piece of military apparatus is ready for instant use. You will poise your occupation troops on all borders so that immediately upon the withdrawal of American forces we can take over in a matter of hours."

He turned to the propaganda chief. "I don't have to tell you, Davlovsky, what we need in the way of releases. We want photographs of the open box, blow-ups of Godofsky as a great Russian hero with the Order of Lenin, international news releases on the power potential of the bomb, range, area of destruction, effects, and so forth. And start suggestions that Americans are no longer welcome in Europe and Asia.

"You, Kukor, you will make arrangements for the occupation of continental America, set up channels for immigration.

"You, Bronin, your job will be to organize Russian business and industry to the point where they can take over American and European potential as soon as they are available.

"I want reports from all of you daily on what progress is being made and what ideas you have. You all have my authority to commission and commandeer whatever personnel and material may be necessary. Nothing, you understand, nothing must be left undone."

The Leader stepped away from his chair, pushed it neatly into place, turned, and set his hands on the back of it. He gazed down at the table. "Comrades," he said, *"I give you a world of Soviet Socialist Republic!"*

The date was July 31, 1963, exactly two weeks before the expiration of the twenty-seven days set by the Alien, and it is perhaps significant that it took only thirteen days from the first contact of the Aliens for the world to find itself on the brink of war.

27

Three days after the Russian council of war, the President of the United States presided over another historic meeting in the White House at Washington, D.C. He stood at the head of a table in the council room, surveying the Prime Minister of Great Britain, the Chancellor of West Germany, three of the most prominent scientists of these nations, and Jonathan, Eve, and Professor Bochner. Before him on the table lay half a dozen newspapers, their headlines proclaiming Russian success in opening the box. Below the headlines was printed almost the entire story of the Alien interview with the five people of Earth. The President pointed gravely to the papers and to a sheaf of dispatches lying next to them.

"By now," he said, "you must all have heard the story which broke about two hours ago. Most of you know that the Chancellor and the Prime Minister have been conferring with me for the past two days. I've asked them to be present at this meeting because I feel that everyone in this room will have a significant part to play in whatever action must be taken in the future. The gentlemen to my right are scientists–Professors MacDonald, Oberdorff, and Neuhaus. I think their names are familiar to all of you. For the past three days they have been working together to try to open the boxes you see before me. They are seriously concerned, as we all are, that Russia has succeeded where we have failed." He nodded toward Jonathan, Eve, and the professor.

"We were hoping, now that there seems to be no further need for concealment, that one of you might enlighten us as to how this was accomplished."

Jonathan, Eve, and the professor exchanged glances. Then the professor got slowly to his feet and crossed around the table to within reach of the capsules. He turned to the President.

"Mr. President, do you know which of these boxes is the one taken from me?"

The President picked up one of the boxes, glanced at a paper glued to its bottom, and silently handed it to the professor. The professor held the box in the palm of his hand for a second and looked toward the group of scientists. His face was grave.

"Watch!" he said.

Every eye focused on the box. Abruptly, it clicked open. The table buzzed with consternation and surprise, which the professor interrupted, glancing at the scientists.

"You must not feel too discouraged, gentlemen. No force on earth could have opened this particular box but my mental projections. No one but Mr. Clark can open this other. By the same token, only the Russian soldier, Ivan Godofsky, could have opened the box in Communist hands. Each of them is keyed to the electrical emanations of its owner."

The Chancellor leaned forward tensely. "Then the Russian story is true? The Aliens expect us to use those capsules so that they may take over the earth?"

The professor nodded. "It is true. Perhaps you understand now why we refused to speak. We were not acting under orders from the Alien, but neither were we prepared for the announcement which he made. When it *was* made, all of us fled in panic from the questions we knew were bound to be asked. Apparently, all of us reached independent convictions that world-wide chaos was preferable to world-wide destruction. You see, two facts were not included in the Russian releases. One is the fact that the capsules' life expires in twenty-seven days. The other is that the five of us made a pact aboard the space ship to conceal the existence of the weapon. But due to sheer stupidity in my case, and to an unfortunate accident in the case of Miss Wingate, the existence of the boxes was discovered. Since you seem convinced that Su Tan is dead and that her capsules were destroyed with her, it seems fairly obvious that Ivan was unable to conceal his possession of the box any further."

There was a deathly hush in the council chamber. Then Professor Neuhaus leaned across the table and took one of the capsules from the professor's hand. He examined it thoughtfully. Finally he looked up.

"Did it ever occur to any of you gentlemen," he said softly, "that this whole thing might be a giant hoax?"

All eyes leaped from the box Neuhaus was holding to the scientist's face. "There is no denying," he continued, "that the people from space are up to something. Their star ships did appear and there is no doubt that their science far surpasses ours. But this," he turned the box slowly in his fingers, "this, I for one, do not believe. Can anyone believe it without evidence? Perhaps this is the whole key. Might it not be that the space ships, the broadcast, the interview with the professor and this young couple were all part of a plan to make us believe that everything they said was gospel, even to the extent of a box designed to operate on the brainwave of its owner, and for the contents to disintegrate when those brainwaves ceased to flow. But think what a relatively simple scientific accomplishment this is compared to what the Alien asks us to believe about the capsules which the boxes contain."

He shook his head again. "No, gentlemen, I say once more, I do not believe it. What better way could the Aliens have of starting a war of attrition here on earth than to place these boxes in our hands and let us believe that they will do everything the Aliens say they will do?" He returned the capsule to the professor, who quickly replaced it in the box–and snapped the lid closed.

The people around the table stared at Professor Bochner. He had distracted them from Neuhaus–but what Neuhaus had said could very well be true. The Prime Minister turned toward Jonathan. "What do you think?" he said. "Do you believe it's a hoax?"

Jonathan bit his lip and laced and unlaced his fingers in front of him. "It could be," he said. "I don't think it is, but it could be. I suggested the same thing during the interview with the Alien. I asked him how we could be sure that this whole thing was not a fake. He replied that there was no way in which I could verify it. He said he could cause a gigantic explosion on some barren planet or even on our moon if he wished, but that, if I really disbelieved, I would convince myself that he had merely created an optical illusion for my benefit, and so the demonstration would prove nothing."

The Prime Minister nodded. "And he was right. The only way in which we can test the truth of the Alien's word is to test one of the bombs, and, from the standpoint of the free world at least, the test is impossible."

"Why?" said Oberdorff. "We've got a free testing area with a radius of more than fifteen hundred miles at the Pole, and our last checks indicated that the radiation in the area is negligible."

The Prime Minister turned toward the scientist. "But you forget," he said, "that this area for testing atomic missiles was evacuated, of necessity, before the first tests. And, for this test, we need a human life. If it is a hoax, it has been worked out to the tiniest detail. We cannot put a human being in the test area when we have every reason to believe that the life of that human will be the price of our mistake."

The German Chancellor frowned. "But, in the interests of world security, wouldn't a single life or a group of lives be expendable? After all, we use live ammunition in our war exercises. A few casualties are inevitable."

"They are," agreed the President, "but those casualties are accidental. We don't put a helpless soldier in front of a squad practicing bayonet drill. We use dummies. Men are killed preparing for war, by accident, as they are killed crossing the street or getting out of their bathtubs. We don't plan it; it happens."

The Prime Minister nodded in assent. "Furthermore," he said, "what reason could we give for risking anyone's life when we have no provocation? We cannot claim national security as the reason, because, while the bombs are always a potential danger, there has been no immediate threat to our security."

The President stood up. "Gentlemen," he said, "these are grave problems, and in need of immediate attention, but they are problems which cannot be decided without thought. I am sure that the professor, Miss Wingate, and Mr. Clark will want to weigh the course of their future actions carefully in view of the present developments. I'm sure that you, Mr. Chancellor, and you, Mr. Prime Minister, will want to confer with your aides and your ambassadors. And since the news of the Russian developments will very soon be on the streets I think you will want to contact your own governments as quickly as possible. Therefore, I suggest that we adjourn this meeting for at least six hours." He looked at his watch. "It is now four o'clock. Could we all meet here again at ten this evening?"

There was a murmur of assent and everybody filed out. The President was alone in the emptiness of the Council Room. He sat there for a long, long time, staring straight ahead. Finally, with an effort, he started toward the door. The youthful buoyancy of his gait was gone. Dark circles were under his eyes and deep lines of care were etched into his face. Since the advent of the Aliens, the President had become an old man.

28

At nine-twenty that same evening, Jonathan, Eve, and the professor received an urgent message requesting their immediate attendance in the conference room. They arrived to find the meeting already convened. The President was standing, looking tense and drawn. When they were seated, he wasted no time on ceremony.

"Gentlemen, our worst fears have been realized. Twenty minutes ago the Russian ambassador delivered to me personally a note demanding the withdrawal of all American forces from Europe, Asia, Africa, and continental waters in their vicinity. The withdrawal is to begin within forty-eight hours. We are to confine our sphere of influence to Continental United States. The alternative, you can guess. If, within forty-eight hours, we do not vacate West Berlin, Wake, Formosa, and other bastions which we have throughout the world, the Russians will launch their missiles against the North American continent. Congress will meet in one hour.

"Unless we comply with the Russian demands, gentlemen, it means war, a war in which we are at a disadvantage. The Russians have only three bombs to our six, but their target is a great deal smaller. I am faced with a decision of accepting the ultimatum or of launching our bombs first in the faint hope of knocking out their capsules. If, however, I take this course and their capsules are sufficiently diversified so as to be untouched, their retaliation will wipe out the United

States of America. Since the Russian box is open, it is highly probable that their three capsules are at this moment in the hands of Russian agents at widely separated points of the globe, because, as we have heard, anyone can launch the bombs. If I could bring myself to strike first, which I sincerely doubt, and providing that the professor and Mr. Clark would permit me to do so, which I also doubt, it would be a miracle if we destroyed all three of the Russian capsules. I have no choice but to comply with the Russian proposal."

"But you can't do that," the Prime Minister raged. "This Russian dictator is a madman. He is another Hitler. He is an irresponsible epileptic. This is only the beginning of his blackmail. Pull your forces back to America and you make yourself an even more inviting target. You put all your potential where he can destroy it at one blow!"

The President sighed. "I am aware of that, but there is no choice other than race suicide, which is precisely what the Alien expected. It appears we have only one hope. If we can begin our evacuation within the forty-eight hours and then delay its completion by doing everything in our power short of war to drag out that process, perhaps we can hold out until the deadline when the bombs cease to be lethal. There is a bare chance that if we seem to be complying with the Russian demands, they will hesitate to use the bomb until it is too late, and satisfy themselves with destroying our prestige throughout the world and occupying our foreign bases. I do not believe this, you understand, I only say it's a remote possibility." He looked around the room.

The German Chancellor frowned. "We have an agent in the Kremlin. I wonder if it would help . . ."

The Prime Minister looked up sharply. "Assassination?"

"Yes. We all know this must be the Great Leader's idea and his alone. If there was a hope of saving millions of lives, it would be justified."

The President shook his head. "I agree it would be justified, but I doubt it would help. True, the original blueprint for this must have come from the Leader. Only he would have the insane recklessness to jeopardize the world at one stroke. But the Prime Minister and I have both met him. He is mad–as Hitler was mad. But he is devastatingly shrewd. No one works under him who isn't hand-picked and I have heard that even they are forced to undergo periodic narcosynthesis to test their loyalties. They submit to regular psychiatric treatments calculated to make them fanatical worshipers of the Leader. It is almost impossible for them to doubt him. To destroy him would, I feel, accomplish nothing. The whole plan must be too far advanced for it to falter now, even if the Leader himself were killed."

The Prime Minister nodded a reluctant agreement. "There are many Russians who hate the Leader and detest the police state he has set up, but the majority of the people have swallowed the lies he has been pumping into them. They have no knowledge of the true facts. As the President points out, psychiatry guarantees the devotion of his generals and ministers. Propaganda guarantees the rest of the population. They will support him to the end. They look upon him as the Leader, Godhead, Savior, and heaven knows what else. An attempt on his life, even a successful attempt, would almost certainly provoke the very catastrophe we hope to avoid."

Oberdorff raised his hand. It was a surprising gesture and probably an unconscious one. The President nodded in his direction. "We still have not considered Dr. Neuhaus's suggestion that the boxes do not actually contain weapons. Until we know this, we may be giving up the world for nothing."

"I agree," the Prime Minister broke in. "The professor or Mr. Clark must permit us to launch one of the capsules at the Pole."

The President faced the three at the end of the table. "Will you help us?"

Professor Bochner turned to Jonathan and Eve. Jonathan nodded. The professor turned back to the group. He tugged at his right eyebrow. "We will help," he said. "I will reopen the box and I will launch the capsule to the Pole coordinate." There was an explosion of relief, which the professor cut off by raising a hand. "On one condition I will do this." The room fell silent. "On condition that you give me permission to examine freely the other two capsules."

The President glanced sharply in the direction of the Prime Minister and the Chancellor. "Professor," he said, "your conditions are difficult. It seems the only advantage we have in this battle for survival is that we possess six bombs against the Russian three. Since they provide a target area that is many times greater than ours, we are already at a disadvantage. We must use one of the capsules to check its deadliness, and if you begin experimenting with the other two and, in so doing, destroy them, we weaken whatever bargaining power we may possess."

The professor shook his head. "As bargaining power, you may still use them. The Russians need not know that I am examining the other two. But, other than this, as you yourselves have pointed out, the capsules are useless. We will not launch them first, because you could not bring yourself to do so, and we, who have the ultimate responsibility, have already decided we will not permit it. If Russia launches her capsules, America will be destroyed. It is thereafter a futile and irreligious gesture to destroy most of the rest of the world's population in reprisal. One or two bombs will be quite sufficient to destroy Russia as a world power and to preserve the freedom of those who are unharmed by our quarrels. No, Mr. President, I insist on my condition. The bomb for the Pole you may have, but I must be given permission and facilities to work on the other two."

The President looked deeply disturbed. "Professor Bochner, with all due respect to your genius, what can you hope to accomplish when the considered opinion of all these other brilliant men in your own field has already pronounced the situation hopeless?"

The professor blushed. "You will forgive me," he said, as he regarded his fellow scientists at the opposite end of the table. "I did not mean to impugn the abilities of men like Oberdorff, Neuhaus, and MacDonald. But you must not forget that I was aboard the space ship. I know something more than they know, however little that 'more' may be. And I have somewhere an idea which I cannot bring into the light but it has, I know, something to do with the capsules, and I shall not rest until I have had a chance to examine them. I shall welcome the assistance of these men, but you must permit me to conduct the experiments in my own way. You forget, Mr. President, that I can do what the others could not. I can *open* the box."

The President was never a man for quibbling when the cards were on the table. "Very well, Professor, you shall have your permission and your facilities. And, in return, you will launch a capsule at the Pole coordinate."

The Chancellor cleared his throat. "Gentlemen," he said, "we have the weapon and we have the proving ground, but we have yet to find the test material."

The President nodded. "It is a crucial problem, but one which can scarcely be decided at this moment. I have called a special session of Congress and I am afraid that the House is waiting. Let's give ourselves a deadline. Today is the second of August. If this test is to be of any significance, it must be made within the forty-eight hours during which we are required to begin our withdrawal from Europe and Asia. Perhaps, by a tentative agreement to withdraw, we can persuade the Russians to extend us another twenty-four hours' grace, which will give us time to arrange every possible scientific check at the proving ground. We could then set the test hour for, say at random, 10:00 A.M. on August 4. Agreed?" The President glanced toward the scientists.

Neuhaus nodded. "Most of the equipment is ready now. In twenty-four hours we can have everything checked and in position, and designate observation posts outside the danger area."

"Good. Now, gentlemen, I must leave you. We will meet again at seven tomorrow morning, but if there are any urgent communications, you will find me in my room after midnight." The President arose from the table and left the room.

The others made no move, with the exception of Karl Neuhaus, who, a few moments later, excused himself and quietly took his departure.

29

During the remainder of the night and the morning following the emergency meeting in the White House, events moved rapidly on the international as well as the local scene. The American ambassador in Russia delivered a note into the hands of the Great Leader, protesting vehemently against the unethical and warlike threats which were being used to force the withdrawal of American troops from areas outside the North American continent. The note stressed that the Americans possessed six capsules to the Russian three, and made it clear that the Americans would retaliate with all six of these weapons in the event of an overt act of war.

In a further attempt to forestall the crisis, the note made a typical diplomatic counterproposal that the Russians make a similar withdrawal from Berlin, East Germany, and all points outside the continental limits of the U.S.S.R., but, at the same time, agreed under protest to the evacuation demanded by the Russians. It went on to explain at length that the beginning of such an evacuation was not possible within the allotted forty-eight hours, and demanded thirty-six more hours before they could possibly comply with the Russian ultimatum. No reply had yet been received to this note, which had been presented in the late hours of the morning.

On the domestic scene, frantic preparations were being made for the launching of the capsule at the Pole. Crews of scientific experts were flown to the test site and teams of surveyors checked and rechecked the position of an observation post fifteen hundred and five miles from the true Pole. Tractors were set to work clearing an area a hundred yards in width and a mile long, whose outer edge was a segment of a circle with its center at the pole. This cleared area was later to be dyed a violent red. Inside it crates of animals, insects, and biological specimens were set up and labeled. Architects drew up plans for heated observation posts situated on the edge of the five-mile limit beyond the danger area, and, in addition to the customary scientific equipment already located in this danger area, extra television cameras, high-powered telescopes and binoculars were rushed to the scene and set up around the post. Squadrons of observation planes were briefed in the area they must patrol outside the lethal area of the bomb.

The scientists had already decided that if the bomb were truly lethal, its power would be confined to the area designated by the Alien. So far, everything else he had said had proved to be true. Either the bomb was a fake and would do nothing whatsoever, or it would do exactly what the Alien said, no more and no less. Preparations were made with the utmost secrecy and those involved in the preparations were led to believe that the tests were for the latest atomic weapon.

The reactions of the world when the Russian revelation of the true nature of the contents of the black boxes appeared in the press were astonishing. Perhaps it was due to the fact that the public was already exhausted by days of hysteria, panic, and rioting. Perhaps it was due to the fact that the imminent threat of war, no matter how frightful that war might be, was something that humanity understood. It now seemed apparent that they were faced with a tangible enemy and a concrete force. They were no longer afraid of invasion by the Aliens; they were solely concerned with the immediate problem of the preservation of their own lives.

Whatever the reason, the rioting stopped, the panic abated. The angry mobs which had surrounded the White House and made passage through the streets of the capital difficult and dangerous melted away. The damage to transportation facilities and industries, the growing famine in parts of the country, and the outbreaks of disease due to failing water supplies and lack of medicines were things which could not be rectified in a matter of hours or even of days, but a start was made and the restoration of authorized law enforcement agencies began to put the nation back on a weak but gradually strengthening footing.

At seven o'clock in the morning, a tense group appeared in the White House conference room. Few of them had slept. They came to the table with weary faces and bodies leaden with fatigue. At precisely five minutes past seven, the roster was complete except for Professor Neuhaus. The President sent an aide to check on his whereabouts and proceeded to acquaint the rest of the company with the events of the night and the American note which had been put into Russian hands. In the whole picture, there was only one bright factor, the partial restoration of order throughout the nation.

When the President had finished, he pushed aside the sheaf of reports in front of him, poured a cup of coffee from one of the steaming pots which were set at regular intervals around the table, and began to stir sugar into it almost absently. After a few seconds, he raised his head, without touching the coffee he had poured, and surveyed the group.

"Gentlemen," he said, "we are now faced with the problem of finding a human life to be risked in our experiment. I have given this matter considerable thought during the night, as, I am sure, have most of you. The obvious choice would, of course, be the life of a criminal who had been condemned to death. However, within the next forty-eight hours no such death sentence is to be executed, and so the problem is extremely serious. We cannot move up a sentence which has already been passed and set for a later date because, by so doing, we would deprive the criminal in question of the right to a last-minute reprieve, which some of you may not know is a possibility under American law.

"Furthermore, there are other difficulties. We could not arbitrarily use such a prisoner unless he volunteered his services. This would involve considerable publicity, which is precisely what we hope to avoid. The same objections can be made, though perhaps with very slightly less validity, to the use of some unfortunate citizen with an incurable malady or someone with a life expectancy of a matter of weeks. We could, undoubtedly, get hundreds of volunteers simply by telling the people the facts, but this would be dangerous and, at such a late date, somewhat impractical."

The door opened and Neuhaus entered, nodded a mute apology and slipped into his seat.

"Yes, gentlemen," the President continued, after acknowledging Neuhaus's gesture, "we are faced with a problem to which I and none of my advisers have been able to offer a practical solution. It has been suggested that we might use an anthropoid for the test, but it would be a dangerous expedient. The Alien particularly specified that the bomb would attack only human life. If the ape failed to die, we would have accomplished nothing. We would still not know whether or not the capsules were lethal to human beings."

There was a movement at the end of the table, and Professor Neuhaus arose from his chair, "Mr. President, may I say a few words?" The President inclined his head and resumed his seat.

"Gentlemen," Neuhaus began, "I came here to tell you that the problem of finding a test subject has been solved." He unbuttoned his cuff and pulled up his sleeve. He pointed to a minute red mark on the inside of his forearm just above the wrist. "Two hours ago, gentlemen, I injected myself with a poison which will cause my death within sixty or seventy hours."

There was an instantaneous explosion of surprise. The President was on his feet, but his voice could not be heard above the uproar. Neuhaus held up his hand, until silence descended on the room.

"I know everything you are going to say, but, before you say it, please allow me to speak. I have thought about this quite carefully. I did not make this injection in a moment of childish abandon, nor as a gesture of dramatic heroism. I made it coldly and intellectually in the interests of science. I was tempted originally to make up a lie that I was going to die anyway within a few months, and so was the obvious choice, but I knew that you would discover it was not true, and so I decided to place you in a position where you could not refuse my offer. I don't wish to make this sound like a Hollywood movie, gentlemen, but, having made this injection, I think it only fair to point out to you, in my own interests, that my death is now inevitable, and the death from this particular poison is not a very pleasant one."

The silence in the room could have been cut with a knife. "You see," Neuhaus continued, "I realized that you would not accept me if I volunteered my services. You would talk all sorts of rot about my being important and invaluable, forgetting that no one is indispensable, and that, of all the people in the world, I must bear the strongest responsibility for this test. Furthermore, should I live through it, I am one of the few people who could analyze his reactions, which a criminal or an ordinary citizen would be unlikely to be able to do."

The President opened his mouth to speak, but Neuhaus held up his hand again. "Please, Mr. President, allow me to finish. I want you to remember that it was I who first put into your minds the idea that this whole thing was a hoax. It was I who first expressed the belief that the bomb would not work." He smiled somewhat ironically. "I have to be shown! It is my firm conviction that this test must be made and, as it was my word that precipitated this experiment, it is only fair that it should be my privilege to make it possible. I beg you not to make a further issue of this. I have told you, and I reiterate, that this poison is fatal; there is no known antidote against its virulence. I am very normal in most respects, gentlemen; I do not particularly relish the idea of giving up my life. The least you can do is allow me the satisfaction of giving it in the manner I choose."

He sat down. There was nothing anyone could say.

Eventually the President spoke. "Professor Neuhaus," he said, "in the light of what you have just done, I cannot tell you how deeply we regret that you have taken such a drastic step. But, inasmuch as you have done so, you have left us no way in which to prevent you from fulfilling your objective. A life such as yours is a terrible price to pay for any kind of knowledge.

"If there is anything that the American people or I can do, if there is any request that you would like to have granted before that time, you have only to ask."

Neuhaus shook his head. "Thank you, Mr. President. No."

"In that case," the President said, "I think there is no point in continuing this meeting. The test is confirmed for ten o'clock tomorrow. I have made arrangements for all of you scientists to be at the proving ground tomorrow morning. The Prime Minister, the Chancellor, Miss

Wingate, Mr. Clark, and Professor Bochner will remain here, in case of any accident. We cannot risk their lives to no purpose."

The assembly rose. Neuhaus, looking strangely embarrassed, made his escape.

30

The morning of August 4 dawned bright and clear. By seven o'clock in the morning, MacDonald, Oberdorff, and their fellow scientists were in their observation posts making last minute checks of their equipment. Eve and Jonathan had been forced at the President's command to remain in Washington. He had not had the same success with Professor Bochner. Klaus had adamantly refused to launch the capsule unless he was given permission to be at the observation post. He had guessed that in these last hours Neuhaus would not want to be alone, and he had been correct. The two of them had stayed awake through the entire night and morning, quietly talking scientific theories, exchanging views on the microcosm and the macrocosm like two old friends who had met after a span of many years.

At 9:00 A.M. they were interrupted to synchronize their watches; at 9:30 A.M. they emerged from their room into the post. Neuhaus chatted quietly with the personnel, stared through the thick plate-glass window at the marking towers, perfectly visible in the clear air five miles away. He gazed at a TV viewer trained on the point marked by a single flag one mile inside the lethal area where he was to be stationed. At 9:35, he shook hands with everyone.

He thanked Professor Bochner warmly for his company through the night. "I'm only sorry," he added with a warm but slightly ironic smile which was so characteristic of him, "that we couldn't continue.

Mind you, I don't say I believe everything the Alien told you, but it's fascinating. Think of it! Thirty thousand intelligent worlds out there and we are chained to the earth. Tragic. Good-by, Klaus."

He donned the jacket and parka of his electrically heated suit, to complete the ensemble which had been given him, wrung Professor Bochner's hand once more, and descended the short ladder from the observation tower to the snow-packed ground. Every eye followed his erect figure in its bulky snow suit as he crossed the intervening distance to the waiting helicopter. His breath hung in a white trail in the biting cold. At the door of the helicopter, he turned and waved a hand toward the tower. As one, the men in the tower waved back.

He entered the aircraft, which lifted vertically and then moved forward toward the danger area. They watched it till it dropped, a black speck, onto the white snow beside the lonely little flag, six miles from their point of observation. Gazing through the telescope, Professor Bochner saw Neuhaus descend from the plane and stretch an arm back into the plexiglass cockpit to shake the hand of the pilot. The time was 9:45.

Immediately, the plane lifted again and began returning to its base. The men who had specific duties to attend to sat down at the complicated panels in the post.

The seconds ticked by–9:50, 9:53, 9:55. Professor Bochner's eye was glued on the TV screen. Neuhaus looked as though he were waiting for a bus. He was swinging his arms against his sides, probably to keep warm. A hundred feet away were the cages of the test animals and the insects. The professor felt a tap on his shoulder. The man who had been designated as the official firer said quietly, "I think, Professor, it is time we went outside." The professor donned his own parka and jacket and took the black box which the man handed him. They walked out onto the small balcony which had been erected around the tower. The time was 9:57.

"Will you open the box?" the man said.

The professor took off his glove and held the box in the palm of his hand. The sudden cold nipped at his fingers. He looked at the box and began to concentrate. Nothing happened. The box remained closed.

The man saw the look of consternation on the professor's face. "What is it?" he asked anxiously.

"It won't open," the professor said in a low harried voice. "The trouble is, I don't really want it to open, so it doesn't respond."

"Professor," the man said softly, "remember that Doctor Neuhaus is destined to die anyway. The death he has chosen for himself is pretty horrible. This at least will be clean and instantaneous. Remember, too, that the future of the world may depend upon your opening this box now."

The professor looked at him. The man was right. To fail Neuhaus now would be criminal. He fixed his attention once more on the box. Perhaps five seconds passed in what seemed to both of them an eternity. Then suddenly the box snapped open. The time was 9:58:30.

"You may begin now," the man said. "And I am to remind you of your instructions. You will say everything but the last figures of the final coordinate at once. You will say the final coordinate on the printed digit 2, as I drop the last of the time cards."

The professor nodded. He tried to take one of the capsules from the box, and found his fingers were numb. He transferred the box as quickly as he could to his other hand, pulling on his mitten with his teeth. With his warm left hand, he was then able to remove the capsule, when he had returned the box to his right glove. He closed the box containing the remaining two and slipped it into his pocket. He held the capsule in his hand. The firer nodded.

The professor pulled the pin and spoke the coordinates of the true Pole except for the final figure. The time was 9:59:40. Five seconds ticked by, and the firer began to flip the numbered time cards. Fifteen–fourteen–thirteen–twelve–eleven. At the lonely flag inside the danger area, Neuhaus looked at his watch, and the observers at the TV monitors saw him wave a last good-by. The firer's cards kept snapping down, second by second. Ten–nine–eight–seven–six–five–four –three–

Two!

The professor spoke the last coordinate and the capsule disappeared. On the instruments, nothing happened. There was no explosion, there was no sound. On the seismograph, nothing changed. But at the tiny flag inside the lethal area, in a billionth of a microsecond, a battle was fought and lost. Countless billions of invisible rays flashed through the open mesh of massed molecules which formed the outline of Professor Neuhaus's body. Unerringly, each sought as its target one of the atoms which formed the basis of his physical entity, smashed with irresistible power into the nucleus in the atom's heart, destroying the delicate balance of its electromagnetic field. In that billionth of a microsecond, the microcosms which were in toto the form of Professor Neuhaus became a hundred different elements as electrons were battered out of their orbits, reaction induced counterreaction. And suddenly there was nothing.

On the hard-packed snow there lay a gold signet ring and a watch which had belonged to Karl Neuhaus. Beside them in an empty heap lay the clothes which had covered him.

Karl Neuhaus had lost his gamble. There had been no poison in his veins. The mark of the needle on his forearm and the elaborate story had both been part of a desperate and successful effort to force his country to accept him as the guinea pig.

In the observation tower, the men scanning the instruments shook their heads in wonder and confusion as their instruments failed to react. But the men monitoring the TV screens straightened up, their eyes meeting in silent affirmation of horror. There could no longer be any doubt that the Alien had spoken the absolute truth!

31

Professor Bochner had his laboratory on a small, highly secret, and well-guarded island in the vicinity of Puerto Rico. He, Jonathan, and Eve had been housed in hastily erected quarters. All of the attention and care in construction had gone into the laboratory, which was as thoroughly equipped as time and money could make it. A full week had passed since the test at the Pole, and the professor and his colleagues, living on benzedrine and black coffee, had worked around the clock in an attempt to discover the secrets of the bomb. Their efforts had been fruitless.

In the interim, the world crisis had reached a new high. Russia was openly arrogant and triumphant. Despite every attempt to delay the operation, America had eventually been forced to evacuate Germany and her other bastions beyond the North American continent. Russia had solemnly agreed to perform a similar withdrawal, but it was already apparent to the world that she had no intention of keeping her word. Two hours after the last American soldier had left Formosa, the island had been subjected to a ruthless attack by the Red Chinese. Within twenty-four hours, Nationalist defenses had crumbled and Formosa was in Red hands.

The Russian satellite of East Germany had occupied all of Berlin and West Germany, and Communists were poised on the French and Belgian border. A Russian flotilla was steaming toward deserted Wake

Island. American prestige had collapsed, and, perhaps for the first time in their history, the nations of Europe and Asia were realizing the true significance of the Communist power which they were going to be forced to embrace.

But America in many respects is a mighty nation. As her prestige crumbled throughout the world, and she found herself a lonely sanctuary for free thought, her will to resist increased a hundredfold. Like the tiny British island that stood alone against the might of the German war machine, she drew courage from desperation and found hope in a situation that seemed hopeless. Her recovery from chaos was wrought of courage and ingenuity. Already, transportation was restored, disease checked, famine lifted, and factories began to turn once more. A state of national emergency existed, and, while there seemed little to do in the face of the immediate danger, every possible preparation was made for war on the atomic scale.

In their own sanctuary far from a target area, should the Americans launch their capsules, the Great Leader and his followers reveled in triumph. And the Leader himself, unknown to his military chieftains, laid plans to destroy America at the last possible minute before the expiration time of the capsules.

Ivan was being treated like a royal guest. He lived in the lap of luxury, in a splendor which left him slightly ill at ease. To have servants perform for him services which he had always performed for himself made him nervous and uncomfortable. He was shown articles in newspapers declaiming the adulation in which he was held by the Russian people. But the true state of affairs of the world was carefully kept from him. It was explained to him that the Leader and his advisers had been forced to move to this remote outpost, where they all lived together in one enormous villa, because of the immediate danger of American attack on Russian soil. It was not explained to him that the possibilities of this attack were provoked by the Russians themselves.

And yet, Ivan was far from easy in his mind. Not only was he disturbed by the crisis in the world and the fact that he had broken his pledge to the other four people who had been given the bomb, but there was an undercurrent of something else in the air which disturbed him even more. He could not quite put his finger on the reason for his uneasiness, but in actuality it was caused by the demeanor of the Leader and his council, whom Ivan had occasion to see from time to time. He had not yet correctly read their manner as one of self-satisfaction and triumph in evil, but there is a certain aura of guilt about any human being who convinces himself of the rightness of a criminal act when he knows that that act is indefensible. Even the Leader himself was not completely immune to this virus, and it was this aura of conscience if you like, this indefinable something that made their voices a little too loud, their gestures a little too abrupt, and their laughter a little too forced, which Ivan sensed but did not fully comprehend.

He was not stupid. He realized that, regardless of the honors which had been heaped upon him, he was being treated with the utmost courtesy because the bombs were only lethal as long as he remained alive. And yet he was not sufficiently suspicious or shrewd to consider this the only reason for his having been catapulted into opulence and fame. It was impossible not to remember that he was the only Russian citizen who had contacted the Aliens, and it was undeniably true that he was the only Russian defense against foreign aggression.

But, despite the luxury of his surroundings and the height of his fame, he was lonely. No one visited him. He had no one to talk to. He had nothing to do, and his servants seemed strangely reluctant to be drawn into conversation. Since Ivan had had no experience with servants, he did not suspect that they had been sternly forbidden to fraternize with him, and thought their taciturnity natural to their profession. To pass the time, he took long walks in the villa gardens onto which the doors of his suite opened. He had no knowledge of the fact that while he brooded in solitude, the Great Leader was preparing to use his capsules to dominate the world.

On the other side of the world, on the island off Puerto Rico, the professor too was beginning to find himself a lonely gladiator in the battle against time. After a week of fruitless struggles, he had been forced to admit that he and his fellow scientists had accomplished precisely nothing. They were no nearer to knowledge of what power caused the capsules to operate than they had been in the beginning of their experiment. The scientists were urgently needed at Oak Ridge and Los Alamos, as America girded her loins for an atomic war. That afternoon, the professor had shaken their hands as they departed by air for the mainland.

It was little comfort to him that Jonathan and Eve also remained on the island, because he was so preoccupied with his work and so tired in those brief hours when they persuaded him to relinquish it that he was in no condition for social amenities. Perhaps of all the people immediately involved in the gathering storm, Eve and Jonathan fared the best. The realization that every moment might in fact be their last made them savor each drop of time. They were never free of observation by the armed soldiers who patrolled the island or the tactful guards who followed them wherever they went. But they learned to accept the surveillance and for brief periods even managed to forget it. They were useless in the laboratory and, until the Russians made some further move, had no responsibilities. Yet the fact that Jonathan possessed three capsules made it imperative that he be guarded and available. Exactly what use he was to be, should the Russians attack, no one seemed to know, since it had never been decided whether or not he should launch the capsules if America was attacked. Perhaps the very fact that he and Klaus were alive and in possession of capsules was felt to be some kind of deterrent to an overt act of aggression.

On this particular afternoon, he and Eve lay on the sands of the beach, still caught up in the wonder of each other. One of their guards had taken a few moments off and the other, standing in the shadow of the palms, turned his back. He decided if the world ever got out of this he was going to get into some other profession.

In the laboratory, the professor sat on a stool before the work bench, his head in his hands, filled with hopeless dejection. Still gnawing at the back of his mind was the evanescent wisp of a thought which he could not isolate. He knew with uncanny intuition that this sensation of having forgotten something which had plagued him for weeks was the key he so frantically sought. But what was it? Why couldn't he bring it into the light? What perverse psychological quirk kept insisting that the thought was there and yet denying him access to its secret? The robust little man who had left Heidelberg slightly more than three weeks previously was no longer recognizable. He now weighed less than a hundred pounds. His clothes hung on him like the rags of a scarecrow. Great dark hollows underlined his eyes. His cheeks were sunken. His gait was slow and shambling, and his hands shook from lack of sleep and overdoses of benzedrine. In the last twenty-four hours he had developed a tic at the right corner of his mouth which jerked the muscles spasmodically every few seconds. He had scarcely had his clothes off for eight days.

Maybe, he thought, if I bathe and rest it will come to me. Maybe I'm too tired now. He made his way to his quarters and drew himself a hot bath. He slid into it gratefully. His body soaked in the soothing warmth and his tired muscles seized the moment to relax. His head fell forward on his chest and he jerked it upright with the realization that he must not fall asleep here. He bathed laboriously, fighting every second the desire to give way to slumber. Finally, he got out of the bath and weakly pulled the towel from the rack. He walked naked, drying himself, into the next room and sat down on the edge of an iron cot. It was the last thing he remembered.

Five hours later, Jonathan, not finding the professor in the laboratory, looked into his room and found him sprawled on the bed, completely naked, sleeping as if in a coma. He covered him gently, noting sadly the way the ribs showed through the wasted flesh. The professor slept for eighteen solid hours.

He awoke at ten o'clock on the morning of August 14. Without pausing for breakfast, he drew on a pair of trousers and, without stopping for shoes or shirt, rushed out of the building toward the laboratory. Eve, coming up from the beach, saw his strange figure in its outlandish costume as he climbed the stairs to the lab. Anxiously, she called after him. He gave no sign that he had heard.

For days she and Jonathan had been troubled about him. The hot-eyed wildness he had displayed when Eve had tried to persuade him to leave his work for nourishment or rest had frightened both of them, and the alarming rapidity with which Klaus had lost weight had given them serious cause for concern. They felt that, if he continued like this, he had not long to live. Seeing him now, scurrying through the door, she feared the worst and hurried into the laboratory after him.

The professor was bending over one of the capsules. "Go away," he said. "Go away. Can't you see I haven't much time?"

Eve looked at him for a moment and then ran out. She rushed

across the yard and pounded on Jonathan's door. At his muffled, "Come in," she opened the door to find him standing at the mirror wiping lather off his face. As he saw the stricken look on her face, he dropped the towel and came to her.

"What is it?" he said.

"I'm afraid for the professor."

"Why? What's the matter?"

"I saw him running across the yard half dressed. When I called him, he didn't answer, and, when I followed him into the lab, he shouted at me to go away, that he hadn't much time."

"Well, he hasn't," Jonathan agreed grimly.

"Maybe he's sick."

"I doubt it. He probably woke up discovering he'd wasted a night sleeping and now hates himself and the rest of the world because of it."

"I hope you're right, but I think you'd better talk to him."

Jonathan was buttoning the shirt he had put on during the interchange. "All right," he said. "Let's go."

With Eve running beside him to keep up, he strode over to the laboratory. The professor was seated on a stool in the middle of the room, staring straight ahead of him. Eve glanced at Jonathan. "You see," she whispered.

Jonathan said nothing. He crossed the room and walked around the professor until he could see his face. The professor's eyes were blank. The tic was pulling mercilessly at the corner of his mouth. Jonathan put into his voice an ease which he did not feel. "Professor!" he said. The professor did not move or blink. "Klaus!" Jonathan said more loudly. Still the professor gave no sign that he had heard. Eve stood beside Jonathan, her face lined with worry.

"Relax," Jonathan said to her. "Don't jump to conclusions." He touched the professor gently on the shoulder. "Klaus!"

The professor started, and awareness flowed back into his eyes. "Klaus, are you all right?"

"All right? Of course I'm all right," the professor snapped angrily.

Jonathan smiled. "There's no need to be angry, Klaus. I just wanted to make sure. We were worried about you."

"Worried? Why?" the professor demanded belligerently.

Jonathan smiled more broadly and pointed to the professor's emaciated rib cage. "It's not like you, Professor, to be so informal."

The professor glanced down at his half-naked figure and the anger went out of his eyes. "I'm sorry," he said, more in his usual tone, a little confused and embarrassed. "I didn't realize. I was in such a hurry to get to the laboratory. You know I slept for eighteen hours?" His tone implied that the offense was unforgivable.

"You needed it," Eve said softly. "It's a wonder you didn't sleep for a week. You couldn't have gone on any longer without collapsing."

"But it's unforgivable," the professor continued. "Don't you see there are less than twelve hours left before the expiration of the twenty-seven days?"

"But that's wonderful!" Eve exclaimed. "It means we've almost won."

The professor shook his head doggedly. "No, it means just the opposite. It means that we are on the verge of annihilation."

"What!" Jonathan said.

The professor glanced at him challengingly. "If you were going to launch the bombs against someone else, when would you do it?"

Jonathan looked nonplused. "Well, I don't know."

"You do, if you think about it. You would launch them at the last possible moment, so that your enemies would have no time to retaliate. This is exactly what the Russian is doing. The pattern is all too clear. He began by forcing the withdrawal of all American forces into continental United States. Why? So that he could destroy in one blow as much of America and American potential as is humanly or inhumanly possible. What other reason could he have for making such a dangerous demand at this moment? If he knocks America out without demanding this retreat, he leaves nuclei of American strength all over the world, upon which other nations can build a defense when his three bombs are gone."

"I can't believe it," Eve whispered. "It's too inhuman."

"You do not know, my dear, the mentality of dictators. Someone said, 'Power corrupts and absolute power corrupts absolutely!' You heard the Prime Minister describe the Leader's rages and attacks of epilepsy. You have seen the ruthless manner in which he has used his knowledge of the capsules. And you, my dear, being English, should remember the lesson of Hitler. It is my firm conviction that unless something happens to prevent it, in less than twelve hours the Russians will launch their weapons. That is why I cannot spare those eighteen hours. It is a question of life or death."

Then without warning, the professor's whole being underwent a startling metamorphosis. His body froze, his eyes glazed with the force of inner concentration. His lips moved in painful but inaudible articulation. Abruptly he jumped down from the stool and began padding about in his bare feet, his head bobbing, his mouth working. Gradually his mutterings became intelligible, but the words were meaningless . . . "life or death . . . life or death . . . life or death . . . life or death . . . life or death." Then he stopped dead, his head thrown back.

In the back of his mind the gnawing ceased. The idea he had been pursuing so long began to swim into the surface of his consciousness. As it came through, like a magnet it pulled the other pieces of the jigsaw into place. He stood still, letting all the ramifications float through his mind. Then he closed his eyes. He stood there motionless, as if in a trance. Eve made an anxious movement and Jonathan caught her arm, motioning her to silence. They stood there, the three of them, like statues–the two younger ones with their eyes fixed on the emaciated figure before them.

An eternity later, the professor's lips moved slightly. "Of course," he breathed softly to himself. "If it's anywhere, it's *got* to be there!" Suddenly he opened his eyes and, turning, scurried across the lab and plunged waist-high into a stack of unopened equipment. Recklessly, he hurled boxes, cartons, and crates in every direction. Finally, there was a triumphant cry. He emerged carrying a carton marked modeling clay. He ripped it open on the way back to the bench, dug out two double handfuls of the gray material, and flung the rest of the box away.

Eve and Jonathan watched him in open-mouthed consternation, but the professor was oblivious. Working with feverish eagerness, he plumped the clay down on the bench. The change that had come over him was miraculous. There was new strength in the body, new fire in the eyes. He smoothed a portion of the clay with a spatula, then took a soft brush, dipped it in oil, and bathed the surface of one of the capsules. Then he rolled the capsule across the clay until the impressions on its surface were left in the clay. He removed the capsule, pulled down the corners of the mold, and set it under a heat lamp to dry.

He disappeared and came back with a box containing a quantity of soft black powder and blew it over the mold he had made. Then he set the tablet at an angle against the back of the bench and examined it carefully with a magnifying glass.

Jonathan and Eve barely heard the soft exhalation of breath, but there was no mistaking the look of triumph in his eyes. He straightened up slowly, seeing them again for the first time.

"Why is it," he said, "that one always overlooks the obvious?" He extended the glass to Jonathan. "Look."

Jonathan bent over the tablet. Under the magnification of the glass, a mass of symbols leapt out at him. He straightened up, handing the glass to Eve. "What is it?"

Klaus glowed. "It's a message couched in the language of mathematics."

"You can read it?"

Klaus shook his head. "Not the way you can read a page of print, but I can decipher it eventually, I'm sure."

"But how is it nobody discovered it before?"

Klaus shrugged. "Who can answer? There is some excuse for the others; they couldn't open the box, but for me . . ." He shook his head. "I don't know. I was looking for something complicated. I took it for granted the tracings were functional. They can't be read by the naked eye, and in any case, until they were transferred to the clay, they were upside down and backward, as things are in a mirror. I never suspected they might be a message."

Eve stared. "But what gave you the idea just now?"

The professor was getting impatient. "It's too complicated. I'll tell you later."

Jonathan picked up the tablet. "Just one more thing, Klaus, and then we'll leave you alone. You've got an idea what this is all about, haven't you?"

Klaus tugged at his eyebrow. "Yes, an idea, but that's all. I can't tell you any more until I have worked on it." He took the tablet from Jonathan. "Now get out of here, both of you."

Jonathan smiled. "All right, Professor. If there's anything you need, let us know."

The professor nodded silently, already studying the tablet. Jonathan and Eve had reached the door when his voice stopped them.

"Jonathan!"

They turned. "Yes?"

"Do you have your capsules?"

Jonathan hesitated. "Yes. Why?"

"I think I'm going to need them."

Jonathan glanced at Eve. "Why?"

The professor spoke without looking up. "This message is incomplete. If I'm correct, it will take reliefs of all three capsules to finish it. One of mine was used at the Pole."

For some strange reason, Jonathan had a vague feeling of uneasiness. He fingered the box of capsules in his pocket but didn't withdraw it. Klaus glanced up at him.

"What's the matter, Jonathan?"

Jonathan sighed. "Nothing, I guess." He crossed the laboratory, took out the box of capsules and laid it on the work bench. "Here you are and–good luck."

Klaus nodded. "Ah, yes. Thank you. Don't forget to open it."

Jonathan threw another look at Eve. Her face wore a worried frown. He hesitated again, then picked up the box. It clicked open. He set it back down.

"There it is."

The professor, engrossed in the tablets, seemed to take no notice.

32

The professor had not been talking idly when he explained his convictions that the Russian leader would launch his capsules at the last possible moment. There was, of course, no guarantee, but, inasmuch as he had not yet done so, it was the only logical assumption to make. If the Russian were ever to act, it had to be before 10 P.M. Puerto Rico time tonight. He glanced up at the laboratory clock: 4:55 P.M. Five hours! Five hours in which to beat the Russian at his own game.

The professor plunged back into his work. The three tablets were propped in front of him and he had almost completed the task of copying their symbols onto a large sheet of paper. The significance of some sequences he had already grasped, and the thought of their import filled him with a terrible excitement. The minutes sped by as if Time itself was conspiring against him. At six-fifteen, he glanced up again and was overcome by a familiar feeling of lightheadedness and nausea. He had slept for eighteen hours and worked for seven more without eating. Memory of the Brooklyn fish store forced him to waste almost twelve precious minutes eating the sandwiches and drinking the thermos of coffee Eve had left at the door.

The minutes marshaled themselves into hours. The hours slipped by. His desk became littered with sheets covered with formula equations. The perspiration ran in rivulets from beneath his armpits and coursed down his naked torso. Droplets from his dripping forehead began falling on the paper. He tied a handkerchief around his head and went back to work.

The clock ticked—the pencil sped across the pages—the symbols ranged themselves into coherent form. But there was so much, so much!

By seven-thirty he was convinced that it couldn't be done in time, and then the key hit him all at once. The shortest distance is always the straight line—the direct approach. By nine, he almost had it all. But he couldn't believe what he solved. He went over it again. It checked. It had to be! And yet, if he could believe his calculations, the potentialities of the power he held in his hand were far, far beyond his wildest expectations.

By 9:40 he had won. He did not pretend to understand the science upon which the capsule operated, but the tablets had shown him that his suspicions about their nature were justified. He knew now what else this mysterious power housed in the golden shells could do, and he had discovered the tiny mechanical adjustments, which a child could have made, to transform these capsules into something whose potential was so much greater that it staggered the imagination. With two of these capsules it was now possible to blanket the world!

At 9:46, he began making the adjustments to one of the capsules. The tic which had plagued the right corner of his lip had ceased its insistent spasms, and his hands were no longer shaking. As the seconds raced on, the professor finished the adjustments and set two capsules on the work bench before him. It was done.

He sighed and wiped the perspiration from his forehead. The capsules were now ready for launching. They lay on the work bench, the living fire in the core of the jewels winking back at him prophetically. He wondered if he would have the courage to launch them. What if his calculations were wrong? What if he had made a mistake? What if their potency were not what he thought? What if, in the sureness of his convictions, he had made the symbols read what he wanted them to read? What if, instead of changing the weapon, he had destroyed it?

The large laboratory clock said 9:59:30. He picked up the capsules and walked out to the porch surrounding the laboratory.

The Great Leader stood close to the long wall of the banquet hall on the second floor of the villa. Before him, tacked to the paneling was an enormous map of North America. On the map were three circles of clear plastic, their edges overlapping. They covered the entire continent of North America from Panama to Alaska. Their centers were pinned to Vancouver, British Columbia; Houston, Texas; and Fort Chimo in Northern Quebec. On each circle in wax pencil were the latitude and longitude coordinates of the points to which the circles were pinned. The Leader stretched out a pudgy hand and spun each of the circles in turn. His face was covered with a thin film of perspiration, and behind him the crowded room was deathly still. He withdrew the hand from the map and picked up the open box of gold capsules from the stand next to him and turned to face the group. The atmosphere in the room was electric, almost explosive. Tense faces gazed back at him. Every pair of eyes was riveted to his figure. He let his own eyes range over the group. They stopped briefly on the figure of Ivan Godofsky. Ivan was seated almost directly in front on the aisle which extended from the Leader's position to the French doors opening onto the second floor balcony. The boy was flanked by two grim-faced guards, each of whom had a hand on his shoulder, and behind his chair was a white-gowned physician. In contrast to his appearance only a few days earlier, the boy looked desperately ill. His cheeks were sunken, his eyes wild, and his face had a feverish flush. He stared back at the Leader with an almost insane hatred. The Leader looked away and consulted his watch. "Five minutes. Everything is ready?"

General Zamki's voice came from behind Ivan. "Our troops will move the movement the third capsule is released."

In the silence that followed the statement, Ivan made a choked, gasping sound and half rose only to be pushed back into his chair by the guards. The Leader didn't even look in his direction. He stepped down off the low podium and moved toward the balcony opposite him. When he reached it, he set the box of capsules on a black velvet stand next to the railing. He took one of the capsules out of the box and cradled the golden shell in the palm of his hand. He stared at it as if mesmerized, then raised his head slowly. He touched the tiny spindle at the end of the capsule and he said, "In less than three minutes, comrades, the world will be ours."

The words hung in the charged air like tangible entities, reverberating in the consciousness of the listeners, freezing breath in the throat, blood in the veins, until each was a captive of the instant. Then abruptly the Leader pulled the spindle. There was an inarticulate, barely audible murmur, a muffled shuffling as men strained beyond the limit of mere perception. One of the guard's hands slipped from Ivan's shoulder and the pressure of the other lessened perceptibly. They were momentarily oblivious to his existence. Ivan lunged. He was halfway across the room before the spell could be broken, and then everything happened at once. One of the guards drew his gun. Everyone was shouting. Men stumbled over one another, some in an effort to get out of the way, others to stop him. Over the confusion, the Leader screamed, "Don't shoot, you fool!"

The crash of the gun came halfway through the sentence. Ivan staggered as the bullet hit, but his momentum sent him plunging into the Leader. The capsule in the Leader's hand was knocked loose and arched over the balcony into space as he staggered. A second later, the velvet stand splintered into fragments as Ivan lurched against it. The Leader made a wild grab for the box of capsules, but with his last remaining strength, Ivan thrust him away. The box followed the single capsule into space. Ivan collapsed. There was a stunned, unbelieving moment of shock. A tiny wisp of smoke still drifted from the muzzle of the guard's gun. A slow trickle of blood from Ivan's back began to ooze across the floor of the balcony. The Leader was trembling and shaken. He leveled a finger at Ivan's body. *"Fools! If he dies, the capsules are useless!! Useless!* Look after him!"

He ran across the room pushing men out of his way and making strange animal noises in his throat. He burst through the doors of the banquet room and pounded to the top of the staircase. He had taken the steps down when a great hollow roaring began deep in the recesses of his mind. It brought with it a pain such as he had never known. He staggered as if he had been struck, clutching at the banister for support. The pain grew until the agony was excruciating. The Leader crumpled with his head against the rails, whimpering. There was foam at the corners of his mouth, but he willed himself to his feet. Half walking, half falling, he stumbled down the stairs, forcing himself across the foyer as the waves of agony shuddered through him. The roaring in his head was reaching a crescendo by the time he got to the lawn. He could no longer walk, but he could still crawl. His vision was blurred, but he could still feel. He dragged himself across the grass until he was beneath the balcony. The pudgy fingers soaked with perspiration fumbled wildly over the sod until they touched a capsule. He drew it to him, pulled the spindle. The agonized mask of his face cracked in a terrible grimace of triumph.

"Latitude," he croaked hoarsely. "Twenty-nine degrees, eighteen minutes, north. Longitude. . . ."

Jonathan and Eve came up from the beach through the dark shadow of the palms. Behind them the moon had laid a veneer of liquid silver over the ocean and across the sand. As they broke into the moonlit compound, Jonathan glanced at his watch.

"What time is it?" Eve asked.

"Ten o'clock."

"Shall we go and see the professor?"

"Yes, and if he hasn't eaten that food you left, I'll hold him while you push it down his throat."

The laboratory was a great black shadow against the background of trees, except for the open doorway where a flood of orange light poured out on to the veranda. As they came nearer they heard the sound of a human voice. "Now he's talking to himself," Eve said.

Jonathan grinned responsively and pressed her hand lightly. "This time let's not jump to the conclusion he's crazy."

They came up the steps of the lab and looked in. The room was empty. Probably nothing could have given them more of a shock. His absence, at such a crucial moment, was stupefying.

Eve glanced at Jonathan worriedly. "But I heard his voice," she said.

"So did I. He must be in the back of the building."

"Maybe he's on the veranda," Eve said.

"What in God's name would he be doing out there in the dark?"

"I don't know, but there's one way to find out. Let's go see."

They turned away from the door and started to walk around the veranda that encircled the building. Away from the door, the shadows were black and heavy. They had almost reached the corner of the front section of the porch, when they heard the professor's voice speaking again. The voice this time was loud and guttural, but there was no possible mistaking what it said.

"Latitude 38° 18′ North
Longitude 94° 27′ West."

For a moment, the enormity of what he had heard held Jonathan transfixed. Then he catapulted into action. He charged around the corner of the porch to the back of the building, his eyes seeking the white blue of the professor's body in the darkness.

"Klaus!" The professor made no response. Jonathan seized him and began shaking him convulsively. "Klaus, where are the capsules? Listen to me. *Where are the capsules?*"

The professor's eyes met Jonathan's. "I have launched them."

Jonathan's voice broke. "Do you know what you've done? DO YOU KNOW WHAT YOU'VE DONE! *THOSE COORDINATES WERE THE HEART OF THE UNITED STATES!*"

He heard Eve's gasp of horror behind him as the professor's head bobbed unresistingly. "I have blanketed the world."

Jonathan dug his fingers cruelly into the frail shoulders beneath his hands. He was choking with anger. "I ought to kill you," he sobbed. "I ought to kill you now."

Eve saw the look on his face and screamed. Jonathan didn't hear her. He transferred his hands to the professor's throat and began to squeeze; the veins stood out on his naked forearms and Klaus struggled helplessly in his grip.

And then it happened. A great hollow roaring began deep in the recesses of Jonathan's mind bringing with it a pain he had never known. It grew until the agony in his head was excruciating. The strength drained out of him, his fingers relaxed their hold, and he let his hands drop away from the professor's throat. He stood there shuddering as wave after wave of pain washed over him like a bath of fire. And then, mercifully, the agony began to diminish. It went slowly, leaving him weak and shaken. He clutched the banister of the porch bathed in perspiration. He came out of it as a man comes out of a faint, dazed and wondering.

Eve was looking up at him, her eyes shining with tears, her voice anguished. "Jonathan, Jonathan, what is it? *What is it?*"

He swallowed. "It's all right now." Then he saw Klaus. Klaus had done something. What was it? Oh yes, he had launched the capsules. Jonathan turned the thought over in his mind. It was wrong to launch the capsules, terribly wrong, but somehow he no longer wanted to hurt the professor. He no longer wanted to hurt anyone. The anger was gone as if it had never been and he was filling with a peculiar and unknown tranquillity. Abruptly a thought struck him.

"But, Klaus," he said, amazed at the gentleness in his own voice, "then the capsules didn't work!"

Eve caught it. "But, of course," she said, and her voice thrilled with a freshness it had never known, a freshness from which all anxiety and tension had been drained, "if the bombs had worked, we'd all be dead by now."

Then the professor's voice came out of the darkness quietly. "I think," he said softly, "I think they worked very well."

33

Eve, Jonathan, and Professor Bochner sat hunched around the radio set in their living quarters. They had been there for almost five hours. From the receiver came the voice of a radio announcer which bore absolutely no relation to a normal commentary. The voice was delirious with joy, hoarse from hours of babbling half incoherently into the microphone. There were times when the announcer was obviously crying, times when his voice shook with emotion, times when it soared on the wings of uncontrolled excitement. The words he was pouring out to the listening millions were being repeated in a hundred tongues over every means of communication the world could muster. The recordings of his broadcast and many others are today the most prized possessions in the Library of the World Federation.

". . . ladies and gentlemen, here it is. The bulletin we have been waiting for. It has been irrevocably established that the Great Leader is dead. The Iron Curtain is gone, splintered into a million fragments incapable of reparation. Delirious crowds are celebrating in Moscow, Peiping, Prague, and Warsaw. The entire world is now in the grip of a jubilant celebration unparalleled in its history.

"Reports are still coming in confirming the sudden and inexplicable deaths of tyrants and evildoers in high places throughout the globe. Hospitals are filling to capacity with victims of shock. All the cases have shown the same symptoms prior to their hospitalization. Strange, medically unknown roaring in the head coupled with severe tremors and acute pain. Medical authorities are still trying to analyze the reasons for the collapse but as yet no official diagnosis has been forthcoming. The most prevalent explanation is that we have been bombarded by invisible rays from outer space. I know it's unbelievable, fantastic, but it is true that the rays killed every leader known to have been a confirmed enemy of human freedom. But they also stunned others without seeming regard for importance, position, or age of the individual. The most unlikely people have fallen victim to the epidemic—gossip columnists, thieves, preachers, psychiatrists, senators, plumbers, merchants; there have been attacks in every profession. And yet, it now appears that those who did not meet death in the first moments are destined to recover. There has been not one single fatality among the shock victims admitted to the hospitals, and reports have come in that those who experienced only minor unpleasantness are already recovered.

"From every corner of the country, statistics are arriving which indicate that a great spiritual revolution has overtaken the nation. Wrongs are being redressed in the most forthright manner. In Las Vegas, more than two thirds of the divorce applicants have expressed a desire to discontinue their cases. In California, the governor issued pardons to five convicts who have been sentenced to death. In New Mexico, rioting prisoners have returned the guards they were holding as hostages, unharmed, and have returned peaceably to their cells. The death rate in the prisons is relatively high, lending credence to the theory that there may be some connection between moral righteousness and the manner in which the individual was affected by the phenomenon of the rays, epidemic, or whatever you like to call it.

"There are happier ramifications of this spiritual revolution. All over the world, people are tearing down fences and burning them in public places. In Indochina and South America, opposing armies have laid down their weapons and are fraternizing, and on the streets, I am told, every man is smiling and meeting his neighbor's eyes. Hospitals and charities have been inundated with floods of cash, checks, and offers of assistance. Today, for the first time in history, every man is his neighbor's friend. I suppose it can't last, but, oh God, how I hope it does!"

The professor leaned over and turned off the radio. He sat there for a long time, his head bowed. Then he straightened up slowly to look at Jonathan and Eve. In his face was a peace and happiness seldom seen on a human countenance.

Eve put her hand on his. "You knew, didn't you?" she said gently.

The professor's eyes were moist. "I hoped," he said.

Jonathan bent toward them. "It was the capsules."

The professor nodded, his voice was husky. "Yes."

"But how?" Eve whispered.

"I don't know. I merely worked out the formula on the capsules which told me how to convert their energy into a beneficial power. For the rest, I had to trust in the Aliens. I suppose it was a terrible risk to take, but, somehow, I knew it would be all right."

Eve sat back in her chair and looked at the professor worshipfully. "I think," she said finally, "I'd better make some coffee."

Jonathan and the professor sat in preoccupied silence while Eve bustled about the hot plate. Once during the interval when the coffee was drawing, Jonathan switched on the radio as if to reassure himself that it had not all been a dream, and when the ecstatic voice of the announcer burst through, he switched it off and relaxed in his chair.

After a while Eve brought the cups and set them on the rough board table and then filled them to the brim with strong aromatic coffee. Then she, too, sat and for some time the silence continued unbroken. It was an eloquent silence wherein each of them savored in his own way a sensation of deep and moving tranquillity, an ineffable peace and inner harmony. It was as if each of them had been reborn, and in that rebirth had found himself stripped of the fears and anxieties which are a part of the human mechanism. Strangely, there was no need to discuss this metamorphosis. Each was aware of the others' sensations, for the aura of harmony was almost tangible.

Eventually Eve raised her eyes to the professor. They were filled with a soft bewilderment. "But how did you know what to look for? What gave you the idea that the capsules could be altered?"

The professor raised his cup and sniffed it appreciatively. It was still too hot to drink. He set the cup down again. "It all fell into place this morning," he said, "because of something I said in my excitement.

It was the phrase I used at the end of the sentence that set me off. I said it was a question of life or death."

Jonathan frowned and glanced at Eve. She shook her head. The professor smiled. "That phrase doesn't have a familiar ring?"

"Well, yes and no," Jonathan hedged, a little confused. "Everybody's heard it a hundred times."

"That's the point," the professor agreed. "Everybody's heard it so many times and under so many different circumstances that it took me weeks to realize where I had heard it before, or a phrase very similar to it, under circumstances of crucial importance."

"Where?" Eve said.

Jonathan's face lit up. "The space ship!"

"Yes," the professor said, "aboard the space ship."

Eve was lost. "But I don't understand. What has this got to do with the capsules?"

The professor's face took on a mischievous expression. "If I may borrow a phrase from the mystery novels, the clue lay in the wording of the phrase. As we were about to finish the interview, the Alien said, 'you hold in your hands the power of life and death.'" Their frowns indicated that they still did not understand. "I'm not surprised that you don't catch it. I've been worrying over it for almost a month. The trick is that the Alien didn't say, 'you are holding in your hands the power of life or death.' He said, 'life *and* death.'"

Jonathan's eyes widened in startled comprehension. "I see! The phrase might have meant that the capsules could be used for good as well as evil. But do you mean to tell me that on evidence like this, which might have been a slip of the tongue, you drove yourself to the verge of collapse?"

The professor raised a forefinger and rubbed the side of his nose absently. "Hardly. But once the idea was implanted, there were all sorts of indications that it was correct."

"What indications? Where?"

"In the Alien's talk with us there was a very strong clue. Thinking about it now, I can't understand how I missed it. He told us that their morality did not permit them to invade, destroy, or attack any other race or intelligent life form, even at the risk of the total destruction of their own. Then he went on to say, somewhat later, that, although they were constantly running into races of ruthless killers in the Galaxy, their science had so far enabled them to deal with these races. Now, if they could not attack these psychopathic peoples and were not permitted to destroy them, they must perforce have developed some means of diverting or eliminating their aggressive instincts. When you think about this, the thesis begins to develop from the vaguest possibility into almost a kind of probability. Then Jonathan gave me another clue. I was so involved in my own rhetoric explaining the mores of the Alien that I missed it."

Jonathan looked puzzled. "I gave you a clue?"

The professor drained his coffee cup and set it neatly back on its saucer. "Yes, you were very bitter at the time and if my memory serves me right you said, 'If this Alien is so all-fired chock full of loving kindness, how come he just happened to have a lot of shiny human exterminators lying around to give to us?' or words to that effect."

Eve's face brightened. "I think I've caught up at last. If they were as moral as they seemed to be, it wasn't logical for them to possess a force which could be used only as a destructive weapon."

"Exactly. Almost any power–fire, electricity, explosive, atomic fission, and so on–has two diametrically opposed uses–as a weapon of destruction or as a valuable asset to peace and life. It seemed logical that these capsules, regardless of the advanced nature of their science, should follow the same pattern. The problem was to discover how to convert this energy into useful channels. Then I remembered that the Aliens had taken their plan to the Galactic Council. I felt sure that a beneficent Council of the Worlds would have insisted that any weapon put into our hands must bear instructions as to how it might be used for good, if anyone on this planet took time off from their general preoccupation with killing one another to look. Once I had reached this conclusion, the rest was only a matter of time–and a kind of heavenly accident!"

He sat back in his chair. The tic had disappeared, the tension of fanatic purpose which had driven him had gone out of his eyes. A touch of his customary rosy color had returned to his cheeks and the thatch of white hair stood out around his bald pate in amusing but improbable tufts. He looked once again, with the twinkle back in his eyes, like a benign but somewhat tired little sprite.

Eve and Jonathan regarded him for some time in affectionate silence. Then Eve leaned across the table and refilled his cup.

"It still seems impossible. The thinking of an entire world changed in a few minutes. How could it happen?"

The professor shook his head. "If we knew more about the origin of human emotion, about what makes one man good and another man evil, we could make a better guess. But I don't find the effects of the capsules as implausible as you." A shadow crossed his face, making it look tired and drawn. "You see–I saw the power at work when Dr. Neuhaus died. It was focused on the human mechanism. It effected total disintegration, which means that every cell in the body, probably every atom, was smashed–yet the animals, the insects, the birds surrounding Neuhaus were completely unharmed. If the power could be set to attack only human cells, it obviously could be set to attack specific kinds of cells."

Jonathan frowned. "Meaning . . . ?"

The professor tugged at his eyebrow. "I'm only theorizing, of course, but think of it this way. When you are angry or frightened, your glands pour adrenalin into your bloodstream. Temporarily, at least, your body is different from what we would call normal. And even if there were no external symptoms, an instrument could be made to determine the extent of your fear or anger by the percentage of adrenalin in your bloodstream. Now, supposing that the evil man, which is not really very far from the angry man, has another kind of secretion–supposing his brain cells or his bloodstream, or perhaps every cell in his body, has a higher percentage of this malignant secretion than the average. The Alien power certainly could be set to attack those cells where the secretion index was above a certain level. With those high above the basic norm, so many cells would be destroyed that the attack would be fatal. With those with somewhat less, it would be highly painful." He glanced at Jonathan with a twinkle. "And in the case of those who were briefly possessed by violent impulse, it would be only temporarily unpleasant."

Jonathan blushed and looked down at his hands. The professor smiled.

"On the other hand, the explanation may be even simpler. Perhaps what we call 'evil' in men is only the instinct of aggression developed to an abnormal degree. And it is possible that aggressive impulses are the product of a certain segment of the brain, like the speech or memory centers. It may be that the capsules merely attacked this segment of the cortex and killed our aggressive instincts. It's too soon to tell, but we may discover we now live in a world where competitive sports do not exist."

Jonathan started. "But wouldn't that mean the end of progress? Without the aggressive instinct, we'd have no stimulus to advance."

"I don't see why. Men will still climb mountains to see what it's like on the other side. They'll still build because of need. They'll still search to satisfy curiosity and they may even learn to create for the satisfaction of the soul and the betterment of their fellows. Competitive sports are only a reflection of a competitive world. They prepare men to fight, and we have made 'fight' a proud word in our language. Wars are won, someone said, on the playing fields of Eton, but Christ won a world with love. I for one will be profoundly grateful if man has found a reason for excellence not confined to his desire to feel superior to his fellows."

Eve sighed. "I suppose I ought to feel elated, but I can't help thinking what all of this means to the Aliens–in a few more days their world will be finished."

The professor nodded gravely, his face troubled. "It's a terrible thing–millions of years of learning wiped out in a few hours!"

Jonathan stared at them and a gleam came into his eyes. He straightened up. "Well, why don't we do something about it? We've got vast uninhabited areas which we can't use but they might–deserts, jungles, polar caps. With their knowledge, they could probably build cities under the seas."

The professor faltered. "But there is no time——"

"There are a few days. Isn't it worth trying? There are no barriers between nations now. For the first time in history, there is no fear–no suspicion–no mistrust. We could get the leaders together in forty-eight hours!"

Eve came alive, glowing with excitement. "He's right, Professor!

And, once we had them assembled, you could persuade them. I'm sure of it. They'd listen to you!"

Klaus sat up abruptly. He began tugging his eyebrow and massaging his head at the same time. "You *may* be right. They must be monitoring our radio broadcasts–we would only have to transmit an invitation——"

Eve leapt to her feet, her eyes shining. "Oh, Professor, we *have* to do it!"

The professor nodded his head excitedly. "You are right, my dear. *We have to.* There may be another chance!"

The President of the United States stood up and faced the United Nations. His face was grave, but possessed of a deep tranquillity. "Gentlemen," he said, "I need not remind any of you that for the past twenty-four hours we have been broadcasting our invitation to the Alien on every available wave length, in the hope that every human being within reach of a receiver may hear his reply. If we have succeeded in reaching him, we have asked that he answer our invitation at midnight. It is now three minutes of that hour. As of fifteen minutes ago, every radio and television broadcast in the world went off the air to leave reception free. Since Professor Klaus Bochner has been almost the sole instrument in bringing us together here in complete harmony for the first time in history, it is only right that he should extend the final invitation. Professor Klaus Bochner . . ."

The thunder of applause ended abruptly when the President waved his hand and pointed to the clock. It stood at one minute to midnight. In the center of the room, the professor leaned toward the microphone. His voice came echoing through the chamber ringing with sincerity and hope.

"People from space, this is the people of Earth calling. We offer you our hospitality and our sanctuary as long as you may need it. We offer you trust and hope now and in the future. This invitation comes to you from every nation and every race on the planet Earth. If you hear us, we ask you to reply in fifteen seconds."

Every eye in the vast assembly turned to the great clock above the podium. The stillness was absolute. The seconds ticked away——

eleven-ten-nine-eight-seven-six-five-four-three-two-one. A rich, resonant voice reverberated through the room. It said:

"People of Earth, we accept your invitation. We come in gratitude and love. We bring you greetings from thirty thousand intelligent worlds which are waiting to meet you—among the stars!"

EPILOGUE

Today, in the year of our Lord nineteen seventy-three, it is possible to look back over the intervening decade with a glow of pride in the knowledge that man has at last found the road to his true and perhaps glorious destiny. Today, international boundaries are lines of demarcation between races and cultures, not thresholds to suicide, and in the vast Neuhaus Center in Switzerland, over which a gleaming spire towers in permanent memorial to the scientist who gave his life for humanity, there is at last a seat of world government and a president of the World Federation.

The latest developments in the realm of microphysics have already taken us to the planets and may soon take us to the stars. We no longer have a northern or southern polar cap and our deserts are blooming in exotic splendor. The Aliens who inhabit these areas still inspire us with something akin to reverence, so I think we may be forgiven for the childish wonder with which, after ten years, we still view their tremendous size, their other-worldly coloring, and their fantastic contours. By 1980, they will have completed their reconstruction of the Martian atmosphere and have turned its arid deserts into the same kind of paradise they have created here on earth. They will leave this planet with the wholehearted love and gratitude of all humanity, for it is their genius and unassuming generosity which has taken us into space, increased our life span by twenty-five years, and helped us to forge, for the first time, an abundant and enduring peace. And yet, great as their contributions have been, I think we will not be sorry to see them go. Our relations have never once been strained, but I think we want to go the rest of the way on our own. Wherever it is we are going, we want to be able to say when we arrive, "We got here by ourselves."

It is still difficult for the children in our history classes to understand how, after centuries of conflict, the nations of the world were able to get together in the brief four days which remained before the Nova of the Alien sun to invite the star voyagers to share our planet. Yet, unshackled from the chains of mistrust and fear, we have already proved that man is capable of even more redoubtable achievements. Poverty and famine no longer stalk the formerly overpopulated areas of the world. Our factories, homes, and transportation facilities are running on the fulfillment of an ancient dream of cheap and unlimited atomic power. We do not have paradise, but we do have peace and love and plenty, which, any way you look at it, is a pretty fair beginning.

It is frightening, too, in our present security, to remember that at one point the fate of the world rested on the genius and humanism of one man, Professor Klaus Bochner. And in this realization, it is inevitable for us to wonder if the selections made by the Aliens of the five people to whom they gave the capsules was entirely random. It seems too much of a coincidence that, among the world's billions, one of its five representatives should have been not only its greatest intellect but one of its most simple and sincere human beings. On this point, the Aliens have steadfastly refused to enlighten us.

They have also refused to explain how the capsules operated in The Transformation. And even now, ten years later, we are no nearer to the solution of that problem.

The only concrete conclusion we can accept is the obvious one: The Transformation actually took place, and for this the human race will be eternally grateful. It is probably the first time in history that global justice, however terrible, was meted out in exact proportion to the culpability of the individual. Furthermore, the justice seems to have a long-range effect. We still have occasional cases committed to the hospitals where the symptoms are spastic collapse preceded by a hollow roaring in the head. We call it Power Sickness. But this time, thank God, it is curable.

As I said, we have not yet reached the stars, but by this time next year we expect to have our first representative in the Galactic Council and to take our place in the political structure of the cosmos. We are very proud of the fact that we are the youngest world ever to have been granted admission and we are equally sure that our representative, Professor Klaus Bochner, will carry his commission like a banner.

Ivan Godofsky is a highly honored delegate of the Russians to the World Federation, and Jonathan Clark is the head of the World Press. He and Eve have three fine sons and the tests have shown that there is a daughter on the way. They have enrolled their eldest son, Jonathan, in the school for deep space pilots (class of '84), and the twins, Ivan and Klaus, are showing an astonishing predeliction for the study of microphysics. They have thrice blown up the basement of the Clark household, to the despair of Eve but to the delight of their godfather, Professor Bochner, who insists that they have only one more explosion to go before they break his record.

Perhaps, since this story began with Jonathan, it is only right it should close with him, or something of him. One year to the day after The Transformation, a book appeared on the newsstands of the world, authored by Jonathan Clark.The opening of the book seems like a fitting close for this chronicle. Jonathan wrote, and his words have since been translated into every known language of the globe—

AT A FEW MINUTES PAST TEN ON THE EVENING OF AUGUST 14 IN THE YEAR 1963, FOR THE FIRST TIME IN HIS HISTORY, MAN STEPPED OUT OF THE GRIME AND REACHED FOR THE STARS!